★

Many thanks to Paul Godden, and author Declan Conner, for their help with the cover format.

For Chloë,

'I hope you enjoy
the story.'

Best Wishes,

Jane
x

MFahy

2017

The Palace 'over Yonder

Woebetide Wood

stream

this way to
Bert
Bottomley's
Bungalow

Lookout Tree

Little
Upham

The Brambleton's

The Patch

footpath

The Willow Tree

Talking Cows

Trader's Row

Prickly Hawthorn hedge

Mould Cottage

Well

To Pottage's

A magpie's-eye view

Copyright © Text M. J. Fahy 2013
Copyright © Cover & interior M. J. Fahy 2013
First published 2014 by © Stirring Stick Publications via CreateSpace
Illustrated edition published 2016

ISBN-13: 978-1497374386
ISBN-10: 1497374383

(Also available as an eBook)

M.J. Fahy's
The Magpie King

(Book One)

For Lee, Emily, and Charlie

~CHAPTER ONE~

The Giant Milk Bottle

Not all faeries are pretty, some are downright ugly. Tatty Moon wasn't ugly. She could best be described as plain-looking, except for the white wings sprouting from between her shoulder blades. Freckles speckled her nose and cheeks.

Frustrated, she watched as her friend, Willum Patch, tried slotting the reeds together. She gestured at him to hurry. In reply the elf made a silly face and tugged the mouse closer, muttering all the while. Then, with fumbling hands, he began connecting the hollow reeds to make a long pipe.

'Hurry, Will,' hissed Tatty. 'You're makin' a right meal of it!'

The mouse was harnessed to a wooden cart. It rolled forward, barging into Will. He dropped a reed and Tatty heard him curse. He picked up the stray reed and jammed it into the end of another. Out loud he yelled: 'It's this stupid *mouse*, he won't hold still!'

Just then, the rodent let out a loud squeak and pulled back on the reins. 'Ow! What's the matter with you, Mealy? Pack it *in!*' he snapped, yanking hard on the bridle. Finally, the mouse stood still long enough for him to grab the last reed from the back of the cart, completing a long length of rickety pipework. 'Finished,' he called shakily.

'Come on then,' said Tatty, standing on top of a massive milk bottle, which stood upon a humungous doorstep, 'pass one end up to me and let's get a move on, it's gettin' late.'

Straining with the effort, Will lifted the pipe.

The furthest end snaked upward and Tatty caught it. She thrust it through the foil lid of the bottle, then frowned. *What's Will doing, standin' there? Annoyin' Mealy by the look of it*, she thought. The mouse had been in a jittery mood for ages. It had taken them twice as long on this milk run than usual. She watched him grab the mouse's bit and push backward; Mealy wouldn't budge, but jerked his head instead, lifting the elf off the ground for an instant.

'Will!' Tatty yelled.

'All right!' he snapped back. He sucked hard on the end of the creaking pipe until milk siphoned down it, then choked as a torrent gushed out, drenching him. Somehow, he managed to guide the spewing pipe into the top of an empty baked bean tin in the back of the cart.

It was as the milk began to fill the tin that Mealy's squeaks became more desperate. Sadly, the milk was louder. The mouse sniffed the air, then filled his lungs and squeaked at the top of his voice, displaying long, curved yellow teeth.

'Mealy, hush will you – you numpty! You'll wake the *Biggun's!*' Will yanked on the mouse's bridle again, but this time Mealy reared up on his hind legs and plunged forward.

★★★

The cat, Delilah, hated being hungry more than anything. She was hungry all the time, though you wouldn't know it to look at her. The local vet had put her on his 'obese' list long ago. Her stomach growled. It was early morning and breakfast wouldn't be for ages yet. She had stalked each front garden she passed, just in case a small creature fancied a quick death. Catching and eating her own prey was a distant memory, but one that she hadn't completely given up on.

Delilah watched the curious little group from the cover of a sprawling rhododendron bush. The cat could almost *feel* mouse bones snapping between her teeth. A long string of drool plopped onto the dusty earth, leaving a dark stain. Oh the sweet joy of flesh and tendons tearing, nothing could compare … apart from, maybe, being hand-fed something fishy from Mummy-person. She quickly swallowed another build-up of saliva and slithered from beneath the rhododendron like a hairy slug, reaching a stone birdbath in the middle of the lawn. She tried to hide behind it, her stomach sticking out either side, and waited a moment to see if she'd been noticed. All clear – though the mouse appeared very jittery – even jitterier than mice usually were, and mice were the jitteriest creatures *ever*! That's if she could catch the rodent. Most creatures were too fast for her nowadays, but the mouse did seem weighed down with all that stuff? It was certainly possible, she supposed … She crept from behind the birdbath, bunched her hind legs beneath her, and launched. In a fraction of a second she was almost upon her prey.

★ ★ ★

Mealy had the scent of the cat in his nostrils, so scurried away in a blind panic, dragging the cart and elf like trailing toilet paper stuck to the sole of a shoe. The reed pipe pulled taut, toppling the bean tin and emptying milk over Will, drenching him for a second time. The milk bottle fell too, smashing to hundreds of pieces on the doorstep.

Tatty shot skyward and hovered over the cottage's thatched roof, watching helplessly as Will bounced along the concrete path, trying desperately not to get dragged beneath the cart's wheels. Tatty could see his arm tangled in the reins. There was no use trying to shout either, he wouldn't hear. Sparks flashed from the luck-stone hanging from his belt. *Ha, lucky! That's a good one,* she thought. *He would've been better off with a bud of white heather in his pocket, same as everyone else, instead of that great lump banging against his hip all the time, leavin' big bruises …* Before she could think of a charm to cast, Will, Mealy, and the cart, disappeared beneath the fence.

CHAPTER TWO

The Willow

Snakecatcher Lane began as an ordinary lane, but once past Pottage's General Store it changed to a rutted track, which led to a wooden gate. On the other side of the gate was a ramshackle, oak-beamed dwelling. Nobody knew who had named the place Mould Cottage, but its bricks were prone to sprouting the odd patch of mildew if the weather was especially damp.

Mould Cottage was home to George and Hilda Parsons. Though the elderly couple couldn't be described as *actual* recluses, they did keep to themselves most of the time, going out only to do their shopping at Pottage's, or to collect their pensions. Hilda had lived there all her life. Before the old cottage first existed there had been other dwellings on the site, each one occupied by Hilda's various ancestors.

The couple were childless. George was an only child, and Hilda's sister had died in infancy, so they worried about what would happen to Mould Cottage in the future. Of the two, Hilda worried the most. George would try to put his wife at ease, but he'd noticed that she was getting very absent-minded. Back in the spring she'd gone out to feed their chickens with a striped tea cosy on her head instead of her usual moth-eaten brown beret. They'd laughed about it at the time, it had seemed such a silly mistake; but lately, Hilda's memory was worse.

Only the day before she'd started making a pot of tea and had put the kettle on top of the stove, turning on the gas without actually lighting it, filling the kitchen with explosive fumes.

With luck, George came in from the garden a few minutes later and had flung open all the windows. Hilda, happily unaware of the danger, simply asked George if he would like a nice slice of malt loaf with his cup of tea!

On this particular summer morning, George and Hilda pottered about their little garden, weeding and pruning the plants. After, they sat and rested on a bench, turning their wrinkled faces toward the early sun, enjoying the birdsong – until a blaring siren cut through the peace and quiet.

'What in blazes is goin' on, George?' asked Hilda, wearing her beret in spite of the heat.

George patted her hand. 'Nothin' to worry about. 'S just a fire engine, or amb'lance, or somethin'.'

'Oh.' She thought for a moment, staring at the bottom of the garden. 'George?'

'Yup.'

'What'll happen when we die?' She turned to look at her husband.

He sighed. 'Not sure … S'pose we goes to heaven.'

She dug him in the ribs with her elbow. 'Naw, you know, not what happens to us, that don't matter. But, what about this old place?' She pointed towards the fence. 'And *them*?'

He gulped, his stomach bunching into a tight knot. 'Oh, them.' He tried to keep his voice carefree. It was a speech he made often. 'They've been around a lot longer than us; I daresay they'll still be here long after we've left this Earth. I wouldn't worry if I was you. They can take care of themselves. Got more sense than the rest of us put together, that lot.' He held Hilda's hand and stood. 'Come on wife, up you get. Let's go an' have a look, see what they're up to, shall we?'

George pulled a pair of opera glasses from his pocket. They

weren't much of a replacement for his old World War Two binoculars, but they would have to do. He had lost his binoculars the year before. He'd only dozed off for a few minutes and when he'd gone to pick them up they'd vanished. Mind, he could guess where they'd got to, same as all the other odds-and-ends that had gone missing over the years …

Hilda sighed, letting her husband help her up and lead her past the old well, on past the chicken coop and across the parched lawn. They came to a wooden fence at the bottom of the garden and leant on the top rail, peering through gaps in the bushes on the other side. Hilda bobbed this way and that, trying to get a decent view.

'Keep still, Hild',' George whispered, pushing his spectacles onto his forehead and squinting through the opera glasses, 'thought I saw somethin' over by the willow.'

'Budge over then,' grumbled Hilda, 'an' give me a turn with those 'noculars.'

The wild land beyond the fence couldn't have been more different to the tidy garden the Parsons tended. At almost an acre, it had returned to nature, with a stream at the far end whose banks were so overgrown that it was now barely a trickle. Wild, rambling, currant bushes hung low with overripe fruit. Scabby apple and pear trees hunched like wizened old folk. A clump of stunted beech trees stood halfway down and slightly to the side of the garden; between these and the Parsons' wooden fence was a gnarled old willow tree.

The willow had been little more than a large twig when Hilda's mother accidentally sat on it as a four-year-old child. She'd been heavy enough to split the sapling down the middle, so that it grew with two separate trunks. Twisted and knotted, the willow appeared sinister, with both trunks reaching from the earth like grasping arms. One trunk had died long ago, but life still went on inside. The hollow shell was now a home. Small creatures always take advantage when looking for somewhere warm and dry to raise their young.

It's only nature's way, after all.

CHAPTER THREE

Giddy Up

Minutes before the loud siren blare which would startle Hilda Parsons, a figure emerged through the shimmering heat-haze like a cowboy from an old Western film. Bert Bottomley, postman of Upham village for the last umpteen years, sat astride a 1970s Chopper bicycle instead of a horse. A horrible squeaking followed Bert up Springle Street's gentle slope: it sounded like a giant, rabid mouse.

It was a nuisance that squeak.

Bert frowned. *I'll have to pop a drop of oil on that wheel when I get home,* he thought. It wouldn't do to wake his customers too early, what with the festive season in a few months' time, not if he wanted his lovely Christmas tips. He smiled as he remembered the dear little envelopes stuffed with money. Last Christmas he'd collected over two hundred pounds, not bad for an average-sized village. There had been enough to buy Dot, his wife, her main Christmas gift. As usual she'd wanted it spent on the cat. She'd chosen one of those daft, cat-gymnasium thingummies. Bert shook his head in bewilderment at the cost of a few bits of cardboard platforms and tubing, all covered in cheap carpet. And what a waste of money it turned out to be: all Delilah had managed so far was to take a few feeble swipes at the plastic fish dangling from it!

Bert puffed his way up the hill. It was hot again. There had been no rain for weeks. Though it was still only seven o'clock in the morning, beads of sweat speckled Bert's podgy face. He imagined drinking lemonade with ice, could almost feel it dribbling down his chins. *Bliss.* There were only another five letters to deliver; then he'd be able to head home and flop into his comfy armchair to watch the cricket match on TV. He smiled to himself – then groaned as he remembered that Dot had cancelled her planned shopping trip to Pratchester. She would be with him *all* afternoon. 'Fiddlesticks!' he yelled aloud, as he recalled trying to watch the previous week's match with his wife's silly interruptions:

'Ooh! That daft bloke's just knocked those little sticks down, Bert, clumsy great lummox!' Dot had giggled and clacked her knitting needles together annoyingly.

A vein in Bert's temple throbbed at the memory.

'Why's he thrown that ball so hard? Don't they have health an' safety in cricket, Bert?' She had stared at him, blinking questioningly with spider-leg-lashed eyes.

Bert continued pedalling, shaking his head in despair.

'Fancy those men wearin' WHITE to play a game on GRASS!' Dot had said. *'I mean, it's not rocket science is it? Their wives must be saints, what with havin' to wash that lot after every match. Mint humbug, Bert?'*

Bert had had to pinch his lips together at that point, to keep from blurting something rude.

He sighed. He would just have to bite his tongue and ignore her, because if he said anything, Dot might not cook his dinner. And Bert really loved his dinners.

At last, he reached the top of the hill. He slowed to a halt and planted his feet on the ground. He always got a thrill from the next part of his round, even though he was about forty years too old for such childishness. It was a good thing it was still early: less chance of being seen. He glanced about; then viewed the steep downward slope with a shiver of excitement. After checking his postbag was secure in the bike's front basket, and with his bottom spilling over the sides of the saddle like uncooked pizza-dough, Bert pushed away from the tarmac.

The Raleigh Chopper gained speed quickly. Bert Bottomley leaned back and giggled, enjoying the rush of warm air up the legs of his shorts and through what was left of his hair.

'Giddy up,' he said.

CHAPTER FOUR

Why, Delilah?

No, it was no use – mice were too fast – even when dragging *stuff*. Delilah watched the mouse disappear beneath the fence. She couldn't follow, the tummy forbade it. Jumping over the fence was out of the question too, Delilah didn't *do* fences: she might blunt her claws, and those had to stay sharp to rake down the back of Daddy-person's chair. Besides, there was so much milk pooling on the concrete that chasing the mouse any further would have been plain silly. And it was creamy milk too, not that watery stuff Mummy-person liked.

Delilah was so busy lapping up milk that she didn't notice the door of the cottage open. When a large whiskery chinned woman wearing a nightgown came out onto the glass-covered doorstep, she still carried on. She also failed to hear the woman grind her teeth in anger, or see her reach through the doorway for a stiff-bristled broom. Even as Delilah saw the woman for the first time, she still couldn't stop lapping.

Her tongue was a pink blur.

Outraged, the woman swung the broom and bellowed: 'That'll teach you to keep pinchin' my milk, you nuisance!' The broom thudded into Delilah's rump. 'What am I supposed to put on my muesli in the mornin's, eh? I'm *sick* of it I tell you! Sick! Sick! *SICK*!'

It was lucky Delilah had plenty of padding on her nether-regions, otherwise she might have been seriously hurt. The cat shot across the whiskery woman's front garden, yowling with fright and leapt through a privet hedge – wiping the smile off Bert Bottomley's face as he hurtled down the hill, pretending to be a jockey. A black and white blur flashed in front of Bert's front wheel. He braked – too hard! A single thought popped into his brain: *Delilah*.

Bert sailed over the handlebars. Strangely, he thought that flying felt scary, but at the same time quite *thrilling* … He imagined himself as a gymnast, or a famous actor from an action film, moving in slow-motion. Those people almost always landed on their feet. Sadly, Bert was in the 'Almost' category, landing on his back in a ditch, driving the air from his lungs in one long Whoosh! The Chopper flipped, ending on top of him. Orange spots danced in front of Bert's bulging eyes. The last thing he saw before he passed out was a black tail with a white tip disappearing through the hedge near his head.

He jolted awake and tried to move, but a pain in his ankle rocketed up his leg. He stifled a scream; then lay still and let his thoughts wander … *It was strange how that tail had looked so like Delilah's? But it couldn't have been, could it? Dot's cat was much too lazy to have wandered this far from home, surely?* However, Bert couldn't think of any other black and white cat in Upham, only Mrs Dingle's Ambrose, and he'd died six weeks before at the grand age of twenty-two-years and nine months exactly.

Bert groaned. Where was he again? *Oh, yes … Delilah.* What were the chances of being killed by a cat anyway, a gazillion-to-one? Suddenly he laughed aloud. He knew his wife's cat disliked him, but this was ridiculous! No, it couldn't have been Delilah. He'd been mistaken. It must have been some other cat, probably a wild one. They were a nuisance, feral cats, spreading their diseases everywhere. *Have to phone the council … get the pest controller to sort 'em out.* Who would have thought it? Death by cat! Bert laughed again. A felony, that's what they called a criminal offence in America, wasn't it? Though this case was a feliney … His eyelids grew heavy, so he closed them, still smiling. *Not the cat's fault … yours. Going too fast, as usual … silly old fool, and at your age.*

The heavy bicycle dug into his thigh. He had a look. *No, that can't be right*, he thought, blinking. He was lucky, he'd never worn glasses, never needed them. But he still couldn't believe what he was looking at!

There's a little fairy-thingy on my arm!

He clasped a hand over his mouth to keep from screaming. *Concussed, that's all … Or, or, maybe there's a speck of something in my eye…?* With his free hand he rubbed them and looked again.

She was still there.

It seemed to Bert that she wore a look of concern on her little freckled face. *Freckles!* What an earth was he thinking? Whoever heard of fairy-whatchamacallits in the first place, let alone ones with freckles! The more Bert stared, the more he reckoned that freckles were a cause for concern.

He watched, frozen, as the thingamajig walked up his arm and stood inches from his face.

'I saw it all,' she said, in an odd birdlike voice with a definite local accent. 'It was that cursed cat, runnin' out in front of you like that. Crafty things, cats. Are you badly hurt?'

Bert groaned. Vomit rushed into his mouth. He swallowed.

'Did you hit your head, or are you just daft?' she asked.

Bert stared, silent.

'I asked if you were hurt. Don't you understand Hampshire?'

Bert screwed his eyes into tightly scrunched slits. Maybe if he counted to ten? *Yes, I'll count to ten; then she'll disappear:* 'One – Two – Three – Four – Five – Six – Seven – Eight – Nine and *TEN*!' His eyes snapped open. The thingy was still there, but she'd backed off a little. Now she was staring at him as though he was a weirdo. She looked up the lane suddenly; her white wings flicked outward, dazzling him, so he flung an arm across his eyes, shielding them from the glare. In his fright he forgot about his reckless speed, telling himself that it *had* been the stupid cat's fault all along and it *had* been Delilah. *Stupid, stupid cat!* That's when Bert had started tunelessly singing: 'La, la, la, la, la-la-

lahhhhhhh–'

'Are you all right?'

That's strange, thought Bert, *how the little thingy-whatsit's voice has gone all deep like that?* He removed the arm from his face. A large shadow loomed over him.

He shrieked.

'It's all right, mate,' said a young man in oily blue overalls. 'I was on my way to work. Spotted you lying here, thought you might need some help. Bike looks a bit of a mess, doesn't it?'

Bert stared silently at his other arm. The fairy-thingamabob had vanished.

The young man looked worried. He tried speaking louder, and slowly: 'CAN – YOU – STAND?'

Bert winced. 'I can't stand you shoutin' into my ear 'ole like that – that's what I can't stand. Just 'cause I'm older than you doesn't mean I'm *deaf!*'

The man ignored Bert's scowling face and removed the bicycle, placing it nearby. Then he dialled 9-9-9 on his phone, even though Bert told him that he didn't want any fuss and to 'just take me home to Dot, she'll have me right as rain in no time.'

The young man didn't appear to be listening, and finished making the call. 'They're on their way; I have to go to work now. Sorry I can't wait 'til the ambulance gets here. It won't be long. See you, and good luck.' He got into his van and drove off.

As he waited, Bert scanned the trees and hedges for signs of the fairy-whatsit. She seemed to have disappeared.

No more than ten minutes later, an ambulance arrived with its blue lights flashing and sirens wailing. Bert always hated drawing attention to himself. He wished they'd turn the racket off! A hurt ankle was hardly an emergency. The ambulance crew put Bert onto a trolley, and strapped his ankle. They insisted that he go to hospital for a check-up, 'to be on the safe side.' A paramedic placed Bert's bike on the grass on the other side of the lane for safe-keeping, where it was promptly run over and crushed by a dustcart, squeezing past the ambulance in the narrow lane. Bert's pride and joy was now a crumpled heap.

'Nooooo!' Bert wailed.

Alerted by the siren in the usually quiet lane, people in nearby cottages came out to stare, including the whiskery lady. They each agreed that Bert was being rather silly, wailing over a hurt ankle. They weren't to know that he wept for his bicycle, ridden with pride since the summer of '74.

The dustmen apologised and loaded the remains of the Chopper into the dustcart, while the ambulance crew loaded the remains of Bert into the ambulance. The whiskery lady took Bert's postbag, promising to deliver the last few letters inside. Bert tried to smile at her, but his chins wouldn't stop wobbling. He cast a last lingering look at the dustcart as it disappeared around a bend in the lane. 'Bye, old friend,' he whispered as the ambulance doors closed.

★★★

Sitting on a pile of letters inside a post box, Tatty Moon watched intently. She couldn't help but feel responsible for the Biggun's mishap. If she and Will hadn't been after milk, there wouldn't have been a cat to cause the accident in the first place. The Biggun had appeared devastated at the loss of his bi-sickle: she could feel his grief still lingering over her like a veil, even after he was taken far away in the noisy motor-vickle.

It was no use; she would *have* to try to do something to put things right. She realised there was only one person who had the skills to help: *Aggie*. And after she'd met with Agatha Pottage, she would try to find Will.

She flew out of the post box and headed towards Pottage's General Store.

CHAPTER FIVE

Hide~and~go~seek

A sour cloud wafted around Willum Patch. The milk had dried in the heat, leaving his hair and clothes cardboard-stiff. Hours had passed since Mealy wrenched the harness off and disappeared down a rabbit burrow. When Will finally managed to pull the cart from the burrow's entrance, he'd called into the darkness for ages, trying to entice the mouse out with promises of treats, then to a sound thrashing, but nothing had worked. He'd almost stepped into the burrow, but hot and cold sweats, and a feeling that he was going to pass out, stopped him. He'd backed away, gasping, and lain down in the shade of the cart for a long time after.

While he rested, Will thought back to the time when all this nonsense had started. Not that he'd had many funny turns. Twice he'd fainted. Twice, that was all … it wasn't many when you really thought about it. The first time was when one of his younger brothers had locked him in the outdoor privy. The hole cut in the plank seat had let out a horrible gurgling sound. He'd been very young, barely out of napkins and convinced that something with pointed teeth lurked down in those smelly depths. He'd kicked and clawed at the door to escape. Then he'd fainted; luckily, well away from the grumbling pit.

The second time was long ago too, though he'd been cons-iderably older; but it had been worse, mainly because it took place out of earshot of anyone – anyone who cared, that was– and had lasted much, much longer …

Back then, he'd played hide-and-go-seek with another elven child: *Burnley* Snot*grass*, and remembered how he'd stupidly climbed into his parents' stove, holding the door ajar and trying not to giggle while the bigger elf checked under the table, and even inside his mother's cooking pot, just to make sure Will wasn't curled up in the bottom.

If only the soot hadn't made him sneeze.

Will shuddered, remembering the sly look on Burnley's face as the bully pretended that he hadn't known where the smaller elf hid, calling Will's name over and over, and then barging the stove door closed as he passed. Once shut, the door could not be opened from the inside. At the time, Will was certain he would be burned to death as soon as his mother lit the stove. Of course, she would have seen him as soon as she loaded it with firewood, but in his panicked state Will's common sense fled. He'd beaten on the door until his fists ran with blood; and he would never forget Burnley's cruel taunts: 'I never knew you were such a snivellin' baby, Patch; otherwise I wouldn't 'ave agreed to play with you! Never mind though, eh? If you die your parents will hardly notice, what with all the other brats they've got to feed! You never know, they might even thank me for doin' them a favour. And by the way, about our game of hide-an'-go-seek – I reckon *I'm* the winner, don't you?'

It was at this point that Will had passed out.

Later, Will's mother, Daisy Patch, had opened the stove to find him curled into a ball, unconscious. Unsurprisingly, Master Snodgrass had not been allowed to call on Will any more; though Burnley much preferred the company of other bullyish types.

Tatty had tried to help Will overcome his fear. But there were only so many times a person could put up with being called a fart-bag or pus-bucket, so she eventually gave up.

Will shook his head, banishing the memories. What was the

22

point in dwelling on things you couldn't change? He stood, gripped the shafts of the cart, and began the long walk back to Little Upham. Even without the weight of the bean tin, the wagon grew heavier with each step. *Curse the cat! I hope its teeth an' claws fall out!*

They should have been home ages ago. He hoped Tatty's grandmother wouldn't yell too much. Nan Moon scared him. Even without opening her mouth she scared him; though sometimes she was capable of overwhelming acts of kindness. Sadly, few of these were ever directed towards him.

Blisters covered his palms, and flies buzzed around, attracted by the sour milk. One annoying bluebottle landed on top of his head and vomited, then sucked up the cloudy liquid with its spongy proboscis.

'Yuck! Get off me, you vermin!' he yelled, unable to shoo it away.

'That's no way to speak about me, is it?' Tatty landed beside him. She looked at the slurping insect with disgust. The bluebottle swivelled its faceted eyes towards her and buzzed threateningly, so she pointed at it and murmured: 'Begone with you.' The next instant it was whisked skyward as if attached to a long piece of elastic. Then she showered them both with an insect repellent charm, one that would last at least eight hours. Happily, the rest of the flies buzzed off too.

They walked together, each taking a cart shaft. Will had to tell her the mouse had vanished. He blushed crimson when he admitted that he hadn't been able to enter the burrow. She just grimaced and shrugged.

'Where were you, anyway?' he asked. 'You've been gone ages.'

'Um … only on an errand. I had to see Aggie.' She looked away.

Sighing, he studied his dirty, torn breeches. 'Ma's goin' to kill me when she sees the state of my clothes.'

'Nah, she won't even notice. Your clothes are always filthy.'

'Thanks,' Will said, realising that he stank too: sweat and sour milk had combined to create a special aroma – one he never wanted to smell again.

Tatty wore a glum expression. 'Imagine how Nan's goin' to be when she finds out we've lost Mealy.'

Will shuddered at the mention of Tatty's grandmother. In contrast, her grandfather, Victor Moon, known to the children of Little Upham as Papa, was very mild-mannered. Will couldn't remember a single time when he'd heard the old gentleman raise his voice. 'Mealy'll come home eventually,' he said, trying to run his fingers through his clogged hair and failing. 'After all, he won't want to miss his dinner. You know how greedy he is.'

'Mm,' Tatty murmured.

★ ★ ★

Morning ticked slowly towards noon. At last they dragged the cart beneath the towering hawthorn hedge surrounding Mould Cottage. Mealy's stable, just a hollow in the roots of the Willow Tree, looked lonely without the mouse curled up inside his nest ball. Grooved channels around the iron tethering ring, made by his gnawing teeth, brought a lump to Tatty's throat. She hoped the mouse was safe, all alone out there in the Bigguns' world. They left the cart outside the stable and went around to the willow's oak door, on the other side of the tree.

Will pushed dirt around with his toes. 'Would you like me to come inside? You know, to explain?'

'No, there's no point in both of us gettin' into trouble,' said Tatty. 'You'd just as well get off home.'

For the first time, Tatty noticed a violet-coloured light coming from Will's body, bathing him in a hazy glow, and when she'd said that he needn't come inside with her the light had grown brighter. The glowy thing had started only a few weeks before, along with an irritating itch in her left palm. She wasn't able to see someone's glow all the time, the light would snuff out after a few seconds, and not everybody had a glow. It also seemed that the nicer the person, the nicer the colour of their glow was. Burnley *Snot*grass had a glow: a muddy, greenish one, the sort of slimy colour found at the bottom of stagnant ponds. Tatty hadn't told anyone of this new happening, she didn't need the fuss it would cause.

The glow surrounding Will flickered then and went out. 'Well, as long as you're sure?' he said.

Tatty laughed. 'Just go. And you can uncross your fingers too.'

'But how–' He brought his hands from behind his back and stared at them, silent. He walked backwards. 'Right. Better go. See you sometime tomorrow?'

'Yep, tomorrow.' And he was gone, kicking up plumes of dust as he ran, so that his feet appeared to be on fire. Once he had vanished from sight, Tatty lifted the door latch and went inside the Willow Tree.

She'd forgotten it was baking day.

CHAPTER SIX

Baking Day

Nan Moon sucked raspberry jam from the front of her apron. Strands of grey hair peeped from beneath her frayed mobcap. Emerald wings hung down her back, their veins pulsing with shimmering blood, cooling her. Tatty was envious of those wings. They caught the sunshine, sending green spangles of light bouncing off every surface. Her own wings were such a boring shade of white. White wasn't even a proper colour. *Colourless, just like me, with my pale skin, freckles, and mousy hair.* She stood against the wall and her grandmother did not look up; *hasn't even noticed I'm here …*

Nan scraped pastry scraps from the table into her hand and pointed at a trapdoor in the floor beneath the table. It sprang open and she threw the scraps into the deep hole. Another flick of her finger shut the trapdoor with a Clunk! The sound brought her out of her tidying trance. She looked at Tatty with big owl eyes behind her thick spectacles. 'Where on Neptune's kneecaps 'ave you been, child? Gallivantin' about with that boy instead of comin' straight home, I shouldn't wonder.'

Tatty said nothing.

'Don't stand there with your mouth open – hand me that cloth; pie's about ready.' Nan snatched the cloth from Tatty and opened the

26

stove. A sudden blast of hot air made her step back. A moment later, a light tapping sounded. 'Well?' said Nan. 'The door! The door, child. It won't open itself.' Tatty hurried to the door and yanked it open.

Outside, looking nervous, were two elves, each clutching something.

'Won't be a moment,' puffed Nan, 'just gettin' the last one.' From a shelf in the stove she lifted out a golden pie and carried it to the table. Next, she flipped upside down, fanning the pie with her wings to cool it. With her nose brushing the ceiling, she flicked a cobweb away at the same time. 'Should've got 'ere earlier,' she called. 'I had so many folk waitin' in line that I couldn't count 'em all … must've been dozens. Early bird catches the worm, you know. Oh, there were *so* many disappointed faces that I baked a few more pies out of the goodness of my heart.'

Goodness has nothing to do with it, thought Tatty.

'This is definitely the last one of the day.' A mischievous glint flashed in Nan's eye. 'So you'll have to fight for it.'

One of the elves, Mr Pickle, looked decidedly nervous. Tatty didn't think he looked very confident at winning fisticuffs, even though the other elf was only Mrs Snodgrass. As Nan came to the door, he offered his trade item for her to inspect. The tips of his sharp ears quivered.

'Mm, what've we got here?' said Nan, holding the pie in one hand and taking something from the elf with the other. She turned the cracked leather this way and that in front of her face, and frowned. 'Would I be right in thinkin' that this is a toad harness, Mr Pickle?'

He nodded enthusiastically.

'But, Mr Pickle, I 'ave no need of a *toad* harness. I've a perfectly good mouse out in the stable–'

Tatty felt an urgent need for the privy.

'–so I won't be requirin' this.' Nan shoved the harness back into his hands. 'Bah, *toads!* Such idle creatures!'

Mr Pickle's ears drooped. He gazed longingly at the pie.

Losing patience, Nan turned to her other customer, Petunia Snodgrass – or *Snot*grass, as she was called by the local children; unfairly, because she was a nice person and couldn't help being the mother of the bullying Burnley. Everyone knew she'd tried her best to sort her son out, but short of committing murder, nothing had worked.

Nan saw the objects clutched in Petunia's hand. 'Ooh, Petunia, what've you brought?'

'Wooden spoons, Mrs Moon, carved by my 'usband.' Petunia's golden curls bounced.

Nan took the spoons and inspected them. 'And very talented he is too, if I may say. The carving on the 'andles could be compared to Alf Patch's – almost.' She put the spoons into her apron pocket and handed Petunia the pie.

Tatty agreed with Nan, about Mr Patch being an excellent woodcarver. Will's father could whittle a spoon from a rough twig in the time it took her to write down her name.

Mrs Snodgrass's face glowed with pride; she cradled the pie as if it were an elven babe. 'Oh, *thank* you,' she gushed.

Petunia had hardly finished speaking, when Nan muttered, 'Regards to the family,' and slammed the door in her customers' surprised faces. Almost immediately it was barged open by Papa. Inside his wheelbarrow sat an apple so big that he couldn't fit it through the doorway.

''Bout that then, wife,' he called cheerily.

Nan scowled at the deep gouges he was leaving in the door-frame.

'Think I'll shrink it,' he said, seeing her expression. He pointed a finger at the apple.

Nan was quick to stop him. 'No, you won't! You're not usin' magic and that's that. You'll be whinin' later on that you've no energy; then you'll sit in your rocker moanin' about all your aches an' pains. Go and fetch your saw – cut a bit off the side.' She turned to Tatty. 'He *always* has to get the biggest.'

In no time Papa had hacked a chunk off the apple. He wheeled the barrow through the doorway and dumped the fruit beneath the parlour window. 'It's a beauty, isn't it?' He pushed the barrow outside and wiped a handkerchief over his shiny bald head.

Tatty was about to explain that Mealy was lost when her mother, Marigold, bustled indoors carrying dirty laundry. She dumped the smelly bundle next to the fire, over which hung a big black cauldron. 'Phew,' she gasped, 'another scorcher again today. Anyone fancy a cuppa before I get started on that lot?'

'Not for me,' said Nan.

'Or me, thank you, Ma,' said Tatty.

'What about you, Pop?' asked Marigold, as Papa charmed his bone pipe down from the mantelpiece. It floated to his outstretched hand. Though he didn't smoke any more, he liked to sit and polish the pipe, sometimes even coaxing a tuneful whistling out of it.

'Cup o' tea would be like nectar,' he said, smiling.

Marigold put the kettle on the stove. 'You'd better eat somethin', Tatty. You were gone early this morning.'

Tatty sat at the table. 'I – I'm not hungry,' she stammered. Her face felt hot.

'Nonsense,' said Nan. 'You'll have somethin' to eat and that's final … Out all mornin' long with nothing inside you – preposterous!' The old faery ladled two beetle eggs out of a pan and onto a plate, which she shoved in front of Tatty. Next, she turned to her husband, who sat in his rocker, resting his feet on the apple. 'And Victor, would you go and stand the milk in the stream to cool? It'll spoil if it's left out in this heat.' She squinted at the sun shining through the window. 'May already be too late.'

'Right you are.' He sighed, unravelling his skinny frame from the rocking chair and flexing his crumpled brown and gold wings. With a blue crackle and a loud POP, he disappeared. The pipe dropped to the floor.

'Oh, I *wish* he wouldn't do that,' said Nan. 'It wears him out usin' unnecessary magic. But will he listen to me, of course not.'

Tatty spoke, but no one heard. So she repeated herself, louder this time: 'There isn't any milk.'

Nan turned slowly and pushed her spectacles up the bridge of her nose. 'No milk? What do you *mean* no milk?' Her expression was as stony as her voice. 'The whole of Little Upham has been waitin' for that milk.'

Tatty swallowed. 'Well, it was like this … Um, me and Will, we–'

'Oh I might 'ave known *he'd* 'ave something to do with it!' Nan snapped. 'Bad luck follows that one around like a bad smell. It was a waste of time Agatha givin' him that luck-stone, if you ask me.'

Marigold nodded.

'I've never been one to discriminate, Tatty,' Nan said through pursed lips, 'but I'd rather you had a few more faery friends. Hangin' about with elven kiddies is all well an' good, but they *are* prone to some very impish ways.'

Tatty gritted her teeth.

A bright blue flash signalled Papa's return. He fanned his face with his hand. 'Phew – I'm boilin'. Can't seem to find the milk?'

'That's because there isn't any,' said Nan.

'Oh, that's a shame,' said Papa, smiling. His smile vanished when he looked at his wife, so he plucked his pipe from the floor and pretended to inspect it.

'It was the cat's fault,' Tatty cried. 'If it hadn't been for that great lump we'd 'ave been all right!'

'What cat?' Marigold turned; her red hair and orange wings flashed like fire. 'Were either of you hurt?'

'We're both fine,' Tatty mumbled.

Marigold sat beside her daughter. 'Tell me exactly what happened.'

'Well, we were … actually, *Will* was chased by this big cat … And the milk spilled … Will was soaked through … We managed to get the cart back in one piece. It's out by the stable.'

'And what about the mouse?' asked Nan, in a dangerously pleasant voice.

'He went down a rabbit 'ole,' muttered Tatty, spooning beetle egg into her mouth.

'Oh dear,' said Marigold.

The pointed tips of Papa's ears began to twitch. He started humming to himself.

'A *rabbit* 'ole!' shrieked Nan.

'Oh dear,' Marigold repeated.

'A *rabbit* 'ole!' shrieked Nan again, just in case no one heard her the first time. The ladle she'd used for the eggs flew from her hand. Papa caught it, then took his wife by the shoulders and guided her to a chair.

She sat.

'Now,' said Papa, 'I don't know what all this kerfuffle's about, I really don't.' He looked at each of them. 'You all know as well as I do that Mealy's the greediest creature on Mother Earth. Once he gets hungry he'll come 'ome by himself. He knows when he's well off, that one.'

Nodding, Nan and Marigold had to agree.

Everything seemed almost back to normal. So Tatty blurted out rather more than she should have: 'You should've seen the size of that cat. The bloomin' thing made a Biggun fall off his bi-sickle. Course, I had to make sure he wasn't dead. And it's all right, I didn't tell Will. He doesn't know anythin' about the Biggun.'

Silence pressed in on Tatty's eardrums. Dread crept from her toes to the top of her head. Even the mild-mannered Papa looked shocked.

'Oh, Tatty,' he groaned. 'You were seen by a *Biggun?*'

'But I had to make sure he wasn't dead! He *looked* dead ... It would've been our fault! I had to check – to make sure.'

'You know our laws, Titania.' Nan rarely used Tatty's proper name, except during a telling-off. 'We must never ever, speak to, be seen by, or otherwise have anything to do with the human race. It always ends in disaster – *always*!'

'The young'uns aren't hurt, that's the main thing,' said Papa. 'Tatty shouldn't have shown herself, but what's done is done – no good crying over spilled milk.' He laughed at his pun. 'In a day or two the cows will be back in the meadow next door, so we'll get our milk straight from the udder like we used to. It's getting too dangerous to go snoopin' around the Bigguns' homes anyway … askin' for trouble.' He placed a hand on Nan's shoulder when she started to protest. 'I know – I know, gal. We said we'd stop collectin' it that way when the first cow started to talk. Trouble is they *always* do – can't stop it. No, it's only natural that a bit of magic rubs off on 'em.' He smiled. 'Why, don't you remember, I told you only last week that Mealy said 'is first word. Not much of a word really, but there you are. "Twaddle", is what it was as I recall. Anyway, I'll have a quiet chat with 'em once they're back, ask 'em if they wouldn't mind cutting out the talkin' when the Biggun's around. I'm sure they won't take offence.'

'But that doesn't alter the fact that the girl's done *wrong*, does it?' Nan insisted. 'In my day I'd have been pinned to the scullery door by my wings if I'd been seen by a Biggun. That's how folk learned their lessons back then.' She turned to Tatty. 'You're lucky I'm not strict like my father was.'

'Mm, very lucky,' Papa mumbled.

Nan said, 'You'll stay in your room for the rest of the day and think on what you've done. Let's hope no one finds out or else we'll all be in trouble. Right, that's settled then – we'll say no more about it.' She slapped her hand on the table and continued to say more about it. 'After all, the law's the law. We have 'em for a reason. Misfortune befalls those that flout 'em!'

Tatty knew that arguing would be pointless. She got up and went through a curtained doorway, which led to a dark stair-less shaft. Wondering what a flout was, she flew up into the gloom to her bedchamber. Pushing open double doors, she wandered to the circular window and peered through thick glass. It was stuffy so she opened it, letting in even stuffier air.

Near the window stood a washstand with a basin made from the top half of a stoat's skull. Tatty tipped water into the basin from a skin pouch hanging on the wall. Once she'd washed her hands and face, she let the dirty water out and it gurgled down a bamboo pipe wound around the outside of the willow, eventually dripping onto the parched soil near the tree's roots.

She lay down on her bed and stared up at the spyglass, hanging from the curved ceiling. The rest of the afternoon dragged into evening, and then into deepest night. Despite being bone-tired she was still wide awake, wondering what had happened to Mealy, and if Aggie had found the Biggun's bi-sickle yet?

CHAPTER SEVEN

Desiccated Toads

The Council rubbish dump was lit by a full moon, so Agatha Pottage could see quite clearly. Her Familiar, Chorley, a raven, helped look for the bicycle too. The huge black bird circled overhead, wings swooping through the warm night air. Agatha thought that as it had only been dumped early that morning, the bicycle should still be near the surface and not yet buried in the rubbish. After only a few minutes, Chorley spotted it. He called to Agatha with a hoarse croak. She hurried over mounds of litter to where the shaggy-throated bird sat, perched on one of the Chopper's handlebars.

'Well done, you clever, clever boy,' she said, stroking his head.
He hopped on to her shoulder as she heaved the bicycle free. She laid it on its side and examined the wreckage, peeling a mouldy yoghurt lid off the saddle. 'Dear, dear, dear, it's in a right old state, isn't it?' Agatha tapped her chin. 'Tatty wasn't exaggerating when she said how damaged it was. Still, I'm sure we can sort it out.' She reached into the pocket of her long, black, cardigan and brought out a rather shrivelled and crisp-looking object.

It was a toad.

Or rather, it had been once, long ago, but now it was dried out to such an extent that it was completely mummified. 'This should do it,' said Agatha, rubbing the corpse between her hands so that desiccated toad sprinkled over the bicycle. Her lips barely moved as she whispered the ancient incantation.

Once touched by toad flakes, the mangled bicycle uncurled like an arthritic spider waking after a long sleep. Clunking, popping and scraping made Agatha's teeth hurt. Chorley hid his head under one wing. Any damage from the accident was put right, while chipped and flaking paint from before remained as it was. Both burst tyres inflated with loud hisses. Within thirty seconds the yellow Chopper was fully restored.

Agatha stood back to admire her work.

'Knew that toad would do the trick,' she said to Chorley. The bird's head cocked on one side as he listened. 'It came from an amphora of toads that belonged to Cleopatra. They say she was a very powerful witch, you know.'

Chorley answered with a croaking, 'Toaaaad.'

Agatha lifted the bicycle upright and waited for Chorley to hop into the front basket. Once he was comfortable, she pushed the Chopper over the rough ground until she came to a chain-link fence surrounding the landfill site. She stooped to fit through the gap she'd caused earlier in the evening. On the other side, she turned and pointed a long scarlet-painted fingernail at the ragged hole. Purple sparks streamed from her fingertip and landed on broken pieces of chain-link, pulling them back together so the fence appeared perfect again.

'Home,' croaked Chorley.

'Yes, home,' said Agatha, hitching up her elegant black skirt and hopping onto the bicycle. She switched on the bike's lights and set off down the country lane, until witch, raven, and Chopper, disappeared around a bend. A faint, ghostly whistling echoed through the swirling mist.

CHAPTER EIGHT

De~lousin'

Smelly steam from stewing laundry filled the parlour the next morning. Enchanted, a long stick stirred the contents of the cauldron over the fire. Tatty peered inside, wrinkling her nose at the dozens of stockings and socks all writhing in the scummy water like oily eels.

'Don't touch that stirring-stick,' Nan warned; 'you'll break the stirring charm. Sit down – I'll get you some breakfast.'

Still tired, Tatty sat at the table, where a bowl and spoon waited.

Nan carried a saucepan to the table and threw a dollop of grey-looking porridge into Tatty's bowl. Tatty stared at it and wiped a hot speck of the goo from her eyebrow. 'Thanks,' she murmured, thinking the porridge didn't look up to Nan's usual standard, and that this was probably another way of punishing her. She guessed Mealy still hadn't returned.

'You'll not leave the table 'til it's all gone,' said Nan, turning back to the stove.

Tatty made a face behind her grandmother's back. Her stomach churned at the sight of her breakfast, a rubbery skin already forming on its surface. She spooned a tiny amount into her mouth. It was too salty. She usually had honey on her porridge. *Definitely being punished,* she thought. She'd never be able to eat it all, *not if I sit here till Christmastime.* Not that she'd ever been awake at Christmastime, but that wasn't the point. She needed to get rid of the porridge quickly, so she could meet Will. He had plans today and so had she, plans that wouldn't be stopped by porridge! There was only one place to get rid of the revolting stuff: the trapdoor. Tatty checked to make sure Nan wasn't looking. She flexed her finger slightly and whispered a spell: 'No more lumpy porridge for me, go below and feed the tree.'

The grey porridge rose from the bowl in a writhing, mushy ball. It resembled a mini version of the moon with its cratered surface. Tatty kept her eyes on Nan as the trapdoor under the table opened with a creak. She covered the sound with a cough.

'You want some honey for that cough,' Nan stated, brewing a pot of dandelion tea.

Some honey with my porridge would've been nice, thought Tatty, as the porridge-ball floated under the table, down through the trapdoor and into the darkness below, where it squelched amid the damp tangle of tree roots. With another twitch of her finger the trapdoor lowered with a thud. Tatty dropped the spoon in her bowl with a clatter. 'All gone,' she called.

Nan turned and smiled. 'Now doesn't that feel better? Can't start the day without a nourishin' breakfast inside you.'

The door opened. Papa came in with wood for the fire. 'He's back.'

'Who?' said Nan.

'The bloomin' mouse, who do you think!' Papa laughed.

'Where'd you find him?'

Papa stacked the wood near the cauldron. 'You'll never guess – in the pantry.'

'The *pantry!*' exclaimed Nan, her voice rising. 'Well *somebody* couldn't have locked the door aft–'

They all knew who had visited the pantry last. Papa winked at Tatty. 'No harm done, old gal. I caught 'im before he'd had a chance to eat anythin'. All tucked up in 'is stable now, reckon he'll sleep for days. Poor thing's worn out.'

Tatty jumped up. 'I'm goin' to The Patch, I won't be late home.'

'Right you are,' said Papa, 'but keep your eyes peeled. I saw a lot of magpies over Woebetide Wood. If they get any nearer you're to come straight 'ome, you hear?'

'Woebetide Wood's miles away,' said Tatty.

'I said you're to come straight 'ome.'

Tatty had rarely seen her grandfather look so serious. 'Yes, Papa,' she said.

'Good.' He smiled. 'Off you go then.'

All thoughts of magpies vanished from her mind before she reached the door. Will wanted to go dragonflying. He was an expert at catching the insects. Then, after, it would be *her* turn to choose the activity, and she had a special one planned. Everything would be fine unless Will lost his nerve. They would both have to hide, hopefully nowhere too cramped. She didn't want him having one of his turns.

As she went out the door, Papa said, 'If the magpies get any closer I 'spect Alf will sound the lert.'

★ ★ ★

The flock gathered at the edge of the wood, squabbling and chattering, their eyes feverish with intelligence. But it was a cleverness marred by addled thinking – a madness projected by another; and with more than a little cruelty mixed in, proven by the way the magpies would pick on a weaker bird, harassing and pecking at it until the weakling dropped dead, or flew miles away from Upham, until it was a simple bird once more. The magpies appeared to be listening to something, or someone, tilting their heads from side to side, nodding now and then as if in agreement.

★ ★ ★

Inside the Crow's Nest, at the top of the Lookout Tree, sat Alf Patch. Though Tatty waved at Will's father as she zoomed past, he failed to see her as he peered through the spyglass at something over Mould

Cottage's roof. Moments later, she landed on top of The Patch. The cottage had been made from an upturned wicker basket, weather-proofed by lots of cow dung and mud pressed into the gaps. Sadly, Alf Patch had got his dung-to-mud ratio wrong, so that each time it rained The Patch gave off a strong farmyard smell.

Tatty yelled down the chimney, 'Helloo! It's me!'

Standing in the front garden, Will answered, 'I know it's you. I wish you'd come to the door like a normal person?'

'Wish in one hand, poo in the other – see which one gets filled first,' Tatty sang.

'Nice. One of Papa's sayings, I presume?'

'Of course.'

He sighed. 'Come inside then.' He looked glum.

She landed next to him. 'What's the matter?'

'It's not *fair*. Ma wants us to take Beattie out for a couple of hours. I wanted to go dragonflyin'. I'll never catch anything with that jabberer with us.'

'It'll be all right,' said Tatty. Not having brothers and sisters of her own, she only saw the positive side. 'Come on, let's go an' get her?'

Will's mother, Daisy, was in the middle of delousing one of her six children. She held a small boy by the ear with one hand and tried to catch a darting head-louse with the other. The last louse kept popping up through the child's thatch like a baby bird in a nest. 'Keep still, Charlie-boy, this is the last one.'

'Good job you used that charm on us,' Will whispered. 'I didn't have any lice, nor did Beattie, but she's gettin' in Ma's way.' A jar sat on the table, a dozen head-lice hopped about inside, making pinging noises and doing back-flips. 'She's let them out twice already.'

'Mornin', Tatty,' said Daisy Patch, cheerily, her rosy cheeks shining like waxed red apples. 'Not one of life's most pleasant tasks I grant you, but we should have enough of 'em to pickle, help tide us over in the winter months.' She managed to grab the last shrieking louse, remove the stopper from the jar, and thrust the squirming creature inside. 'Right, who's next?' she asked, rubbing her hands together.

'*Not me!*' a chorus of voices called.

'Tatty! Do Tatty!' shouted Beatrice, with a finger up one nostril. Her eyes gleamed.

Tatty said quickly: 'No, no need. Ma checks me regularly, and I've got an insect repellent charm on.' She saw the look of disappointment on the tiny elf's face.

Daisy combed knots from Charlie-boy's hair. 'Sorry you're to have Beattie hangin' around you for the next couple of hours, Tatty. I hope you don't mind too much? It's just that she's such an imp. I need eyes in the back of my head, I really do.'

'Don't worry about Beattie, Mrs Patch. She's no trouble, are you?'

The child stared back, unsmiling.

'And that's such a pretty dress you're wearin',' said Tatty. 'I love the silver threads in the sleeves.'

Beatrice studied her dress for a moment, and sniffed. She frowned. 'Dem's not si'ver freds ... habn't got an 'anky.' She wiped her nose down her sleeve to prove this fact.

Tatty gulped down a wave of revulsion.

Will laughed. 'Still wish you had a little brother or sister, eh?' He grasped Beatrice's moist hand. 'Let's go, Beattie. Say bye to Ma?'

'Bye, bye, Ma,' said Beatrice as she was led through the doorway. 'Where're we goin' Will–um?'

Will looked into her tiny face. 'Just you wait an' see – it's a *surprise.*'

CHAPTER NINE

Gangergreen

Bert had hated staying in hospital overnight – and all because it took ages for an x-ray. He'd had to put up with doctors pulling and prodding his ankle until it resembled a ripe aubergine. And after all the mucking about it turned out to be a bad sprain and severe bruising. *Complete waste of time!* Plus, he was convinced the nurse in charge of the ward was a witch! The painkilling injection she'd given him for his ankle had been far worse than the injury itself. It had felt like she'd been drilling for oil the way she'd stuck that enormous needle into his bottom! And how she and the other nurses had manhandled him when he'd asked for assistance in the night had been shocking! He'd only pressed his buzzer a couple of times … Well, maybe it *had* been more than a couple of times, but that was their *job* wasn't it – what they got paid for? It hadn't been *his* fault that he couldn't get comfy on that plastic-covered concrete they'd had the cheek to call a mattress. It hadn't been *his* fault they couldn't open the window more than a crack in case somebody fell out, so that he'd needed an electric fan that they'd had to hunt for over an hour for, was it? And he was certain they'd put him in that floral maternity gown on purpose. *Couldn't find any spare pyjamas – what rubbish!* A complete waste of a good cricket match was all it had been, from start to finish.

And Hampshire had won too …

Also, since arriving home, Dot was driving him potty, fussing over him like a mother hen and generally getting on his nerves. There was nothing worth watching on the TV, and his ankle itched under the thick support bandage he'd been ordered to wear.

From his armchair, Bert watched as Dot tottered into the room on high-heeled, pink slippers.

'Let me plump that cushion for you, honey-bun,' she cooed. 'Is that better? Wasn't it a shame you missin' the cricket like that, and them *winning* too? Still, you can't blame Delilah – she's only a cat, after all. And it was just an accident. Strange though, what're the odds, I wonder?'

About the same as you keeping quiet for five minutes, thought Bert. His fingernails dug into the arms of the chair. 'Mmn,' he answered, through gritted, mainly false, teeth.

'Relax,' Dot soothed. 'I know you hate sittin' about. If you rest up properly you'll be back on your postal round in no time, you'll see. We'll have to buy you a new bike. We won't be able to replace your Chopper, but you'd had it since the '70s, so it's high time you had a new one.' Dot bustled about, wiping imaginary dust from the frames of large photographs on the wall. All were of Delilah at varying stages of growth, from early kitten-hood onwards: a cute ball of black-and-white fluff hanging from the back of Bert's armchair, to the one taken just last Christmas, surrounded by shredded wrapping paper. Delilah sat staring at the camera, her pupil's glowing a demonic white.

It gave Bert the creeps, that one, the way the eyes seemed to follow him around the room …

He heaved a sigh. *Poor old bike.* It had been his pride and joy. Not any more, now it was up at the local tip, amongst a load of manky rubbish. The Chopper had been such a big part of his life that he felt it had almost been a living thing. Bert thought he should try to bring it home, give it some kind of proper send off. He felt tearful suddenly.

'Bert, are you all right?' asked Dot, noticing his watery eyes. 'Shall I get you some painkillers?'

Bert was reminded of a giant candyfloss as he looked at Dot, with her stick-like legs and pink-tinted, fluffy hair. The image cheered him and he smiled 'No. I'm fine, thanks.' He watched her rearrange cushions and straighten the cat-owner magazines on the coffee table. She had copies of *Feline Purrfect* and *Clawtastic!* delivered once a month.

Bert's head sagged against the soft cushion.

'Fallin' asleep already?' Dot giggled. 'That didn't take long, did it? We've only been home five minutes. Aw, poor old you. I was goin' to ask if you'd like a drink, 'cause I know how disgusting the hospital tea is. I'm convinced they just dangle a teabag over hot water … Oh, and I'm sorry I didn't bring you any pyjamas, but the nurses said there wasn't any need. If I'd known they were goin' to put you in that – that flowery *tent*, well, I'd 'ave come straight in. Oi, Bert, leave my knittin' needle alone. Stop pokin' it down your bandage! I know your ankle's itchy, but you'll scratch yourself and end up with gangergreen. Right, that's enough tidyin' for today. I'll make a nice cup of tea. Just going to boil the kettle, won't be a mo'.'

Oh go and boil your head while you're at it, thought Bert, unkindly. He wondered how Dot didn't drop dead through lack of oxygen, as she hardly ever seemed to inhale.

Movement caught his attention. It was Delilah, slinking through the open patio doors. She ignored Bert, went behind his armchair, and raked her claws down the back of it, pulling long snags in the pea-coloured material. Bert seethed. *The sheer cheek of it!* And while he was still sitting in the thing, too! *Right, that's it!* He reached down the side of the armchair as Delilah walked to the front. His fingers curled around a rolled-up newspaper: a special cat-swatting newspaper. He missed, thwacking the carpet as Delilah neatly sidestepped. As he leant over the side of the chair, his weight made it topple. 'Blast!' he yelled as he hit the floor. He gasped with surprise as Delilah appeared to grin into his face. Then she retched and coughed up a soggy hairball, which hit Bert between the eyes.

On hearing the thud, Dot rushed into the room. 'What the—

Bert! Oh, my godfathers! What're you doing down there?' Straight away she saw that her cat had been close to danger. 'Ooh, you might've squashed Delilah, you silly, silly man!' She scooped the cat into her arms and smothered it with kisses. 'It's all right, darling, Mummy's here.'

'Never mind De–bloomin'–*lilah!*' yelled Bert, flapping on the floor like a stranded walrus. 'Help me up, woman!'

Placing Delilah out of harm's way, Dot heaved Bert into a sitting position. After more heaving and pulling she managed to stand him up and lean him against the wall. He gave the cat a poisonous look. *It's only tried to kill me – again!*

Dot righted the armchair. Her eyes narrowed as she caught sight of the rolled-up newspaper. She picked it up off the floor. 'What's *this* for?' she asked suspiciously.

Quickly, Bert said: 'I was swattin' a fly. It came in through the patio doors. Blinkin' thing was buzzing around my head.'

'Aw, it must've flown back out,' said Dot. 'You should've called. I would've sprayed it with fly-killer.' She gave a loud sigh. 'Now, sit down and I'll make you comfy.' She fussed with the cushion and the footstool supporting his ankle. Then she said something that sent a shiver of doom down Bert's spine: 'We'll look after Daddy, won't we, Delilah? We won't rest 'til he's all better, and if that means not leavin' his side for one minute, then so be it.'

Bert's eyes swivelled to the cat. It watched from the hallway. *There's that look again! No, no – it – it can't be? Cats can't* really *smile … can they?*

CHAPTER TEN

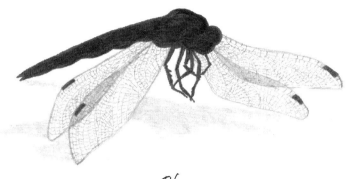

Blue

Bored, Tatty and Beatrice sat on the bank of the stream and listened to its endless burbling.

Will was having no luck roping dragonflies. The ones they had seen were skittish, with the slightest movement sending them darting away. With a face like thunder, Will flopped down next to Tatty and threw his lasso close to the water's edge. 'I knew it'd be a waste of time,' he grumbled.

'Well, you can't blame Beattie for being noisy, she's been as good as gold,' said Tatty.

'I'm not am I?' Will snapped. 'The dragonflies round here aren't worth a light. They're too small!' He chewed on his bottom lip and stroked the luck-stone hanging from his belt.

Agatha Pottage had given him the stone on his birthday, years before, shrinking it to elf-sized dimensions. Tatty watched him caress it and wondered why Aggie had never given *her* anything so valuable.

'Pa told me there used to be dragonflies here centuries ago. They were massive compared to the ones you get nowadays,' said Will miserably. 'Folk used to ride them and everything.' He stared at the stone's mottled earthy colours. 'Don't know why I even bother with my lasso, those days are long gone.'

Tatty stared at the luck-stone. Then a movement out on the water caught her attention. She couldn't speak for a moment, was mesmerised. Somehow she managed to whisper: 'Keep rubbin' that stone, Will. You must be doin' something right.'

He looked at her, confused, and then followed her gaze out over the stream.

The dragonfly was enormous, as big as a hawk: the sort that once flitted over bogs and through tree ferns in ancient times. Will's fingers inched towards his discarded rope and closed around it.

★ ★ ★

He crept through the reeds in the shallows, wading out until the water was waist-deep. Peering from behind a reed, Will could see the dragonfly clearly. It edged closer, wings creating a soft breeze that ruffled his hair. A branch had fallen from an overhanging tree. He hauled himself onto it and stood upright on quivering legs. The narrow branch lurched beneath his feet. He clutched at a thick reed for support, leaning against it while the branch slowed its bobbing. Then, just as Will tried to fathom how he would get the lasso over the insect's head, a searing pain exploded in the centre of his back: The dragonfly had landed on the same reed, and one of its viciously spiked legs dug into his flesh, mashing the side of his face against the rough plant. The pain was unbearable. He found it hard to keep from crying out. Were those his ribs cracking, or the sound of the insect eating? In desperation he ran his hand up one of the dragonfly's legs, as far as he could reach, and gouged his fingernails into the soft gap between its leg and body. The insect suddenly burst from the reeds, flying straight up with Will dangling from its front leg. He thought it was Tatty's voice he could hear, yelling: 'Let go! Drop into the water!'

The dragonfly shook its leg, trying to dislodge the elf. Unable to, it tried to bite him, gnashing its sharp mandibles. Will met its oncoming head with a kick. By swinging, he managed to flip himself up onto the dragonfly's back. The unfamiliar weight sent the dragonfly wild. It twisted and lunged, looped-the-loop, and plunged under low-slung branches to rid itself of the elf. Will thought the luck-stone must be working, because he still clutched his lasso. He whirled the loop above his head in slow circles. He would have one attempt only. There was no way he'd be able to gather up his rope again with-out falling and, looking down, it seemed that the drop would probably be fatal. Hooking his fingers into a crevice and clamping his knees to the dragonfly's sides, Will threw his right arm forward and flicked his wrist. The long rope snaked out at an agonising speed, as if time stood still. Amazingly, the loop slithered over the insect's huge triangular head. Will tugged hard on the rope, pulling it tight.

He'd done it.

Like a magic charm had been cast, the dragonfly stopped its mad flight. Now captive, the insect transformed into a different creature altogether. It made chirping noises when Will spoke soothingly, veering in any direction the elf wanted to go with the slightest pressure from his legs.

They flew downward, close to the stream. 'You're mine now,' he whispered, bending low so that his breath caused a fine mist on the mirrored surface of the insect's back.

★ ★ ★

Beatrice wailed. Tatty hugged the squalling child, though she felt in need of comfort herself. After all this time, Will must be dead. What would she tell Mr and Mrs Patch? As they walked away from the stream to begin the trek home, a familiar voice rang out. She turned in time to see him appear around a bend in the stream, standing upright on the dragonfly's back, whooping like an idiot.

'See, Beattie, there he is safe an' sound. He's naughty, gettin' us all worried like that?'

'Mm,' answered Beatrice. "E's a little imp.'

'Yes,' said Tatty, quickly drying her face on her sleeve.

Will brought the dragonfly to a halt and leapt from its back. 'Not worried were you?' he yelled, laughing.

'Worried? *Us?* Course not. Just wonderin' what took you so

long.'

'Ha, ha, very funny. Seriously, what do you think of him? Great, isn't he?' Will grinned and removed the lasso from the dragonfly's head. It nuzzled his hand to be petted.

Tatty studied the insect's dazzling colours. 'He's all right,' she answered, peevishly, 'but we've been here for ages and I think it's time we got Beattie back home.' In truth, she was annoyed at him for taking such a stupid risk. Weren't their everyday lives dangerous enough already?

'Oh … right,' he said. 'I'll just tell Blue to go.'

'Blue?'

'Yes, I know, it's simple, but he seems to like it.'

'I likes it too,' said Beatrice.

'How're you goin' to catch him again?' asked Tatty. 'He's an insect, with an insect's brain, he'll forget all about you in a second.'

'No he won't. Accordin' to Pa, these olden-time ones are very loyal. Once they've been caught they only ever have one master – and that's me. I should be able to call him in future, to get him to come to me.'

'I'll believe that when I see it,' said Tatty.

Will ignored her and instead whispered something to the dragonfly that she couldn't hear. It flew off and hovered over the water.

They walked back to The Patch, mostly in silence. The only person chatting was Beatrice, who asked Will and Tatty a zillion questions:

'Why're buttercups called buttercups when dere's no butter in 'em?'

'Why're dragonflies called dat? Dey're not real dragons, are dey?'

'Hawse ches'nuts 'abn't got hawses in 'em, hab dey?'

Tatty and Will gave terse replies:

'I don't know.'

'Because they are.'

'Dunno why they're called horse chestnuts – ask Ma.'

Beatrice skipped along, merrily unaware, as very young children often do.

When they entered The Patch, Tatty was relieved to find that Daisy had finished delousing the children. The parasites floated about in a jar of pickling vinegar on the mantelpiece.

'Did you behave, Beattie?' asked Daisy. 'I hope you were a good girl? She wasn't too noisy, was she? Did you catch anythin', Will?'

Before Will could speak, Tatty said, 'Oh Will caught the most amazing dragonfly, Mrs Patch. The biggest I've ever seen, big enough to ride. It was wonderful, seein' him tame it.' She snuck a look at Will and saw the blush spread up his neck. A smile twitched at the corner of his mouth.

They could never fall out for long.

'Good – good. That's nice, dear,' said Mrs Patch, sitting by the window and darning a hole in one of Mr Patch's socks. Her fingers moved like quicksilver. Within three seconds of threading the needle she was finishing the last stitch, neatly snipping the thread with her teeth.

It was a magic of sorts, Tatty supposed, the way elves were good at mending and making things really fast. But it wasn't *proper* magic, which faeries were capable of. Then she scolded herself for feeling so superior. Some said all faery-folk had shared magic equally, numberless years ago, when the beginnings of their kind first fell from the sky trapped inside strange rocks, long before humankind had even been dreamed of. It was funny, she thought, how her race, the Keridd, had grown wings and special powers, while the Dann people, from whom every elf was descended, remained flightless.

Beatrice sat on the floor with her brothers and sisters. They played Spin-the-Spider, something she and Will had done when they were younger. A brown-striped spider was tied to the top of a wooden spinning-top. Its legs were splayed out and it gnashed its mouth-parts in anger.

'My turn – my turn!' shouted Charlie-boy. Will's youngest brother grasped the spider by two of its eight legs and spun it with all his strength. The spider and the top were a brown fuzzy blur as they whirled on the floor in the middle of the elven circle. Beatrice gripped Charlie-boy's arm in excited fear when the top began to slow and wobble. Each child shrieked with relief when the spider's backside veered away from them. 'Please, not me again!' squealed Rosie, with cobweb still hanging from her plaits. Finally, after one last juddering turn, the spider-top halted in front of Charlie-boy. 'Aw, rats,' he mumbled, as silky tendrils billowed from the spider's spinnerets, engulfing him in fine cobweb. On, and on, the white threads streamed, firing outward.

The children laughed themselves hoarse, until their mother interrupted. 'Hurry an' get his face uncovered. *Before* he suffocates! And put the cobweb in my basket with the rest, I'll make you girls some nice silk stockings. Rosie, release that poor creature and put it outside now, will you? Tatty, would you like to stay for a bite to eat?'

'Oh, no thank you, Mrs Patch. I've an errand to run for Ma this afternoon.' She elbowed Will, hard.

'Y – Yes, and I said I'd help,' he stammered.

'Oh, there's a good boy,' said Daisy, getting up and giving him a hug. 'I'm proud to have such a helpful son.'

Will blushed. Outside, he said, 'What was that all about? You nearly broke my ribs.'

'The other day I overheard Ma tellin' Nan that the Brambleton's were having a Grand Cupboard Openin' Ceremony. I don't know what's so grand about openin' a cupboard, but I want to go.' Tatty's face shone with excitement.

'But we *can't*,' said Will. 'Children aren't allowed, it's ladies only at them things. If they catch me, I'll get a thrashin'.'

'They won't catch us. We'll be careful. Anyway, don't you want to know what goes on?'

'Yes. I asked Ma about it, ages ago…' His face took on a dreamy appearance; '…then she belted me with 'er shoe and said I'd find out when I'm older – weird!'

'Come on then. It might've already started. We'll sneak in through the Brambleton's scullery.'

'All right,' he said, reluctantly. 'But if we get caught I'm blamin' you!'

On the way to the Brambleton's, Tatty kept taking to the air, forcing Will to run to catch up. 'Hurry,' she yelled. 'We don't want to miss anything!'

Will was unaware that he mouthed rude words as he thought them.

She turned to face him, hovering. 'What's that you're sayin'?'

'Nothin',' he replied, hurrying after her.

~CHAPTER ELEVEN~

'Matoes!

Agatha Pottage pushed an old-fashioned pram along the hot pavement with a long fuchsia-painted fingernail. In her other hand she held a lacy fan, which she wafted in front of her face. That was the trouble with dressing entirely in black: it did absorb the heat dreadfully. But tradition was tradition.

The pram itself was curiously empty.

Agatha scanned the surrounding homes. Cooper's Close looked deserted. It was a weekday, so everybody appeared to be out at work. The only driveway to have a car parked on it was in front of Bert and Dot's bungalow, at the far end of the cul-de-sac.

Number five, Cooper's Close, was very neat, with perfectly trimmed box-hedging and pretty baskets of flowers. Movement in one of the windows caught Agatha's eye. It was the fluffy-haired wife, Dot. A mildly irritating person, thought Agatha, the way she talked non-stop about absolutely nothing. Whenever Dot had popped into Agatha's shop, Pottage's, it had been a nightmare to get rid of her. Once, Dot was droning on and on about the perfect size of her and Bert's award-winning tomatoes, and how they *always* won first prize in the fruit and vegetable section at Upham Summer Fayre. Much later, Agatha thought she'd learned all there was to know about how much feed tomatoes needed, what temperature was crucial for perfect ripeness, and what spray to use if they were attacked by pests. Agatha would have given anything for a can of pest repellent at that precise moment – to use on Dot! Instead, knowing the woman hated anything with feathers (caused by her young cat bringing twitchy, almost-dead-but-not-quite, little bodies in from the garden), Agatha had made Chorley's cage door burst open, whereby the huge raven had hopped on to the shop counter, fixed Dot with a steely eye and croaked: "M-m-matoes!' It worked like a dream. Dot had fled, screeching something about how all mynah birds should be shot on sight.

She hadn't entered Pottage's since.

Agatha stood behind a bush and studied the bungalow. Dot bustled about in the kitchen, singing away like a budgerigar being strangled. Quickly checking to make sure nobody was watching, and with some carefully selected words, Agatha turned the pram back into a bicycle and took a velvet pouch from her handbag. Inside the pouch was some grey powder: *moondust*. She sprinkled a pinch onto the bicycle to make it weightless. It rose into the air and Agatha grabbed the bike before it floated away.

Dot disappeared through a doorway, giving Agatha the chance she needed. 'Time to go home now,' she whispered. 'Up you go, bike.' She watched the Chopper soar over the front garden, towards the Bottomley's garage. She stamped her foot and the garage door slid upward, allowing the bicycle to float inside. It came to rest leaning against a big gas barbeque. Before she closed the garage door, Agatha thought of something else, the finishing touch. With a POP! a thick paper label appeared out of nowhere and attached itself to the bike's handlebars by a piece of string. Agatha made hand movements as if she were writing a note, and writing appeared on the label, in green ink:

I hope you're recovering well ~
From your little friend,

With kind regards.

Agatha charmed the garage door closed and turned her back on number five, Cooper's Close, nearly tripping over a horrendously fat black and white cat. It rubbed against her legs, weaving a figure-of-eight through them. 'Sorry,' she said, 'I already have a Familiar, Chorley is his name, but if I ever have a vacancy, you'll be the first to know. Now, if you'll excuse me, I'm in rather a hurry. Good day.' She nudged the cat aside and strode along the pavement, fanning her face and wishing she'd brought a shady umbrella. Agatha hoped Tatty would be pleased with her efforts. And it *had* been an effort too, coming out in this relentless sunshine, not at all suited to her witchy skin: genetically designed for storm and shadow.

Delilah stared after the witch and then ambled into the driveway of number five. She wondered if it was pilchards for lunch again … She liked pilchards, but not as much as she liked mice!

CHAPTER TWELVE

The Grand Cupboard Openin' Ceremony

The cottages were fashioned from discarded things: baskets; broken flowerpots; barrels; even a metal watering can: very noisy whenever it rained, though the spout made an excellent chimney.

The dirt pathways and lanes of Little Upham were deserted, with folk avoiding the hottest part of the day. Will and Tatty soon arrived in a small orchard where there were only six dwellings. The Brambles, an old wooden fruit crate, had the words *PRODUCE OF SPAIN* printed over the front door. A huge straw hat served as a roof (the sort seen at family weddings, worn by loopy great-aunts who are stuck in the Middle Ages), complete with a big peach-coloured plastic flower plonked on the side. Unlike the Willow Tree, which had round windowpanes made from rippled glass, The Brambles' windows were glazed with brightly-coloured sweet wrappers nailed tightly in their frames: pretty, but with a tendency to shrink in strong sunlight, so they needed replacing often.

In the back garden, Tatty and Will crouched beneath an open window. They could hear conversation inside. Tatty recognised one of the voices: *Ma's.*

'Do calm down, Violet, dear. You'll make yourself ill. We've a while to go yet. Would you like another cherry brandy?'

Violet Brambleton sounded fed up. 'No I wouldn't! I can't take much more of this hangin' around. Eustace and I have waited for a family of our own for so long. Oh, it's been such a strain, it really has. Ahh … perhaps I *will* have another teensy brandy after all, just to settle my nerves.'

Tatty turned to Will. 'Ma didn't mention she'd be comin' here today. We'll have to be extra careful.'

Will's face looked grey. 'Y – You mean you're still goin' in?'

'Of course,' said Tatty. 'Aren't you?'

'Shhh! – Quiet!' he hissed. 'Um, I am if you are. But I'll completely understand if you change your mind.'

'Change my mind? Why would I do that? I'm goin' now, Will Patch, before your ditherin' rubs off on me.' She crawled through the open back door.

Will gave his luck-stone a quick rub and followed.

They entered a narrow scullery where food scraps lay heaped in a big tin bucket. Shiny ladybird wing-casings were on top of the heap. Fried ladybirds were a favourite of Will's. His stomach gave a low rumble. Just then an elderly faery, sitting near the doorway of an adjoining room, spun around in her chair. Will and Tatty froze, hidden behind a shrew-skin hanging from the ceiling.

'What ish it, Effie?' asked a slurred voice that sounded like Violet Brambleton's.

The old faery peered through the doorway for a moment, before turning away. 'Nothin', thought I heard somethin', that's all. Shall I shut the back door?'

Dread flooded Tatty's veins. Will panicked and grabbed at the back of her shift so that it bit painfully into her wings and half-strangled her. She held her breath.

The same slurred voice spoke again.

'Naw, it'sh too hot. Leave it open for the time being. 'S probably a cockroach. They're a nuisance. I'll curse it later … make a nice broth.'

The parlour buzzed with friendly chat again.

Tatty prised Will's fingers from her shift. She saw that the womenfolk had their backs to the door. She mouthed, 'Come on,' and they crawled through the doorway, straight under a long, cloth-covered table.

The table divided a semi-circle of chairs. On the chairs sat elves and faeries of every age. The table had been laid with all kinds of succulent dishes. There were plates piled high with deep-fried ladybirds; aphid and tomato salad; boiled beetle egg and cress sandwiches. In the centre, on a big platter, lay a golden honey-roasted shrew. Tatty and Will wriggled the length of the table and lifted the tablecloth. They saw the guests chatting, knitting, eating, and nodding off. Sunlight shone through the sweet wrapper windowpane, giving every face a blue tinge.

Tatty was nervous, but excited. The air in the room seemed thick and woolly.

'I've got a headache,' said Will.

'What do you think's going to happen?' Tatty whispered.

'If we knew that we wouldn't be here.' One of Tatty's wings flicked up and hit him on the back of the head. 'Would you mind keepin' those things under control?'

'Sorry!' She giggled nervously.

'Keep your voice down, too,' he hissed. 'Someone will hear.'

A booming voice rang out, making everyone jump. 'COULD WE HAVE ABSOLUTE SILENCE, *PLEASE!*' yelled Miss Pleasant, local midwife and part-time healer. She was square-shaped, with piggy eyes and a purple nose, which Nan reckoned was caused by a certain fondness for 'the drink'. And her apron always looked like it could do with a good boil wash. 'Hush, I said, ladies. Thank you … Thank you … QUIET!' She fixed the gathering with an icy stare, daring them to interrupt. 'As you know, we have met today on this most auspicious occasion to bear witness to the arrival of Eustace and Violet

Brambleton's first child–'

Tatty stared at Will.

'–and some of you may also be aware that I was present at the arrival of Eustace himself.'

Eustace Himself was nowhere to be seen.

Nurse Pleasant stood next to a small iron-hinged door in the corner of the parlour. She laid her beefy hands upon it, moving them lightly over the wood as if examining a patient. The cupboard door bowed inwards and out, as if it breathed. The blue light in the parlour dimmed. The womenfolk murmured and nudged one another.

'It's cooler now, isn't it?' said Tatty. 'Can you hear that hummin'?'

'Hummin'?' said Will. 'That's your imagination, that is. Hang on a minute …' He gulped. 'Look at the cupboard!'

From gaps at the top and bottom of the door, through cracks in the wood, an eerie green light shone out in pulsing waves. The door bowed outward so much that it seemed about to give way completely, before settling back again.

Uneasy now, Will said, 'Whatever's in there seems to want to get out – don't you think?'

Tatty glanced at the womenfolk to the right and left. Food hovered before half-open mouths, all knitting and mending was placed on laps. The air was full of crackling energy.

Will let out a moan. 'Aw, I don't like it – I shouldn't even be here – it's not my *place*!'

'Shurrup,' hissed Tatty, poking him. 'It's too late now.' Though, she too was beginning to wonder if coming to The Brambles had been such a good idea.

Standing with her palms flat against the cupboard and her head bowed, Miss Pleasant was an impressive figure, despite her unwashed appearance. Lavender wings, kept folded before, now spread wide, veins pulsing with sparkling blood. Her eyes were closed and when she spoke her voice had changed: it echoed.

'Oh nature's child, your time is near,
Be wide awake, and do not fear,
The light of day to you we give,
We've banished darkness, so you may live–'

Wind gusted through the parlour, uncoiling Miss Pleasant's untidy bun. Her hair blew around her head like squirming vipers.

Tatty grabbed the tablecloth and held it down.

Struggling with her billowing skirts, Miss Pleasant took a heavy-looking bunch of rusty keys from her apron pocket. Her tongue protruded from between her teeth as she selected a key, which she tried to insert into the keyhole. However, the cupboard had other plans: the keyhole darted about all over the door, dodging the jabbing key, so that deep gouges were left in the wood every time Miss Pleasant missed.

Tatty heard the midwife mutter an unpleasant word.

Then, after another scarring lunge, the key slipped into the keyhole. Nurse Pleasant took a moment to catch her breath, before carrying on with the incantation:

'By opening this cupboard, wide,
We're askin' you to come outside,
We've waited here for five long years,
Wiped away a thousand tears,
Weaved magic 'til our work is done,
Your life today has just – BEGUN!'

On the last echoing word, Miss Pleasant heaved the cupboard door open. It fought against her strong hands, so she had to pin it open with her body. Finally, the door gave a last judder and became still. The green light inside the cupboard was unbearably bright. Everyone had to shield their eyes against the glare. Thick smoke swirled across the floor, sulphurous and choking, rolling up the walls, so that aprons and handkerchiefs were held against noses and mouths. Tatty and Will were lucky to be on the floor where the air was clearer.

Soon the smoke began to fade.

An ugly looking brown thing hung inside the cupboard like a

withered prune.

'What is it?' asked Tatty.

'It looks like some kind of … *chrysalis*,' said Will. 'And I reckon Mr and Mrs Brambleton's child's inside.'

Tatty screwed up her face.

'Don't look so disgusted, it would've been how you were born.'

'Urgh – stop! You're makin' me feel sick,' Tatty said, trying not to gag. She shivered at the sight of the twitching thing. 'What a thought … that I was inside one of those horri–'

'Shh!' Will said, silencing her. 'Something's happenin'.'

The chrysalis began to squirm; lumps and bumps appeared over its surface as the thing inside tried to break out. A split appeared near the top, where a stalk-like protrusion glued it to the top of the cupboard. The split lengthened. Thick green slime oozed out and plopped onto the dirt floor. Next, a small hand appeared, followed by an arm and a shoulder. *It* emerged and dragged its body free of the chrysalis, dropping to the floor with a squelch. The bedraggled child sat cross-legged, exhausted, head drooping. Tiny wings, which had been as crumpled as withered petals, began to unfurl as new blood pumped into them.

Miss Pleasant grabbed the little creature and rubbed it with an old scratchy towel. She filled the cupboard doorway, blocking the view. The child began to bawl at its rough treatment, causing the womenfolk to 'Aaaaaah' in unison.

As Violet Brambleton gulped down another large cherry brandy, Miss Pleasant finished cleaning the child and dragged it from the cupboard by an arm. 'Congratulations, Violet, dear.' She smiled for the first time and thrust the naked child in front of her. 'It's a little boy.'

Violet glowed as everybody congratulated her. She gave a fried ladybird to her new son. He stopped bawling immediately and grabbed the insect, wolfing it down in three massive bites of his very white sharp teeth. He made it clear to his mother with grunts and warbles that he'd like another one.

'Aw, got a good appetite,' said an elf with a soup stain on her dress and an ear-trumpet sticking out of one ear. 'What are you goin' to call 'im, Vi'?'

'Well,' said Violet, 'probably Eustace, after his father and grandfather.' She saw their dismayed looks and added quickly, 'But there's been a Eustace in the family for generations.'

'Oh, that's cruel Violet!' Marigold protested. 'We used to call Eustace "Useless Eustace" when we were young. Please don't saddle the poor child with that dreadful name!'

Everyone agreed with Marigold, but Violet insisted it was out of her hands. She couldn't even turn to her husband for support, as he'd been packed off to his mother's that morning by Miss Pleasant, with strict orders not to return until he was summoned (though he hadn't minded too much, as Violet's moody outbursts were starting to get tiresome. He thought that Violence might be a better name for her, what with all the pots and pans he'd dodged lately).

As discussion over the child's name grew more heated, nobody noticed him take some wobbly steps until he raised a chubby finger, squealed, 'Whassat?' and pointed beneath the table.

Tatty let the tablecloth fall into place and froze, certain they would be discovered.

'Ahh,' said the elf in the stained dress. 'Look at 'im Vi'. He wants another ladybird, bless 'im.'

Violet handed a second ladybird to her golden-haired son. He stuffed it into his mouth, instantly distracted from the children under the table.

As everyone crowded around the new-born, holding recently knitted clothes against him to check they'd fit, Will and Tatty crawled out from under the table, in to the scullery, then back outside to the garden, taking a seldom-used pathway back to the Willow Tree and meeting no one. They stood outside the willow's door, where, a moment later, Marigold arrived, landing beside them with her face flushed pink from the flight. 'Afternoon, Willum,' she said. 'Would you like to come in and stay for a bit of tea?'

'Yes, please, that'd be lovely, Mrs Moon.'

Marigold smiled. 'Excitin' wasn't it, at The Grand Cupboard Openin' Ceremony?'

Before a single thought had a chance to pop into her brain, Tatty gushed: 'Oh yes, *really* excitin' ...' She paused. 'Aw, Ma, you did that on purpose!'

Marigold laughed. 'I couldn't help it. I saw you under the table when Miss Pleasant got started. The tablecloth twitched and there wasn't a breath of wind then. You both took a great risk. I reckon that luck-stone must be working, Willum.'

He blushed. 'Yes, Mrs Moon. Thanks, Mrs Moon.'

'Thanks, Ma, for keepin' quiet,' said Tatty.

'Come on, you two imps,' laughed Marigold, holding the old door open; 'let's see what Nan's cooking up.'

'*Imps!*' said Tatty indignantly. 'We're not *that* naughty.'

~CHAPTER THIRTEEN~

Caterpillar Daydreams

After wolfing down a scrumptious tea, Will felt his stomach was about to burst. Tatty's gran had put on a lovely spread, but she'd watched him with a pained expression when he'd dropped crumbs on the tablecloth. They'd eaten aphid pie, followed by redcurrant tarts; butterfly cakes made with real butterfly extract, making them light as air. He grinned as he recalled how Papa drank his tea from the saucer, holding it at arms-length and sucking up the liquid into a golden column, so that it whirled between his lips as if through an invisible straw. Will was mesmerised. Mrs Moon had scolded her husband for tiring himself out. Minutes after, the old gentleman fell asleep in the middle of eating a cake. It dropped on the floor and Mrs Moon picked it up, grumbled, brushed off specks of dirt and put it back on his plate.

"Old still before I pulverise ya!'

Will froze. The voice was sickeningly familiar. He looked up the track, but saw no one. He looked back the way he'd come. No one there either? He heard a rustling sound. Carefully parting the leaves of a big plant, Will watched Burnley *Snot*grass at play with a feeling of loathing. The bully held a piece of curved glass in one hand while pinning down a struggling caterpillar with the other, trying to burn its skin with the sun's rays. Will let the leaves fall back into place. *What'll I do?* He chewed on his bottom lip. *Just go home, stupid,* he thought, *pretend you didn't see anything.* But he *had* seen something. How could he leave and let the poor creature suffer? It was just a caterpillar, but still … He'd never be able to sleep later if he did nothing. So, before he knew what was happening, Will stood behind Burnley. He prodded the elf on his back. Burnley swung around, releasing his hold on the caterpillar. It wriggled away into tall grass.

'Neptune's Trident, Patch! You made me jump!' snarled Burnley, leaping to his feet. The elf stood a head taller than Will. His handsome face was spoiled by an ugly sneer. 'What d' ya think you're doin', eh – ruinin' my fun!'

Will gulped and his voice shook. 'Why d – don't you p – p – pick on someone your own size, Burnley? Leave d – defenceless creatures alone!' It all came out a bit high-pitched for his liking. Hot tears sprang into his eyes. *No. Don't cry … Please …*

Burnley cackled. 'That's you that is – a defenceless *creature!*' He spat the last word with such venom that droplets of spit landed on Will's face. Will was too scared to wipe them away. Burnley brought his face lower, so that their noses almost touched. 'How's that dung heap you live in then, Patch? Good job it hasn't rained for ages – saved us all from the stink! So, think you can interrupt my game and get away with it, do you?'

'Um – no, not really.'

'Where's your *faery* friend? You know, Moon-face? Not 'ere to protect you today, is she?'

Anger blazed white-hot in Will's chest. 'At least I *have* a friend.' He stood on tiptoe, eyes level with Burnley's chin. 'What friends have you got, Burnley *Snot*grass? Real friends I'm talkin' about – not ones who tag along 'cause they're too scared not to. *None,* that's how many!'

For a moment Burnley stared in silence. Will noticed a vein twitching in the elf's throat and thought it was probably a bad sign.

'What did you call me, you little pus-bucket!?' roared Burnley, grabbing Will by the collar and drawing back a fist. Will shut his eyes and braced himself for the blow.

As expected, pain exploded in his nose and a bright light flared behind his eyelids. Burnley shoved him to the ground. He lay still, pretending to be unconscious. Trickling warmth ran down his cheek. He fought the urge to brush it away.

It was a long time before he cautiously opened one eye.

Burnley had disappeared.

Will got to his feet. He felt his nose run and took a handkerchief from his pocket, which he pressed to his nostrils before inspecting it: *Blood.* He was surprised at how much of the red stuff one nose could hold. He felt a bit sick and fuzzy-minded, but also strangely happy. *Well, who'd have thought it, eh? He, Willum Patch, had stood up to the village bully – and lived!* With his head held back to slow the bleeding, he stumbled rather a lot on his way home.

★★★

The caterpillar watched the elf leave with no memory of having met him whatsoever. It looked away, munched on a leaf, and carried on with its strange daydreams about flying …

★★★

It was late. The table had been cleared. Nan sat spinning a clump of wool, and Marigold knitted socks for the cold months of The Long Sleep. Tatty curled at her mother's feet, thinking how lucky elves were, not having to spend a third of the year unconscious. She was envious of Will's tales of fun in the snow. Not that it *always* snowed – sometimes he spoke of endless weeks of rain and the odour of The Patch's dung weatherproofing. Tatty had seen snow a handful of times. Once, she'd woken on a March morning to find a blanket of whiteness covering Little Upham like a glittering overcoat. It had lasted a whole day, though next morning the spring sunshine melted it all away.

Papa rocked his chair and polished his pipe. He whispered and the pipe began whistling.

Nan knew the melody and her foot bounced along to the

65

rhythm. 'Not too long with that magic now,' she said. 'You hear, Victor?'

'I won't,' he replied with a wink.

It was dark outside. Tatty went to the window and pressed her face against the cool glass, cupping her hands around her eyes to block out the glow from the candlelight. The silhouettes of trees looked scary against the purple backdrop of sky. *Like spiky ogres,* she thought. Not that she'd ever seen an ogre, seeing as how the last one had died out ages before in a remote corner of the Scottish Highlands. She tried to see how long she could stare without blinking. Her eyes began to water. Then THUMP! Something black and leathery hit the glass. 'Ogre!' she cried, and ran to her grandfather. 'Out there!'

Papa's concentration broke and the pipe stopped playing. 'Hush, child,' he said. 'There's no ogres any more, and they never lived this far south anyway. Come on;' he stood, 'let's see what all the fuss is about.' At the window he squinted through the wobbly glass. 'Hah! Thought as much. Come an' have a look, Tatty.'

She went slowly to the window. Papa placed a hand on her shoulder. 'See, there's your ogre. You've seen them plenty of times before. Nothin' but a perishin' Divin' Past! It hit the window by accident, lookin' for its supper, that's all.'

Her heart slowed its hammering. She watched the dark shapes zoom past the willow. They'd always looked so small before. It was the first time she'd seen one so close.

'Don't fret, he can't get in,' said Papa, smiling. 'He wouldn't hurt you anyway, you're too big.' Then he yelled excitedly: 'Look! There goes another Divin' Past!'

She reddened. When she was very small, she'd thought the bats were called Diving Pasts – because that's what everyone yelled when the creatures zoomed through the skies. Nobody let her forget it, even though the joke had worn thin.

'Here 'e comes – another Divin' Past!' yelled Papa, again.

'Shusssh, yes, all right, that'll do, Pops,' Marigold said, trying not to laugh.

Later, after flying up to bed, holding a candle to light the way, Tatty dreamed of a suffocating chrysalis, and watched Will fall head-first down a big hole in the dirt, his mouth open in surprise as he disappeared. She dreamed she ran forward and called his name into the earth tunnel, but there was no answer, just the sound of scuttling footfalls. His luck-stone lay at the mouth of the hole, discarded …

Her pillow grew damp with dream-tears.

~CHAPTER FOURTEEN~

Agatha

Tatty woke with the remains of a dream drifting inside her head, but try as she might she couldn't remember the details. She'd go and see Will, and then visit Pottage's to ask Aggie about the Biggun's bi-sickle. She wouldn't let Will know: she hadn't changed her mind about not mentioning the Biggun. It was safer, for all of them. Looking through her spyglass, she saw Alf Patch up the Lookout Tree. So, nothing had come of the flock of magpies, after all. *Thank the stars.*

Mr Patch had the same unruly black hair as Will's; tufts stuck out from beneath a green felt hat, a little wooden flute tucked in the hatband. Tatty thought he looked tired and thin. Though the Crow's Nest was lined with goose-down and covered with a shingled roof to keep off bad weather, Mr Patch had completed some long watches lately. If a person was wingless, it was an hour's climb up rope ladders to reach the Crow's Nest before the shift had even started. *Poor Mr Patch, stuck up there for thirteen hours a day.* Shifts were decided by pulling names from a hat. Will said his father reckoned the hat had a jinx on it, because his name had been picked out five times in a row now, and if it carried on he'd have no choice but to go to The Palace Over Yonder to have the hat tested.

Tatty tried to remember when the last lert had been called? *It must be over a year ago*, she decided: It was dusk when the warning had sounded. A voice echoed down the hollow deer-bone in the Crow's Nest: *'LERT! LERT! – THIS IS A LERT! – STAY CALM AND GET INSIDE AS QUICKLY AS YOU CAN! – I REPEAT, THIS IS A LERT!'* She had stood in the doorway of the Willow Tree as Nan came barging past, grumbling about how there hadn't been any lerts for ages and what a fine time to call one when she hadn't even had time to lock the pantry, and that they'd all be robbed blind. But her grandmother wasn't grumbling next morning when she learned of old Widow Hensfoot's fate: on her way home after bartering for a bag of barley, she'd failed to hear the weasel approach. Two stripy stockinged legs sticking out of its mouth were the last anyone saw of her. Nan never stopped praising the Watchers now, and their marvellous early-warning system.

Tatty dressed quickly and hoisted the spyglass back up to the ceiling; then plummeted head-first down the shaft before stopping a hair's-width from the floor.

'I wish you wouldn't do that, Tatty. You'll bash your brains out one day,' said Nan, bashing pans about on the stove.

'Wish in one hand, poo in the other – see which one gets filled first,' Tatty chanted.

'That's enough of that talk!'

'But Papa says it all the time ...'

'Yes, and if *I* hear 'im I'll knock his block off!'

Tatty ate her breakfast in silence, before leaving for The Patch. As she went out the door, Nan's voice rang in her ears: 'Don't be gone too long, young lady. I've got an important chore for you later.'

Soon after, Tatty landed at The Patch and knocked on the door. It was opened by Will. 'What've you got planned today? No more sneakin' into private ceremonies, I hope?'

'No, nothin' like that.' She smiled. 'There's somewhere we haven't been for a long time. I reckon we deserve a treat.'

69

'A treat …?'

Tatty whispered, 'Pottage's.'

★★★

They smelled Traders' Row before they saw the place. A curious blend of scents hung in the air: leather; herbs; cabbage; freshly sawn timber; spices, roasted nuts and insects, all mixed with a whiff of stale urine. Shops were crammed together like two rows of crooked teeth. The upper floors stuck out, seemingly unsupported, like they were about to collapse on top of everybody. Tatty and Will entered the main pebble-cobbled street with its central channel to take away liquid waste (which was flung down from the buildings' upper storeys without warning). Most of the shops had rippled glass in the windows, while others had openings with wooden shutters.

They passed *Goldensoles*, the cobbler's. An elf with a grizzled beard stood in holey socks, waiting for his boots to be mended, a grasshopper tucked under one arm as payment. The insect rubbed its back legs together noisily. 'Pipe down,' cried the elf, 'or I'll fricassee ya!'

Next, they passed Miss McCorduroy's dress shop, pushing through the crowd gathered outside. Will paused to stare at the models parading up and down inside. Tatty thought they looked ridiculous in their impractical, sheer, floating fabrics. As they walked on, Will wanted to know what Tatty had brought with her to trade.

'Nothin',' she replied. 'I'll put it on Nan's tab. She gets Papa mint humbugs and brings Aggie some of her jams an' stuff.'

'You can't do that,' Will protested. 'Your gran will go mad. And she'll put the blame on me – you know she will!'

'She won't notice a cone of toffee …' but, suddenly, Tatty wasn't so sure; Nan wasn't easily fooled, and maybe Aggie wouldn't let them put it on the tab anyway?

'It's all right,' said Will, 'I've got somethin'.'

'You have?' Tatty was surprised. Will didn't have many possessions.

He said nothing, but kept walking past a narrow shop that sold

70

foul-tasting tonics and potions. *Tonics for Chronics*, was run by an elven couple, Mr and Mrs Windybank. They had run the shop since 1866. Some of their recipes dated back several thousand years. They wore matching feathered hats and both had sickly complexions even though they traded in medicines.

'Weevil and wild chive tonic – gets rid of foot odour!' shouted Mrs Windybank, who was alone today.

'Gets rid of cheesy feet, but gives you a hairy back,' said Will, giggling.

'Oi, you, I'll 'ave you for desiccation of character!' yelled Mrs Windybank, her eyes wild and feverish-looking.

'Oops,' said Will.

Tatty saw Will rub his luck-stone. *No, not that. He couldn't.* She grabbed his arm and swung him around. 'You've got nothin' in your pockets, Will. You're thinking of tradin' that stone, aren't you?'

He pulled free and shrugged. 'What if I am? I reckon it was only chance that I caught Blue. I mean, how long have I had this stone?' He lifted the thick twine and turned the stone in his hands, poking his finger through the hole in the middle. 'Five years, maybe six? It's never brought me luck before, has it? I bet it'll keep us supplied with sweets for a whole year. And I'm sick of luggin' the thing around with me. I've got a massive bruise on my hip where it bumps against the bone … probably caused me permanent damage.' He rubbed his hipbone vigorously.

'But Aggie gave you that stone for your birthday, remember? It'd be like thowin' it back in her face!'

'Ouch, that'd hurt.' Will giggled at his own joke.

'It's not funny. I mean it, she'll be upset.'

'She won't be upset.' He grinned. 'She's got a soft spot for me has Aggie.'

'Don't whine when she throws you out of her shop,' said Tatty. 'Come on, let's get a move on. At this rate it'll be midnight before we get there.'

As they walked, Will whispered, 'How do you think she 'eard me,' he nodded his head towards Mrs Windybank, 'when we're right over here?'

Mrs Windybank shouted after them, ' I 'eard you, young elf, 'cause I take a tincture of bat juice every mornin';' she turned to passing faery-folk, who paused to see what the fuss was about, 'what gives me hexaggerated 'earing! NOW CLEAR ORFF! – No, no, not you, sir. I was talkin' to them two scallywags over there …'

Tatty became aware that they were being followed, though she'd heard nothing. A tingling feeling started in the palm of her hand.

'I haven't seen white wings like those since I was knee-high to a grasshopper,' said a velvety voice.

Tatty spun around. 'Sorry … were you talkin' to me?'

The smartly dressed, dusty-looking gentleman had snow-white hair tied in a pony-tail; untidy strands fell across his face. His eyes were dark blue and piercing. He smiled. 'Yes, I was addressing you, my dear. Alas, my wings aren't at their best at the moment. The rigours of travel, you see.' He raised his sky-blue wings and clapped them together. Dust and scales billowed from them, making him cough.

Tatty gave a nervous laugh. She couldn't see a glow around the old gentleman, so couldn't tell if he had a kind heart or not. 'Oh – well – um – my ma says that white ones like mine are rare … though I'd much rather have coloured ones.'

'Does she? Yes, yes, coloured ones *are* nice. And where does your mother reside now, exactly? I've rather lost track of her. I'm an old acquaintance, you see.'

Tatty was about to explain that she wasn't allowed to speak to strangers, when Will blurted: 'She lives in the old crooked willow.' He turned to Tatty and nodded – his smile fading when he saw her grim expression.

'We've got to go on an errand now,' Tatty explained, pulling Will's sleeve. 'It was nice meeting you.' To Will she hissed: 'Come on *you!*'

72

The gentleman still smiled. 'And I you, my dear, I you. Farewell … for now.' He vanished in another puff of scales and dust.

'Who *was* that toff?' asked Will as they hurried on.

'I don't know,' muttered Tatty, feeling suddenly irritable.

'Well, he knows your ma?'

'So, lots of people do – she does *laundry*. She probably washes his smalls.'

'Oh, yes – right – laundry.'

They came to the hawthorn hedge. A pathway had been worn beneath it. The dim thorny tunnel was cool after the sunlight, and at the far end the exit shone as a white disc of glowing light. They hurried towards it, spurred on by the thought of buttery toffee running down their throats. Then the tunnel plunged into darkness. There was a snuffling sound. A pair of eyes appeared at the end of the tunnel, like orange lanterns.

'What is it?' Will whispered.

'I know what it is – it's that blasted cat again! It's beginnin' to get on my nerves!'

The cat inserted a paw into the prickly tunnel and felt around, trying to hook them with a snagging claw.

'Can't you do something to get rid of it?' asked Will.

A moment later, Tatty barked like a dog, *WOOF – WOOF – GROWLLLL!'*

Will had to cover his ears.

The barking worked. The cat screeched and fled, tail fluffed up in fright.

He slapped Tatty on the back and laughed. 'That was brilliant – really brilliant!'

After checking the cat had definitely gone, they left the safety of the hedge. A weed-covered footpath separated them from the brick side-wall of the General Store. They ran to the base of the wall. 'Wait here,' said Tatty, before flying up to a small window. She landed on the ledge, peering down into the shop through grimy glass.

73

Tall and pretty, Agatha Pottage stood behind the counter and smiled as she served a regular customer: an elderly man with an overweight Jack Russell Terrier on a lead. According to the rules only guide dogs were supposed to enter the store, but, as she'd received no complaints, Agatha chose to ignore them. 'What will it be today, Mr Marshall?' she said.

'What'll it be – be – be?' croaked Chorley, rocking back and forth on a high shelf.

The old man carried on as though the raven hadn't spoken: 'Some mint imperials and a box of waterproof sticking plasters, please Aggie.'

'Nothing for Stubby today then? He's not ill I hope?'

'Naw, nothin' much wrong with him but old age.' Mr Marshall gazed fondly at his companion. 'Truth is – we're both gettin' a bit long in the tooth.' He smiled at Agatha, displaying a set of ill-fitting, startlingly white false teeth. 'Sadly, he's not allowed treats any more – vet says he's too fat.'

Agatha looked at the little bow-legged dog. He *had* grown very fat, mainly because he had the sort of watery seal pup eyes that cried out for treats. 'Poor old chap,' cooed Agatha. The dog lifted a crooked paw and shivered, trying to win a piece of broken biscuit, which Agatha kept in a box behind the counter. 'No biccies today, Stubby. It's for your own good.'

Mr Marshall paid for his items. 'C'mon lad,' he said. 'Let's go 'ome and have a nice cup of tea. That's one treat you're still allowed – without sugar, of course.' He dragged the dog away from the counter by its lead. 'Cheerio Aggie.'

'Bye, see you tomorrow, Mr Marshall.'

The bell over the door tinkled as they went out.

Agatha tidied stacks of newspapers on a shelf. An article on the front page of a local paper, *The Trumpeter*, caught her eye. She brought it to the counter to read. It seemed there was a huge increase in the magpie population in the area; experts were linking this phenomenon to the recent hot weather. Apparently, people had been phoning the paper's offices to complain that the birds were spattering droppings over their cars; laundry; conservatories, and so forth. Agatha tapped the article with a green-painted fingernail. *Chorley, you and I are going to have to keep our eyes peeled. There is no way this is an act of nature.*

The bell over the doorway tinkled again. But this time it didn't stop. Agatha looked up from the paper. There was no one in the shop.

The tinkling continued.

She went to the window and looked right, down Snakecatcher Lane. All she could see was a fat black and white cat sitting next to the telephone box. In the other direction was the gateway to Mould Cottage. Agatha realised that it must be another sort of customer ringing the bell. She hadn't had any of those for a few weeks, so she quickly bolted the door and turned the sign over to read: *CLOSED*. Then she hurried through a doorway at the back of the shop, which led to her private living quarters.

CHAPTER FIFTEEN

Pottage's

Out where Agatha kept her dustbins, and where she parked her turquoise Mini Cooper car, was a miniature sweet shop. Set into the General Store's back wall, the little shop had a maroon-coloured sign with ornate gold lettering, which read: *POTTAGE'S~ Purveyor of the Finest Sweetes Since 1568.* Tatty and Will pushed open the heavy door. Mouth-watering smells of strawberry; aniseed; liquorice and vanilla, filled their nostrils.

They waited by the counter.

An eyeball in the corner swivelled to look at them. It was brown in colour and human-sized, set into a brass mount and connected to a small TV and recorder in Agatha's flat above the shop. Agatha once told them that the eye had belonged to a pirate named Shrewd O'Sullivan, who gained the reputation of both charm and viciousness. She'd won a card game that lasted for five days and nights. The pirate threatened to slit her gizzard when Agatha demanded all the gold he'd wagered. It seemed he'd pretended his gold bullion reserves were much higher than they actually were. Shrewd O'Sullivan had been powerless against the witch's magic, when she'd taken one of his eyes in part payment.

Tatty fidgeted under the gaze of the eye, not least because Agatha had whispered that Shrewd O'Sullivan's parting shot to her was that he would take the eye back one day, 'Come hell or high water!'

★ ★ ★

Nobody directly enquired as to why Agatha Pottage always wore black. She got the impression that the villagers regarded her as a youngish widow. And if anybody did start to pry, Agatha found that holding a handkerchief to her nose and sniffing a bit usually did the trick. They would wriggle with embarrassment and soon change the subject.

The doorway from the store led into a hallway, with stairs going up to Agatha's flat. She looked into a mirror above a side table and smoothed her bun of white-blonde hair, tucking an imaginary strand behind her ear: imaginary, because Agatha never, *ever*, had a hair out of place. She took a pinch of sparkly powder from a silver snuffbox on a chain around her neck and said, 'Minor,' throwing the powder into the air. It floated down in a pink cloud. When it touched her she began to shrink. Soon she couldn't see herself in the mirror at all. The side table rose like a cathedral above her head. To shrink was painful and dizzying, but, luckily, over in seconds.

Underneath the table, Agatha faced the high skirting board. She pressed a knot in the wood and a low door swung outwards. She ducked through and emerged inside an old-fashioned sweet shop, complete with a long wooden counter lined with lots of narrow drawers. Rows of shelves reached the ceiling, and on them sat thimbles and tiny jars containing shrunken sweets.

'Good morning. It's a long time since I've seen you both,' said Agatha, going behind the counter. 'You're a sight for sore eyes.'

'Urgh, please don't mention eyes, Aggie,' said Will, 'what with that one starin' at us.'

'Sorry,' said Agatha, 'but I need to have security in the place. There are people who would empty this shop if they could. Unfortunately, an imp broke in here recently, and before I'd time to shrink it was in an out with half my stock. I didn't even have to check the TV screen to see if an image had recorded, it had rained that day, you see, so I had all the evidence I needed in the wet footprints across the floor: the long middle toe was the give-away.' She turned her attention back to the children. 'Now, my dears, what can I interest you in today? Humbugs? Cough candy? Sherbet lemons …?'

'Toffee, please,' said Tatty. 'The hard stuff.'

'Yes, the hard stuff,' Will echoed.

'Oh,' said Agatha, looking up at the highest shelf. 'That's a nuisance.'

'Sorry,' said Will.

'We could always choose somethin' else,' said Tatty, helpfully.

'No, don't worry. I can reach it.' Agatha took a pinch of powder from the snuffbox and sprinkled it over her knees. 'Major,' she whispered. A pink cloud puffed around her legs, hiding them for a moment. She appeared to rise from the ground, though her feet were still planted on the floor. Below the knee her legs had stretched as thinly as two pieces of spaghetti, looking as if they couldn't possibly support her weight. But she took the thimble from the shelf with ease and used more powder to return to her legs to proper proportions.

'What's in that powder, Aggie?' asked Will.

'Don't be nosy,' said Tatty.

'Oh, that's all right, I don't mind. Will's not being nosy,' Agatha fought the urge to ruffle his thick, black hair; 'he's curious, that's all.'

'It's still rude to ask. Spells are personal things.' Tatty gave the elf a look that said he ought to know better.

'I *said* I don't mind,' said Agatha, watching a pink tinge creep up Will's neck. 'Um, well, I can't remember *all* the ingredients offhand – they're written down in my spell book, but a few I can recall are: a hair from the mane of a Minotaur … um … two drops of mermaid blood; some ink from the Kraken; a red feather from robin redbreast – that's what gives it the pink colour – plus some other herbs and spices from the supermarket.'

'Supermarket?' Tatty was puzzled.

'Yes, a place where humans get a lot of their supplies,' Agatha explained.

'Oh.'

'Thank you, Aggie,' said Will, smiling at the witch.

'Don't mention it. Now, I don't want to appear rude, but I must get back to the other shop soon. Children come out of school at lunchtime and I always get a few popping in. How much toffee would you like?'

'This much,' said Will, holding up the luck-stone.

'I ... see,' said Agatha. 'I'm not sure I stock that much toffee. You'd probably have to give me a while to get it all together. But then, how would you get it home?'

Will looked through the hole in the centre of the stone. He paled, almost dropping it.

'What's the matter, Willum?' Agatha asked; a smile at the corners of her mouth. 'Did you see my kindred spirit? My Familiar?'

'I – I don't know…'

'Let me have a look,' said Tatty, grabbing the stone from his hand. 'Neptune's navel, Aggie! You look just like Chorley.' Where Agatha's own head should have been, there sprouted a raven's head.

Agatha Pottage laughed. '*Like* Chorley, and yet not. He isn't really a pet. You see, in a funny sort of way, he is me and I am him. He can ease me out of awkward situations if I run into them. We're bonded.'

'Bonded?' said Tatty, unable to drag her gaze away from the weird way Agatha's beak moved when she spoke.

'Yes, you see, Familiar comes from the same word as family. The raven has been my family's spirit guide for eight hundred years. If I choose to I can take on Chorley's appearance, and he mine. It came in very handy long ago when witch-hunts were all the rage. I know stories of Familiars who saved their witches' lives by pretending to be be them on the execution pyres. Then, when the pyres were about to be lit the Familiar would change back to animal form, escape the chains and slip away. Mind you, I've only had to use it a handful of times over the years. Once, when a particularly loathsome boy asked me to the school dance and I couldn't get out of going, Chorley went in my place. Oh, I'll bet conversation was exciting that night! Chorley's not known for his vocal abilities, bless his dear heart. Another time at school – goodness I was naughty – I took the appearance of a raven and snuck through the headmaster's office window to look at the answers to the maths exam. Outrageous really, but maths was always my weakest subject. Everyone was so shocked when I got top marks, I shall never forget the looks on their faces …' She smiled dreamily; then realised she still had work to do. 'You can stop staring now, Tatty.'

Tatty put the stone on the counter. 'Sorry.'

'It's to be expected,' said Agatha. 'You can see ghosts through them too, if you happen to be anywhere haunted. My ancestors used to say luck-stones, or hag-stones, belonged to the very first witches, and that they would string them together to make fine necklaces.' She turned to Will. 'I can't say I'm not disappointed that you'd even think of trading this fine piece;' she picked up the stone and studied it; 'and after I shrunk it to suit your size, too. All for some measly toffee.' She let out a long sigh. 'I scoured Brighton beach for hours to find that particular one – such wonderful properties.'

She stopped Will when he tried to apologise. 'Never mind, I shan't hold it against you. But I *shall* hold the luck-stone here in the shop for safe-keeping, under Shrewd O' Sullivan's watchful eye. I won't take the stone in trade, it's too valuable. It was my gift to you, Will, and it shall remain so. If you ever need it, it will be here waiting. I can't be fairer than that, can I?'

'Thank you, Aggie,' said Will.

'Yes,' said Tatty, 'thanks. If you'd given it to me, *I* wouldn't have wanted to trade it, for anything.'

'But, Tatty, why would I have given the luck-stone to you when you have no need of it?'

Tatty reddened. 'I – I–'

'I always find, as a rule, it's usually best to think before one speaks.'

Will sniggered. 'I'm *always* telling her that.'

Tatty dug him sharply with her elbow.

Agatha Pottage laughed and opened a drawer on her side of the counter. It held a variety of things, each shrunken to fit inside the tiny shop: reels of silver and gold thread; exotic feathers; jewellery; a child's silver christening spoon; a freshwater pearl; insects preserved in amber; shells, and a dinosaur egg. She placed Will's stone next to the egg and closed the drawer.

Tatty was worried. 'Aggie, if you're keepin' the stone here … does that mean we can't have any toffee?'

'Of course you may have toffee,' said Agatha; 'as long as you bring me a jar of your gran's honey next time you come. And I'd like a flute like your father's, Will – if that's all right? Chorley likes a bit of music sometimes, as well as a story, before bed.'

'All right with me,' said Tatty.

'And me.'

'Good.' Agatha quickly scribbled an I.O.U on a scrap of paper. She looked around. 'Mm, where did I put my weighing hands, I wonder?'

Will and Tatty looked about vaguely. The weighing hands were usually on the end of the counter.

'They should be here somewhere? Mind you, it's been a while since I had a special customer.' Agatha drummed her fingernails on the counter. 'Oh, I remember – I put them in the trunk. They'd been misbehaving, kept getting things out of the drawers when I told them not to, and they can be *so* heavy-handed, I was scared they'd break something.' She clapped her hands together suddenly. 'Come along, hands. There's work to be done. Chop, chop!'

In the corner, near the shop window, sat an iron-studded trunk. A thumping noise came from inside. The trunk hopped across the floor, before the lid burst open. Thimbles on shelves rattled dangerously. 'Careful!' exclaimed Agatha, as a pair of huge golden hands floated from the trunk and over to the counter.

Both hands cracked their joints to loosen up.

'If you've quite finished,' said Agatha.

The hands cupped their palms and floated in front of the witch. 'We have an unusual state of affairs, as neither child has anything to place into you; I've taken the liberty of writing an I.O.U. for the items I would like, namely: one jar of honey and a wooden flute.' She placed the note into one of the hands. It dropped down sharply as if loaded with a weighty object. Into the other she poured toffee chunks, until both hands drew level, like a set of kitchen scales.

'I think that's about it,' said Agatha, holding a paper cone that a golden hand tipped the toffee into. The witch handed the cone to Tatty. Before anyone had a chance to say or do anything else, Will grabbed one of the biggest chunks and shoved it into his mouth. While Tatty tut-tutted at his bad manners, Agatha just smiled. 'By the way, Tatty, I forgot to mention earlier, I – um – carried out that little request you asked of me and it went very satisfactorily, thank you. Apparently, *you-know-who's* on the mend, though I don't know if he's made the, um … *discovery* yet.'

'Dishcoverwee – washa' abou'?' slurped Will, toffee stuck in his molars.

'Never you mind, young elf,' said Agatha, tapping the side of her nose. 'We ladies have to have *some* secrets, you know.'

Will rolled his eyes and shook his head.

'Well, I'd better get on. The schoolchildren will be here any moment.' Agatha took the I.O.U. and slipped it into the drawer next to the luck-stone; then she hurried to the door. 'Goodbye, my dears. Do be careful, won't you?' Oddly, she looked straight at Will.

'Bye, Aggie. And thanks for the toffee,' said Tatty.

''Esh, hanksh 'ery mush.'

From the doorway, Agatha watched the children leave the shop and knew with utmost witchy certainty that Willum Patch would be getting his luck-stone back sooner than he could ever have imagined.

CHAPTER SIXTEEN

Talkin' Cows

Only half the toffee remained in the cone. Tatty felt sick and her jaw ached with so much chewing.

'Can't eat another lump,' groaned Will, holding his stomach.

'Me neither.' Tatty prised toffee from her teeth. 'Toffee's a tiring confection, isn't it?'

'Yep.' Will sighed. 'Takes a lot of effort. We should've chosen lemon sherbets or cough-candy twists instead, could've just sucked those.'

Tatty peered into the cone. 'Still, there's some left for your brothers and sisters.'

'Mm. By the way, what was Aggie on about back there, when she said, "I don't know if you-know-who's made the discovery yet"?'

'It's not that I don't *want* to tell you ...'

'I don't believe it! You're keepin' a secret. You don't trust me?'

'Of course I trust you – it's not that simple.'

'It never is with you. I can't believe you'd keep a secret from me...'

She hesitated. 'It's just that ... if anyone found out I'd broken the law, well–'

'You broke the law!' Will yelled. 'When? What law?'

'Never mind what law. I've said too much as it is.'

From behind them came a familiar voice: 'Tatty Moon broke the *law?* Surely not! Ooh, wait till I tell my ma and pa that a member of the respected Moon family's a criminal. They'll never believe it!'

Tatty bristled with anger. 'Clear off, Burnley!'

Burnley had two elves with him: both had been in trouble in the past, and each time their victims were smaller children. The taller of the two, Octavius Brown, had virtually no chin and was as thin as a reed, whereas Drubbett Dirge was a slab of a boy with a flat face and deep-set unfathomable eyes. It was impossible to tell if he was happy or sad as his face only ever wore one expression.

'Shall I clobber 'im, Burnley?' said Drubbett, dully. He cracked his knuckles.

Will gulped. His nose was still tender.

'I can fight my own battles!' spat Burnley. In a friendlier tone, he added, 'It isn't that I'm not grateful for the offer – 'preciate it Drub, really I do. It's just that I'm not sure Master Patch wants a black eye to go with the bloody nose I gave 'im last time he squared up to me. Would ya, Patch?'

Tatty whispered: 'I thought you had a cold? So, Burnley hit you. Mm, so much for *me* keepin' secrets.'

Will reddened. He turned to Burnley. 'You had your fun when we had our, um … *set-to* before. All we want to do is get 'ome.'

'Aw, he wants to get off 'ome to 'is mummy, Burnley – ain't that precious,' Octavius mocked.

'They can both go,' said Burnley, smiling. He faced his friends. 'We're not stoppin' 'em, are we fellas?'

Octavius had disappointment etched on his thin face. Drubbett looked the same as ever.

'No, they can go …' Burnely's handsome face broke into a sly smile, '… just as soon as they tell us which law Moon-face broke.'

'No,' said Will, quietly.

'Oh dear, did – did you say *no*, Patch?' Burnley sniggered.

Octavius said, stupidly, 'Yes, I definitely 'eard 'im say "*no*".'

Drubbett nodded.

Burnley stepped towards Will. He spoke in barely a whisper, which Tatty thought sounded more dangerous than if he'd yelled his head off.

'You *will* tell me, Patch.'

'No he won't tell you,' said Tatty; 'and you can't make him. Now clear off!'

Burnley sneered. 'Or what? You're not allowed to use magic on me, Moon-face, and you know it. It'd be breakin' the *law!*'

A smile spread across Tatty's face. 'You seem to forget, *Snot*grass–' He flinched as she spat the name he hated; '–that I'm well practised at breakin' the law. Once more won't make much difference.'

'You wouldn't dare!'

'Try me.' Her eyes fixed on his. She was ready to use magic if she had to.

Drubbett and Octavius both shifted from one foot to another. 'C'mon Burnley,' said Octavius, pulling on Burnley's sleeve and backing away. 'They're not worth it.'

'Yeah, they're not wurfit,' echoed Drubbett, expressionless.

Burnley broke the stare-out with Tatty first. He laughed nervously. 'All right you two, you win. If you're both scared of a – a *hag* with unnatural wings, who hangs around with a complete pus-bucket …' He followed his companions for a short distance before turning and yelling one last threat. 'I'll see you soon, Patch – when you've lost your bodyguard!'

Will gasped, 'Thank the stars! I thought we were goners for sure.'

Tatty watched the bullies finally disappear amid the undergrowth. 'To think I used to be scared of him … I don't know why, 'cause he's pathetic. It's like he's got somethin' to prove all the time.' A curious feeling crept over her then – while her palm itched like mad across the strange scar which had appeared almost overnight – that Burnley's days were almost over. She was sure that she'd never see him again. As much as she loathed him, she felt sad too. Nobody deserved a violent end, and she knew his life would end in fear and bloodshed. She didn't know *how* she knew, she just did. Like the time she'd had to go to The Patch, even though it was dark outside. Nan gave in to her demands in the end and went along too, only to find Will desperately ill with a fever. Luckily, Nan's swift healing spell had pulled him through. Tatty shuddered.

Will watched her. He looked worried. She grinned and he smiled back. The moment passed. Everything was as it should be again. 'Come on,' she said, 'let's get these toffees back to the others before they end up all stuck together.'

As they walked she explained how she'd shown herself to the Biggun. Will seemed impressed and asked lots of questions. He promised that it would remain their secret.

She believed him.

In the distance, out of sight, the church roof had turned black and white with magpies. They were closer now, and as silent as the graves they watched over.

★★★

Tatty stayed long enough at The Patch to hand out toffee to the children. Will said he'd call on her the next day. She arrived back at the Willow Tree as Marigold dished up dinner. Tatty told them all about Blue and the trip to Pottages, but left out the part about Burnley, so as not to cause a fuss. She was too tired. And Nan would only want to confront his mother and father about their wayward son. Petunia and Padraig Snodgrass were nice, and Tatty didn't want the last memories of their son to be horrible ones.

After the long dusty walk and a large dinner, all Tatty wanted was to lie on her bed and sleep, but Nan had other ideas. 'I want you to go next door to the meadow. The cows are back and we need milk. Folk want me to make custard tarts. Can't make custard tarts without milk.'

'Do I have to, Nan? I'm *so* tired. I thought I'd go to bed early.' Tatty looked to her mother for support.

'Yes, you do have to,' said Marigold. 'You haven't done any

chores at all these last few days. You don't need to take the cart. Nan only needs a few drops in a jug.'

Nan placed a jug on the table, and Tatty snatched it up. She slammed the door on her way out.

It was awkward flying with the bulky jug tucked under one arm. And how she was going to get it home unspilled when it was full of milk, she didn't know? She zoomed across the next door meadow, towards a small herd of Jersey cows. She could hear the cattle murmuring. There were nine cows in the meadow and seven were lying down. When she was close enough she could hear their chatter clearly.

'Oi, Cynthia,' called a bony cow, 'come and lie down yoooooou, or Mister won't put us in the byre!'

The cow named Cynthia carried on grazing, contentedly.

'It's no uuoooooose talking toooo her, dear,' said another cow, chewing a mouthful of cud. 'She's neeoooooow – doesn't speak yet.'

'But she should still know when rain's coming. What is she, soft in the head?' The bony cow lay in the shade of a tree, flicking flies away with her tail. She cast an annoyed, chocolate-eyed gaze upon Joyce, the other cow still standing. 'Joyce! I say, Joyce! I'd have thought yoooooou'd have known better. Why aren't yoooooou lying down with the rest of us?'

Between tearing up mouthfuls of grass, Joyce replied, 'I'll be with yoooooou directly. It's just that – *munch, munch* – I'm starving. There wasn't much grazing in that other field. My milk yield's not what it was.'

'The grazing's not tooooo blame, it's your age, dear,' said the bony cow. 'We're none of us as young as we were.'

'Speak for yourself, Ingrid,' said Joyce, before catching sight of something flitting about. The flitty thing stopped in front of her face. 'I suppose yoooooou want some of my precious milk, doooo youoooo?' Joyce went on, tossing her head, nearly hitting Tatty with her horns. 'I haven't got much tooo spare.'

'Please, I only need a few drops. You see, Nan wants to make custard tarts.'

'Custard tarts? Custard tarts, is it? I wish I kneooooow what yooooou were on about, I really doooooo … All the same, they sound absoluuoooooootely fascinating! And by the way, I reckon that jug's going toooooo hold at least eight or nine drops of milk – a feoooow drops indeed. Well, what're yooooou waiting for, dearie? Come on, before the rain comes; it takes me a while toooooo lie down yoooou see, what with my joints.'

Tatty looked at the cow in disbelief. 'Rain?' she said. 'We haven't 'ad rain for over two months. What makes you think it's goin' to rain?'

'That.'

Tatty turned to look. 'That' was a dark charcoal-coloured smudge in an otherwise blue, cloudless sky. And as she watched, the smudge grew bigger, until it loomed over the far treetops. It moved fast. 'Ah,' said Tatty, 'I see what you mean.' She flew beneath the cow's gurgling, gassy belly and held the jug under one of Joyce's four teats. 'Front left!' yelled Tatty.

The cow lowered her head. 'What was that, dearie?'

Louder, Tatty repeated, 'I said, front left!'

'Doooooo get a moooooove on, Joyce,' said Ingrid. 'Or yoooou'll get caught out. Look, even Cynthia's joined us.' The glossy young cow lay next to bony Ingrid.

'Yes – yes – give me a chance! I'm trying toooooo concentrate.' Joyce strained, passing lots of wind into the sweet-smelling meadow air. Moments later, a drop of milk fell from her udder, followed by another, until Tatty's jug held eight drops precisely. Tatty thanked the cow and said how grateful her gran would be.

'Yoooou should've told me earlier that Nan Moooooon was your granny. I had a sore hooooof once and she healed it. Soooooon after, I started speaking. Anyway, one good deed deserves another. Dooooooo give her my regards.'

'I will, and thanks again,' said Tatty, before soaring into the sky with the jug clasped firmly to her chest. As she flew over the well she stopped in mid-air. She couldn't remember ever passing right over it before. It was like flying into solid silence. The quiet was so complete it seemed to suck the air from her lungs. She tried to beat her wings faster, but they only managed a sleepy figure-of-eight. It felt like she was being pulled down towards the mouth of the well.

A moment later there was noise. *No, not noise: Voices* and they sounded scared. Looking down, she couldn't see the water, just a yawning pit to the centre of the earth. At first the voices were mutterings, but they grew louder and clearer with every passing second: *'Down here, now! – We'll keep you safe! – Now, please! – They're coming! – No! – Too late – It's too late! Look out!'*

Something crashed into her from behind, knocking her away from the voices, sending the jug flying from her arms. It smashed on flagstones, splattering milk in a white starburst. Pain seared her lower back. Somehow, the world had tilted. She faced the ground. Her wings had stopped moving, but she was still airborne? *How?* Then she saw a black wing with a streak of white. Her blood turned to ice. *A Magpie.* But she hadn't heard the lert? She would have heard it being this close to the Lookout Tree. *Mr Patch couldn't be …*

She angled her head to see more of the bird. It seemed huge, blotting out the now iron-grey sky. Other magpies filled the greyness, hundreds more. They started a harsh cackling: Cha-cha-ha-ha-hack – like mocking laughter. Tatty seethed. It wasn't supposed to end like this! She was supposed to die in her second or third century, with children and grandchildren huddled around her deathbed! She could even see it: *the soft candlelight on their adoring faces as I take my last shuddering breaths; my lined face suddenly young again with a last smile plastered on it. Long silver hair fanning out over the pillow, a lock of my husband's hair clasped in my bony hand.* No. She couldn't think of dying – *not yet!* So she began to fight. She beat the magpie with her fists and tried to prise open its toes, hooked into the back of her cotton shift. The bird looked down with glittering eyes and jabbed at her with its beak. An agonising jolt shot up her arm. She ignored the pain. Soon a warm, sleepy feeling crept over her, and she was only half aware of the magpie changing direction. They soared over the roof of Mould Cottage and on towards the faraway wood.

Drowsily, Tatty noticed the other magpies carrying things too: limp, unmoving things … She heard and felt her threadbare cotton shift rip – then she fell. She was free. She watched the magpies getting smaller. One magpie clutched a tattered piece of cloth.

Then it shrieked.

'Got to fly,' Tatty muttered, looking down to see the earth coming up too fast. She had to concentrate, move her wings. Moments from impact, they buzzed to life and took her skyward. She glanced back, to see the magpie plummeting towards her. The wind began to blow, bringing tears to her eyes as she turned homewards. *I won't die,* she told herself; *I won't.* She looked down. *Over Mould Cottage again.* She saw the Bigguns' shutting their hens in. Then the Willow Tree, its branches like arms, reaching out. *'Come on,'* they seemed to say, *'you're almost there, almost home'* … She was dizzy. Her head felt too heavy for her neck, and the magpie was so close, she imagined she could feel its breath on her skin. She went into free-fall, tucking her wings tightly against her back. Her lungs began to burn. She hit the ground and sprinted for the Willow Tree, gulping in big breaths of sweet air. Her head cleared. As she ran towards the willow, long grass seemed intent on slowing her down. She thrashed her way through it. *Open the door,* she yelled inside her head. *The door, the door, the door …*

It began to open. She could see blackness beyond.

Opened wider still.

Papa.

He reached out, and his arm stretched like a length of unfurling ribbon. It circled her waist, reeling her in like a tiddler on a fishing line. She was through the door, falling into more arms. The door slammed shut and immediately something thudded into it. A cackling sound followed, grew fainter; then stopped. Something warm trickled down her arm. She looked. *Blood.* Drops of shimmering brightness fell to the earthen floor. *Red starbursts*. That explained the sleepy feeling. She looked for someone, anyone … Nan, bent over her, a determined expression on her lined face. Then, darkness and blissful sleep …

~CHAPTER SEVENTEEN~

Gnome Night

Heavy clouds brought great droplets of rain. Papa, exhausted after the limb-stretching spell, lit candles in the parlour with a sputtering flame from his fingertip, then sat and watched his wife wash blood from Tatty's arm. The wound hadn't been as deep as they had first feared. Still, the blood loss had worried them. To give Tatty the best chance of recovery, Nan was about to perform a healing spell, something she hadn't done for years, not since young Willum's fever.

As Tatty lay slumped on the rug, Nan held her granddaughter's arm and spoke the incantation.

'Calling Spirits from North, East, South and West,

Come and do what you do best,

Conquer blood, fever and pain,

Make this child *whole* again.'

The raw edges of Tatty's wound came together, until all that remained was a neat scar near her elbow. Checking for more injuries, Nan noticed the mark in Tatty's left palm. It looked like another simple scar: deep, with smooth edges, and red where Tatty had been scratching. It must have appeared recently. *And so it begins,* thought Nan. *Why us? Why our child, when we've already lost one? Not that he was the same as this white-winged …* Nan didn't want to think '*oddity*', but the word seemed to be the only one that fit.

★★★

Funny, thought Tatty, *the things you hear when folk don't realise you're aware.* Before, they'd spoken as if she wasn't there. She'd been shocked at Papa's anguish on seeing her bloodied, torn shift. 'Don't want to lose another … bad enough losin' me only child …'

Marigold had said, 'All right, Pop, let's not talk about it – you'll upset Ma.'

Tatty had wanted to cry out: '*No! Keep talking! I want to hear about my father! Why won't anybody ever talk about him, or let* me *talk about him? I can hardly remember what he looks like!*' but she hadn't. Her eyelids were too heavy to open. She listened as Nan cleared away the bowl and soiled rags. It seemed that her father's name was to be forgotten.

Rufus Moon.

It sounded such a dependable name. Except it wasn't; because he'd gone and got himself killed.

She coughed. Her throat felt dry.

Nan brought water and helped her take a sip. Tatty whispered, 'No milk … Sorry, Nan … dropped the jug.'

It seemed her grandmother needed water too. She made a throat-clearing noise, and when she spoke her voice sounded funny. 'Hush now, silly girl. You're back safe, that's all that matters. Go to sleep. You'll soon feel better. We'll be here, watchin' over you.'

Tatty fell asleep with Nan stroking her hair.

★★★

With the darkness came a creeping chill. Outside, the rain poured down in steely looking bars. The Moons' sat sipping dandelion tea and talked about everyday things. Lightning lit the sky in the distance.

The tea and glowing fire had a reviving effect on Tatty. She asked Papa to tell her one of his stories before bed. 'Tell me one I've never heard before?' She tucked her feet beneath her on the rug. In truth, she'd heard most of his stories more than once, and some as often as fifty times, but she never told him; she would smile and nod in all the right places.

'I'll tell you a tale 'bout a land where it's froze all the time – never thaws out. Have you 'eard that one?' He studied her face to see if she was fibbing.

She replied, 'No, I don't think so.' It was the truth, though a permanently frozen land sounded ridiculous.

'Good,' he said, smiling at Nan and Marigold as they sat mending socks. He began to rock his chair back and forth, taking time to gather the story together. 'Let's see, well, there's a freezin' cold place across The Great Ocean where it's winter all year round–'

Marigold sneaked a look at Nan and stifled a laugh. Nan rolled her eyes.

'–an' there's no trees or grass growin' there – earth's too hard – an' it snows just about every bloomin' moment. This land goes by the name of Tartica!'

'Really?' said Tatty.

'Really.'

''Bout as real as hens' teeth,' Nan snorted, darning a sock so hard it appeared she was trying to kill it. 'Claptrap. Snows all the time – humph! Victor, you an' your tales.'

'Hush, please, Ma,' said Marigold, leaning forward in her chair. 'Carry on, Pop.'

Papa nodded. 'The Bigguns' who live there travel about on sledges pulled by ferocious hounds.' To enhance the story, he muttered a quick spell and his rocking chair began to move. He pretended to ride on a sledge, sliding around the room on the chair's rockers. 'Much – that's what they shouts to their hounds to get 'em movin' – Much! Much!'

As he whizzed about, Tatty and Marigold roared with laughter, while Nan grumbled that he was 'a nitwit'.

Lightning lit the parlour. The flash was followed by a rumble of thunder.

Papa and his chair skidded to a halt beside the fire. 'I know we're cursed with magpies;' Tatty shivered at the mention of the birds; 'but those Bigguns in Tartica 'ave got their own black and white menaces. Their birds go by the name of pingwims. And they're *big*, almost as big as the Bigguns themselves. All the pingwims eat is fish. And 'cause it's night-time most of the year in Tartica, the pingwims have to feel around in the ocean for fish with their great flat feet! How about that then?' He reached across to his wife with a big flat foot and pushed her rocking chair.

She stabbed her thumb with the darning needle. 'Victor! Will you stop with your foolishness!'

'Sorry, gal,' he said. 'Pingwims' eat only fish, but they can still be deadly.' His face looked solemn in the firelight. 'I did hear that, given 'alf a chance, they'll kick you to death if you 'appen to get in their way. Also, they 'aven't got any knees … Come to think of it, they 'aven't really got any legs, either: feet come straight out of their backsides …'

Tatty's head felt heavy, making it difficult to concentrate.

'… lean into the wind an' snow to keep from fallin' over, so …'

Delayed shock and the crackling heat of the fire were making her drowsy.

'… an' the leader of the pingwims isn't a queen, or king for that matter … Oh no, they've got 'emselves an *emperor!* I know, isn't–' Papa suddenly jumped out of his chair. 'Everyone up! Get up the shaft, straight to Tatty's bedchamber!'

They stared at him as if he'd spoken gobbledegook.

'I said *UP!*'

They had never, ever, heard him raise his voice in such a manner. Marigold pushed Tatty ahead of her, with Nan following. They flew up the dark shaft, bursting through the double doors into Tatty's room, where they waited.

'What was it, Victor?' asked Nan, as Papa joined them a minute later, carrying a steaming kettle.

'Outside,' he said, breathless. 'I saw somethin' *big.*'

A flash of lightning lit the room.

Marigold said: 'Oh, it was probably just the lightn–'

'Wasn't the lightnin'!' he snapped.

A bellowing roar came from outside, followed by a loud splintering of wood. Papa ran to Tatty's window and threw it wide open. Rain and wind rushed into the bedchamber. Papa ignored the storm. Tatty stood next to him and leaned out; trying to see who or what was making the din. The driving rain stung her skin. She could make out a shadowy figure below. A crash against the door sent shock waves up the tree, making it judder.

'Come inside, Tatty! Close the window!' yelled Marigold. But Tatty couldn't hear above the howling wind and the howling figure.

Papa shouted into her ear: 'Move over, Tatty! Let's give 'im a taste of *Moon* medicine!' He hoisted the kettle onto the window ledge. 'Oi! Ugly! Up here!'

As the creature looked up, Papa tipped the kettle.

Tatty had to bite back a scream. In the two seconds before the water hit, when a bolt of lightning lit up the night like daytime, she saw it clearly: big saucer eyes, almost entirely white, but with a speck of black pupil. A hump rose between its shoulder-blades, and its arms were so long that its knuckles dragged the ground. A straggly, filthy beard hung below a gaping mouth full of sharp teeth. Thick saliva slid from a pendulous bottom lip.

A shriek filled the air as boiling water sloshed into the creature's face. It clasped a hand over its damaged eye and loped off into the undergrowth. The shrieking grew fainter in the gusting wind, finally disappearing altogether.

Tatty and Papa stood by the window, rain lashing in at them. Shock held them there. It was Nan who pushed past, struggling to pull the window closed against the tugging wind.

'Now per'aps you'll tell me what all this is about?' she said to Papa.

He wiped his hands over his wet head and dried them on his

breeches. He spoke one word and her face paled.

'Gnome.'

After a moment she said to the others: 'Well, we'd best go down and repair any damage … goin' to be a long night.'

CHAPTER EIGHTEEN

Burnley Meets His Match

They'd called Delilah for hours, ever since the storm first hit, but there was no sign of the cat. Usually, at the first clap of thunder, she would hide under the bed until it was quiet again. Delilah had missed supper, too, something Dot and Bert couldn't recall ever happening before.

Dot was frantic: 'She's been run over – I know she has!'

'You don't know anythin' of the sort,' said Bert.

'How can you be so sure? Oh, I knew I shouldn't 'ave been so horrible to that Gypsy fortune-teller. She's gone and put a curse on me, that's what she's done!' Dot wailed.

'Well, you will go and see these weirdos.' Bert closed his eyes as he preached. 'I've told you before, they're all crooks, but do you ever believe me? No.'

Dot chewed her bottom lip. 'Oh, I don't know *what* to believe. It seems such a coincidence that's all. The Gypsy told me I was goin' to have a sad loss, and then Delilah ups an' goes missin'. And I was so *rude* to her, too. Do you think Mr Buckler's been out with his gun again? I saw 'im the other day in the field over the back, takin' pot-shots at anything that moved. He hates squirrels ... Do you think he could have mistaken Delilah for a squirrel, Bert?'

Ruddy big squirrel, thought Bert. 'No, no, dear. I don't think so … um, wrong colour for a start.' Bert had been in a wonderful mood since Dot found his bicycle in the garage, repaired and ready to ride. He could hardly believe it, especially when she'd handed him the little note. He'd memorised it: *I hope you're recovering well, from your little friend, with kind regards.* So, he hadn't imagined the fairy-thingy. He wasn't going loopy, after all. She'd mended his bike! And even though he'd warned Dot about believing in Gypsy curses, he was certainly going to keep an open mind about that sort of thing from now on, though he'd never let on to Dot. *Better let her carry on thinking a couple of the local youngsters mended my bike. She already thinks I exaggerated how damaged it was.* He'd got his Chopper back and still had to pinch himself to believe it. He would have jumped for joy if it wasn't for his sore ankle. The note nestled in the breast pocket of his shirt. His present light-hearted mood had started as soon as he'd placed it there. The skin on his chest beneath the pocket still felt a bit tingly, like sunburn.

Dot said excitedly: 'Bert, I've had an idea. Why don't we call the police, give them a description of Delilah?' She stared at him expectantly.

He wanted to laugh his head off, but managed not to. 'Oh, love,' he said, 'it's not that I don't *want* to find her – I'll bet someone's giving her a big tin of pilchards as we speak. Unfortunately, the police aren't goin' to come out just 'cause your cat's missing.'

She looked at him, aghast. 'Eh? That's not right! We pay our taxes like everyone else. When did we call the police about anything, eh? *Never!* Well, I think we should get our money's worth, that's all.'

As he looked at Dot's face – somewhere hidden under her thick, orange, make-up – Bert felt a pang of pity. It was true he'd never much cared for the cat, but he did care about Dot, even if she did get on his nerves sometimes. The cat meant the world to her, so he vowed he would do his best to find Delilah, alive or … not. He put an arm around her shoulder. 'Tell you what, if she's not back by tomorrow mornin', I'll go round the village and put up some leaflets with her picture on. How about that?'

Dot gazed up at him and gave a wobbly smile.

'That's better,' he said. 'Now, you go and sit down and I'll make you a nice cup of tea.' He watched her totter down the hallway towards the sitting room. Still smiling, he limped to the sink to fill the kettle with water. Bert thought that Delilah going missing had been a bit of a bonus, though it made him feel guilty to think that way, but it meant Dot hadn't asked too many questions about the bike. With her nosy nature, she would have turned into a sleuth to root out the sender of the note, even if it meant questioning the whole village. Luckily, she'd accepted his explanation that the note was from local children.

He whistled happily as the kettle filled.

Later, Bert twirled the snagged loops on his armchair in his fingers. It felt odd without the purring great lump trying to edge him out of his chair, or batting his newspaper when he tried to read. The bungalow felt rather ... empty. Silently he scolded himself: *Must be going soft. Delilah's just a cat ... but still ...*

As soon as she'd finished her tea, Dot went to bed, leaving Bert alone. He opened the patio doors and shuffled outside. It had almost stopped raining. It was as he stared at his swollen big toe that he first noticed the stain on the wooden decking. And next to it, still sodden from the downpour, was a clump of black fur. He knelt to get a better look, touched the stain and held his fingers in front his face – like a TV detective. His fingertips were red with blood, and the clump of black fur looked as if it belonged on Delilah. *Well, well, well,* thought Bert, *looks as if Mr Buckler must've been out shootin', after all!* He and Dot could easily have mistaken a gunshot for a clap of thunder. *But what happened to the body?* He supposed Delilah must have crawled away and died somewhere. They would probably never know ...

Bert went indoors and got the kettle. He took it out on to the decking and poured hot water over the stain until it disappeared. Then he flicked the clump of fur into nearby bushes. He decided not to tell Dot. He would still go out and put leaflets around the village, just in case. Later on, he might even get a replacement for Delilah, a little kitten. But *he'd* train the next one and it would know its place, too.

After a last quick scan around the garden – thinking he detected flitting shadows and scurrying sounds from every nook and cranny – Bert closed the sliding doors and locked them against the drizzly night.

★ ★ ★

Once the human had gone, they emerged from every corner of the garden, sniffing for anything edible to cram into their mouths. Eventually, finding nothing, they disappeared, merging with the shadows.

All but one, that was.

The Gnome carried a prize around her neck like a scarf. She'd had to fight to claim it and she wasn't going to share. Sharing wasn't in her nature. She licked the raw end of her prize. To her it tasted sweet, something to be savoured. She stuffed it under her warty nose and took a deep sniff. It smelled wonderful. The fur tickled and she sneezed.

The black fur sprouted from the severed tail of a cat.

★ ★ ★

Gibbet's eye hurt. He couldn't see out of it any more. His stomach rumbled too. The rest of his tribe had vanished. He should have stuck with them, but he'd been *so* hungry and he was sick of fighting over every scrap. Then he'd got lost amid the massive human dwellings, scrambling beneath a gate to find himself all alone. He'd tried calling the others, but his cries had been carried away by the wind. Gibbet wasn't too bothered though; he knew in which direction the warren lay. He'd be home before daylight; it was still early yet. He needed to feed now. The hunger was terrible. Earlier, he'd thought he had found an elfy hovel, only to find it full of *faeries!* He spat on the ground after he thought *that* word. Nasty, poisonous things those flitty menaces – instant death if eaten! He might still have killed one though, if he'd managed to catch one. Elfies were another matter: good meat were elfies. Those faeries (another quick hawk of phlegm on to the ground) had hurt his eye. *Poor old Gibbet. Poor old eye!* He tried to blink away the thick ooze streaming down his cheek and into his beard. In his dim-witted way, he thought it funny how his tribe were now in the service of a faery (yet another big splat of slime in the dirt), but not the usual type, no. This one was different. Maj…istee, they had to call him. Gibbet still found it difficult to pronounce the word. It annoyed him to have to say it too, because he knew it meant something important, some-thing special. Maj…istee sent them out in the storm to cause trouble, and with permission to kill as they liked. Gibbet wasn't sure why – didn't much care. But Maj…istee could be cruel. He was scared of Maj…istee and his flashy, burny finger. Better just do as he was told. He muttered, 'Make twubble … geddout quick … geddout … quick.'

Something made a pretty sound. He homed in on it. There it was again. His stomach gave a loud growl. He lost the sound, stopped in his tracks and listened to the night noises. There, over that way, chiming through the undergrowth like pretty, pretty, tinkling bells. Gibbet patted his swinging stomach as he loped along. 'Elfies, yacketee-yack … yacketee-yack. Aw dey dowizz yacketee-yack … num – num – num – num, elfies.'

★★★

Little Upham was quiet now. Mr and Mrs Snodgrass had bolted the door and locked all the hatches inside the grass-covered bank. In the children's bedchamber, an argument raged about whether the hatch should be open or not.

'I'm hot and if I want to open it, I *will*.' said Burnley Snodgrass. He took a swipe at his brother, catching the child on the side of the head. The small elf ran to his bed, curled into a ball, and sobbed.

'Wah – wah – wah! Trust you to start snivellin'!' Burnley sniped. Being the eldest suited Burnley: it meant he was always the boss. When his parents weren't around he treated his brother and sister like slaves, getting them to fetch things for him, or tidy up after him. They'd been told to stay silent and not to come downstairs until it was safe. Burnley, like all bullies, was a coward and had spent most of the evening shivering in the corner under a blanket. Now that it was quiet outside he'd soon gone back to his mean ways. He stood with his back to the open hatch. Even his mother, Petunia, despaired of him, telling him often that 'one day you'll meet your match – then we'll see who's boss!' But he hadn't met his match yet. Will Patch had tried to stand up to him. He smirked as he remembered Patch's blood on his knuckles. Fancy Patch trying to take him on like that? *He must have a death wish or something.*

He watched his brother and sister's frightened faces as he pushed the hatch wider for the second time that evening.

'Ma! Pa! Burnley's opened the 'atch again!' his little sister yelled.

Petunia hollered: 'Burnley Snodgrass, if I have to come up them stairs you're goin' to be in deep trouble! Now do as you're told. You're not too big for a thick ear, my lad!'

Burnley made faces at the doorway as his mother spoke. He took off his belt and began flicking it in the direction of the two children. They cowered on the furthest bed, huddled against the earth wall. It was while he mouthed all the horrible things he was going to do to them that a huge filth-covered hand came through the hatch, lifting Burnley off his feet by his fair curly hair. And as he was shoved into a smelly sack, he didn't even have the chance to utter one single swear-word.

Burnley's brother and sister stared silently at the hatch. Then, his sister leapt off the bed and ran to the top of the stairs. 'Ma!' she called. 'Ma!'

'What's he done *now*!' snapped Petunia.

'Um, well, it's just that … I think our Burnley's just met 'is match!'

~CHAPTER NINETEEN~

Sleep

Nan and Marigold's forced cheery voices were getting on Tatty's nerves. A band of pain wrapped around her head through lack of sleep.

'Oh, look,' said Marigold, brightly; 'sleepy-head's awake!'

'Mornin',' trilled Nan. 'And what another glorious mornin' it is. Did you ever see such a blue sky, Marigold?'

'No, I never did.'

Nan took a big flat pan from a hook on the wall. 'I'll make us some nice jigglycakes for breakfast. We haven't had them in ages.'

'Ooh, lovely. What a lovely idea. Mm, I love jigglycakes – they're so … lovely,' said Marigold, as if Nan had suggested turning straw into gold. 'I'll fetch some lovely jam.'

Here we go again, thought Tatty, slumping on to a chair. Her hair was unbrushed; sleep crusted the corners of her bloodshot eyes. *Any hint of tragedy and they act as if everything's normal.*

Papa dragged the table away from in front of the door. 'Poppin' out to get firewood, I shan't be long.'

Every joint in Tatty's body felt like a rusty hinge. Papa left the door open; she could see the mess from the storm. Branches were wrenched from trees, and the Brambleton's hat-roof had been blown off. Some of the villagers had found it. All Tatty could see of them were their feet shuffling along underneath. A shrunken Agatha Pottage stood outside too, waving her arms about in a tidying spell, conducting a towering column of golden leaves, which looked like a spiralling shoal of fish. When Agatha lowered her hands the leaves floated down on to a big pile of branches and twigs.

'Jigglycakes are ready!' called Nan.

Papa returned with the wood. Marigold put jam on the table, ruffling Tatty's matted hair as she passed.

Nan placed a plate piled high with steaming, wobbly, jigglycakes in front of Tatty.

While Tatty pushed the spongy delight around her plate, Papa mended the door, banging and hammering so much that Tatty's headache was soon worse. Her stomach churned at the sight of the strawberry jam. A memory flashed through her thumping brain of pumping blood: *her* blood.

The grown-ups spoke. Tatty paid little attention, but the mention of Burnley's name drew her upright in her chair.

'–that eldest Snodgrass boy,' said Papa, hammering in another wooden peg, 'and old Tom Crabtree from over near Traders' Row–'

'No!' Nan gasped, interrupting him. 'Not *Tom* … We used to play together when we were little …'

'And, sorry to say: Alf Patch, too.'

Tatty shook her head. 'Wh– What did you say, about Mr Patch?'

Papa sighed wearily. 'Missin'. Got to expect the worst.'

'No!' Tatty cried. 'It can't be true.' A searing pain sliced through her hand, through the stupid scar that had appeared out of the blue. *Blue*. She had to see Will. His father was gone now, too. They were both fatherless. She ignored the pain and pushed the chair away from the table. 'I've got to see Will.'

Marigold came towards her. 'I wouldn't, love,' she said gently. 'I expect Daisy will want a bit of peace. It's too early to go over–'

'I'm going.'

Nan pushed her spectacles up the bridge of her nose and stared silently at her granddaughter for several moments. 'Be careful. Take Mealy, you're not strong enough to fly yet. And keep watchful.'

'I will, Nan.' Tatty hugged and kissed her. At the door she turned and saw a brilliant emerald glow surrounding her grandmother.

'If you hear the lert, get under cover straight away,' said Marigold resignedly.

'I will.'

At Mealy's stable, she called to the mouse and found him curled into a tight ball. He opened an eye and blinked, but seemed in no mood for work. Tatty went in the stable and prodded his podgy side. 'Come on lazy-bones, up!' she ordered, dragging on his head-collar. Mealy rose reluctantly and yawned, showing curved, yellow teeth. Tatty put the saddle and bridle on him. As she dragged him from the stable, he rolled his eyes at her in protest. 'Bed!' he squeaked. It was the first time she'd heard him say a proper word.

'No bed. We're goin' to The Patch.' She put her foot in the stirrup and swung her leg over his back; then nudged his sides with her heels. He refused to budge and swung his head around to try and bite her knee. Tatty's anger flared. Grim-faced, she spoke a quick incantation, staring at her right forefinger.

'My finger's short and somewhat thick,

I'd rather 'ave a nice long stick!'

The spell worked immediately. Tatty's finger grew hot and started to itch. It twitched as though something was trying to burrow out from under the skin. It stretched and lengthened. Soon, it resembled a long, flesh-coloured whip. Tatty waved the finger-whip threateningly and the mouse shot forward, scurrying towards The Patch without another sulky word uttered.

It was still early and as she passed the Lookout tree she saw a nervous-looking Eustace Brambleton fly up towards the crow's nest.

He looked paler than usual.

From the outside, The Patch seemed deserted. Flies buzzed dreamily over the cottage, smelly from the recent rain. Curtains at the windows were closed. Tatty shivered. She tied Mealy to the gatepost and went up the path, shrinking her finger back to its usual size before knocking on the door.

Nobody answered.

Try the latch, the door's bound to be locked. It wasn't, and creaked as it swung inward. The parlour was empty. Without the chattering children, the silence felt odd. Though Tatty felt foolish afterwards, she even checked behind the door in case something lurked there. A child's discarded shoe lay in the middle of the floor and a pile of cold, grey, ash sat beneath the cooking-pot in the fireplace. The cottage seemed abandoned.

A muffled sound came from upstairs.

Wind whistlin' down the chimney. But there was no wind. There it was again, louder this time. Tatty went to a step-ladder and looked up at the dark square that led to a bedchamber above. She hesitated, before placing one foot on to the first rung. She climbed, holding her breath so as not to make a sound, and eased her head through the opening. Though the curtains were closed, she could just see the children's sleep-sacks hanging from hooks in the ceiling.

One of the sacks bulged. It was Will's.

Tatty climbed into the bedchamber, went over to the sack, and prodded it. 'That you?'

Will's black hair emerged from the top of the sack, followed by his face.

'I – I wanted … to see you.' She gulped back a sob. 'I'm so sorry about your pa.'

'Thanks,' he murmured, wiping his nose on his sleeve.

'Where's your ma?'

'They've all gone past the meadow … stayin' with my auntie for a couple of days. I couldn't face goin'… seeing as it's all my fault.'

Tatty was puzzled. '*Your* fault? What're you talkin' about?'

'It's obvious, isn't it? My luck-stone. I never should've tried to trade it. And all for a cone of stupid ... *toffee*! Pa's dead an' it's all because of *me*!' Will buried his face in the crook of his arm and let out an anguished howl.

'Will,' Tatty said gently; 'your stone had absolutely nothin' to do with this mess. It could've been anyone's shift up that tree.'

He looked at her, his voice a hoarse whisper: 'But it wasn't *anyone* else, was it? And when was the last time you saw the sky thick with magpies, eh? They're usually alone, or in small groups. No, it's ... my fault all right.'

Tatty caught him staring at the scar tracing a line above her elbow.

'How'd you get that?'

No more secrets, she thought. 'I'll tell you about it after you've slept. You look worn out.'

'Can't sleep. Haven't slept all night ... keep seein' Pa.' Will's face crumpled, but he managed not to cry.

Tatty absent-mindedly rubbed the mark in her palm. 'Has your ma got any dormouse and chamomile tea?'

'No – I don't think so.'

'Look, if you don't get some sleep, you're goin' to be ill, and your ma can't have that. She'll need you to be strong – to help with the little 'uns.' Tatty paused. 'There is somethin' I could try ...'

'What?'

'I could put you into a slumber myself.'

'Could you manage that? What if I don't wake up?'

Tatty stared into his eyes. 'For once, trust me.'

He only hesitated for a moment. 'All right – do it.'

She walked back several paces. *How do the words go again?* Ma had sung the spell to her when she was small, but that was long ago. She closed her eyes and pictured Ma bending over her cradle ... could see Ma's flame-red hair. A moment later the words began to flow easily from her lips:

'Hush, hush, no need to rush,

The blankets are warm – the pillows' plush,'

Not that Will had ever owned a pillow, seeing as how he hung inside his knitted woollen cocoon with its big letter '*W*' embroidered on the front. He yawned and his eyelids began to droop. The sleep-sack swayed, rocking him gently. A smile spread across his tear-stained face. The smile grew wide as orbs of light flew from Tatty's fingertips. They grew bigger; spinning away to circle the curved wicker walls. The whirling spheres looked like planets with stars mixed amongst them.

'Pretty,' he mumbled, as Tatty's faraway voice droned on and on and on …

'Make this place as dark as night,

Wakefulness must now take flight,

Worry not, and slumber deep,

Hasten forward into sleep.'

Will gave a sigh and lost the battle with his eyelids.

The bright orbs slowed and vanished back in to the tips of Tatty's fingers. The room grew brighter and the sleep-sack stopped rocking.

Will snored gently.

Tatty watched him for a long time, and as she watched she cried, remembering Mr Patch. Life was so unfair. Why Alf Patch? Why *anyone?*

When she left The Patch, she mumbled a spell that locked the cottage securely behind her. Mealy, free from his tether, munched on Daisy's home-grown mint, now reduced to chewed stumps. She was too tired to scold the mouse. It took all her effort just to haul herself into the saddle. Hot salty tears blinded her as she rode home.

Luckily, Mealy knew the way.

~CHAPTER TWENTY~

Sir Edwin

Tatty led Mealy into his stable, where he immediately plunged into his nest ball and went to sleep. 'Lucky you,' she said. 'No spells needed here.'

She made her way around the Willow Tree, and had to shield her eyes from a blinding flash. *What's that?* She ran forward to see, and found two elves standing either side of the door. Each wore a green coat with gold buttons. Long boots came over their knees, and furry, striped, bumblebee-skin hats sat on their heads. Curved swords were attached to belts about their waists. The elves were so alike they could have been twins, down to their curly moustaches. They stepped aside to let her pass. Neither spoke as she lifted the latch and went inside.

Nan and Marigold were talking with a well-dressed gentleman. As soon as they saw Tatty they were silent.

Papa just watched the gentleman.

Tatty recognised the stranger immediately: it was the dusty fellow she and Will had spoken to on the way to Pottage's, claiming to be an old acquaintance of her mother's. Ma certainly seemed friendly towards him. So did Nan. When she'd come through the door her grandmother had been giggling. *When has Nan ever giggled?*

The gentleman stood as Tatty approached, and bowed.

'Here she is,' said Nan; 'here's our Tatty.'

He stared.

She studied him too. His hair was long and white. He wore a scarlet waistcoat beneath a black frock coat. Draped across the waistcoat was a silver watch-chain.

Nan and Marigold nudged one another and whispered. Papa just scowled.

'My dear Titania, it is a pleasure to meet you, at last.' He grasped her hand and kissed it.

Behind her back, she wiped the hand on her shift; Papa saw and smirked, rocking his chair back and forth. It seemed the stranger hadn't mentioned their earlier meeting. Tired and irritable, Tatty was in no mood to be pleasant.

'Tatty, this is Sir Edwin Popplewhite. He's come all the way from The Palace Over Yonder … to see *you*.' Nan smiled at Sir Edwin.

'Has he? Why?' All she wanted to do was sleep. A pain flashed through her palm.

Marigold anxiously twisted her apron hem.

Tatty sank onto a chair and rubbed her hand. 'Sorry if I seem rude, Sir, but my friend's … His pa's disappeared … probably dead. So, you'll have to excuse me if I don't bow and scrape.'

'Tatty!' cried Marigold, shocked.

'What?' yelled Tatty.

'Tatty!' cried Nan.

Papa grinned and rocked faster.

Sir Edwin smiled and waved a hand dismissively. 'No matter,' he said. 'Titania has spirit; just what is needed.' He turned to Tatty, his smile fading. 'I have spoken at great length to your family. They tell me you have no idea of your, um … *situation*. I shall try to explain in due course. Right now I must tell you that I've come on something of an errand, for the Queen. She must see you. I know it's a difficult time – I'm sorry about your friend's father – too, too sad. But Her Majesty insists that you are the only person who can help stop this …

unpleasantness.'

Tatty turned to her mother, then Nan, but they were looking puzzled. 'What can *I* do to stop the magpies? And as for the *Gnomes* ... Look, I'm sorry I was rude. Would you mind tellin' the Queen that I'm not up to seein' anyone at the moment? I'm feelin' a bit peaky. Actually, I'm just goin' to bed to lie down.' She went to get up.

Nan placed a hand on her shoulder. 'Stay there, Tatty. There's somethin' me and your ma want to tell you. Should've done it a long time ago, but we didn't, kept puttin' it off. It never seemed the right time, an' then ... we didn't want it to happen, I suppose ...'

It was unlike Nan to be lost for words.

'What Nan's tryin' to say is that you're of royal blood,' said a voice from behind the curtained shaft. Papa came into the room. 'Chosen before you were born, you was. The palace astrologers saw it in the stars, apparently. 'S all gobbledegook to me, mind, all that star-gazin'. Must be somethin' in it though, 'cause you've got the royal wing colour.'

'Royal wing colour? But ... I've got freckles.'

'You must've wondered why you were the only person in Little Upham with white wings,' Marigold said, gently.

Why's everyone tellin' me such horrible lies? 'I did used to wonder why folk would stare,' she whispered. 'Royal. *Me?* Are you sure you haven't been suppin' All Hallowe's broth?'

'No, they haven't,' said Sir Edwin. 'It's quite true. You *will* be our next monarch. *After* the present one passes on, of course.' He smiled, showing very white teeth. 'And we hope that won't be for an awfully long time yet.'

No one else smiled back.

Tatty felt sick. 'But what if I don't want to be queen?'

Sir Edwin said, 'No choice, I'm afraid.'

Tatty slumped in the chair. 'Surely one of the Queen's children will take over ...?' Panic crept into her voice. 'It – It wouldn't be fair, me jumping the queue!'

'Not possible. Once a girl becomes queen she forfeits her right to children,' Sir Edwin explained. 'The next heir is always a stranger, outside the family circle. Chosen, as your grandfather said, by the Universe itself. It's complicated, but that is why we have our astrologers.'

'Well, they've messed it up this time!' Tears streamed down Tatty's face. 'Go an' tell them they've got it wrong,' she wailed. 'I don't *want* to live in a palace – I live in a *treeeeee!*'

'There, there.' Sir Edwin patted her shoulder. 'I know it's come as a great shock, but there is no mistake. The sign on your palm is yet more confirmation.' He took her hand and touched the scar. She snatched her hand away as if she'd been burned.

'What *is* it?'

'Nothing to be alarmed about, plenty of time to explain later,' he said. 'We'd better hurry. The Queen is hosting a banquet this evening, in your honour, Titania. She would like you to stay at the palace for a while ... a few days, perhaps longer ...'

'I can't believe it! Why me? It's not *fair!* And I won't be able to 'ave children. And they were all goin' to gather around my bedside when I – I *died!*'

Sir Edwin, Nan, Marigold, and Papa, looked at each other, bewildered.

Nan said: 'Why, I know folk who'd give their eye-teeth to be in your place, Titania Moon. And they'd cut your throat to get there, too.'

'It really is time for us to leave, if we're going to catch favourable breezes,' Sir Edwin insisted.

'Excuse me,' said Marigold. 'I don't know about anybody else, but I'm not havin' a child of mine goin' to the palace lookin' like an urchin. If you'll wait outside, Sir Edwin–' She prodded him towards the door '–my daughter has to take a *bath*.'

She said that like I never bathe, thought Tatty dully, as Marigold pulled her from the chair; *even though I 'ave three baths a year, regular as clockwork. Spring, summer, and autumn! Only had the summer one back in*

June ... only two months ago.

'Well said, Marigold,' said Nan, 'couldn't agree more.'

As he was shoved out the door, Sir Edwin spluttered: 'I shall be waiting in the carriage. Do be as quick as you can, dear la–'

The door slammed in his face.

Tatty felt trapped. Panic welled up inside her. It was a bad dream. A nightmare.

'Marigold, Victor, get the bath out. I'll draw the curtains.' Nan went to the windows. 'Sir Edwin can wait – takes a long time to boil that much water.'

A small portrait hung on the wall, of Rufus Moon as a child. Below, there sat a human-sized, cracked, china cup (with a portrait of a glum-looking human on the front, wearing a crown). Marigold and Papa dragged the cup close to the fire. Very soon, Nan declared the water inside the cauldron hot enough and tipped it into the cup.

Through all this, Tatty watched in a daze. Once Papa had gone outside, Nan and Marigold helped her into the cup-bath.

'You can't wear this threadbare thing to the palace,' said Marigold, inspecting one of Tatty's old shifts. 'I'll see what I've got in my bedchamber that's suitable.'

Nan gave Tatty a lump of soap and made sure her granddaughter lathered properly. Much later, she said: 'Come on ... time to get out, your wings 'ave gone all wrinkly.'

CHAPTER TWENTY ONE

The Flying Scuttle

Papa opened the trapdoor and tipped dirty bathwater down onto the roots of the willow, then slid the cup back against the wall and flew up the dark shaft and into Tatty's bedchamber.

'My, my,' he said, 'look at you, all done up like a fox's dinner.'

'She looks like a proper young lady,' said Nan.

'No, like a *queen*,' insisted Marigold, placing a circlet of dried Forget-Me-Nots on to Tatty's head.

'Like a prize dollop,' Tatty muttered, wincing as the seams of Marigold's old blue satin dress pinched the skin in her armpits. She hadn't realised her mother had been so tiny. 'Too tight, can't breathe!'

'Sometimes, to look pretty, you 'ave to endure a bit of torture,' said Nan, helpfully.

Tatty glowered.

Marigold packed Tatty a small trunk, but wasn't able to persuade her daughter to wear a pair of satin slippers to match the blue dress. Tatty hated shoes so much that the soles of her feet had the appearance of cracked leather.

'Why don't you go to my bedchamber,' said Marigold, 'an' see yourself in the lookin'-glass. We'll be in the parlour when you're ready.'

Tatty flew down the shaft and into her mother's room. She heard a ripping noise and craned her neck to look.

'Come here, child,' said Marigold's mirror.

The mirror stood open, like a book propped on end. Its carved case was made of bone, which had absorbed lots of magic over the years (It wasn't completely unheard of that inanimate objects could begin to speak, but it was still rare). The mirror didn't like Nan much, and each time she went to clean it the mirror would swear at her in a very unladylike fashion. Nan would grumble that it was 'complainin' that I'm rubbin' too hard. And the *language* – it's disgraceful. I'm not used to hearin' such vileness!' which wasn't strictly true as Nan could curse as well as anybody.

Tatty went over to the mirror. Ma had pinned her shoulder-length hair up off her face. Even her overly large ears had an elegance about them. The only things that looked the same were the freckles dusting her nose and cheeks.

'You look delightful, dear,' said the mirror; 'but then, bathing does help; I do wish you little people would wash more often, it makes all the difference. You know, I *do* like the Forget-Me-Nots in your hair – a lovely touch.'

Tatty smiled at her reflection. Her mother's dress didn't look too tight. She twisted to see if she could see the rip.

'What – What exactly are you doing, dear?'

'I thought I heard a tearin' noise, at the back.'

'Turn around.'

Tatty turned, waiting for the news that the dress was ruined.

'Ah, yes, I can see a tiny tear next to your right wing. I wouldn't have noticed if you hadn't told me about it. Just keep your wings folded and people will be none-the-wiser … especially *you-know-who.*'

'Thanks for saying I look nice.'

'Could have been improved with shoes, but we can't have everything, can we? Have a lovely time, wherever you're going.'

Tatty murmured, 'I'll try.' She flew down to the parlour.

'Don't forget you're representin' the Moons at the palace, Tatty, so don't forget to mind your *P*s and *Q*s. Don't speak till you're spoken to, and don't bite your nails – it's common,' instructed Nan, dabbing at her nose with her apron hem.

Marigold hugged Tatty tightly.

Nan stared at her granddaughter. 'You'll do,' she said, finally.

Papa got up from his rocking chair. 'Of course she'll do, she's a Moon, isn't she!'

'I'll be back before you know it.' Tatty struggled not to cry. 'Wish me luck.'

Papa led her to the door. She laid her hand on the wood. The door felt warm. For the first time she noticed the grime around the latch, where all their everyday touches had become ingrained. The strange scar throbbed. The latch sprang up by itself and the door swung inwards. Tatty blinked in the sunshine. The guards had gone.

'This way, Tatty,' said Papa. 'Sir Edwin's waitin'.' He led her up a slope and past a glade of rhubarb, whose massive leaves were scorched brown in the late-August sun.

Tatty shivered. Papa's arm tightened around her shoulders.

The carriage, surrounded by children, waited in a dusty clearing.

Sir Edwin Popplewhite sat high on a red velvet seat inside a brass coal scuttle. Above, there stretched a red-and-white-striped sun canopy. Both guards stood on a foot-plate at the back, and at the front a long-haired elf held two oars, each ending in a dirty-grey seagull wing instead of a paddle. One of the guards jumped down and opened a door, then unfolded a set of steps. Papa helped Tatty into the carriage. She sat up beside Sir Edwin. Several children climbed the sides of the carriage and hung over the rim, stroking the soft velvet with their grubby hands.

'Get down!' ordered Sir Edwin, flicking a white handkerchief at them as if he was in danger of catching an incurable disease. 'Get down

I say. Keep clear! Sproutly,' Sir Edwin called to the pony-tailed oarsman, 'it's time to drive on. Let us go before we're completely swamped!'

Sproutly lifted the gull wings clear of the ground. He began to pull them as if he were rowing on water. Faery and elven children leaped from the scuttle's sides and stood back to watch, covering their faces as dust filled the air. A tiny elf came close. 'Are you gonna find our Burnley, Tatty Moon?' she called.

The child was Stellar Snodgrass, Burnley's sister.

Other children joined in with more questions: 'Where're you goin'?' called a small boy.

'Who's the old dribbler in the fancy clobber?' cried another.

'Can I come, too?'

'And me?'

'Oi, Tatty ... 'E's not from Little Upham is 'e?'

'Does your ma know you're goin' off with a weirdo?'

'You goin' to The Palace Over Yonder?'

'Is she ...?'

'You are, aren't you?'

'Wanna page, mister? I've always wanted t' see the palace.'

Soon the children's voices were drowned by the whooshing oars. They retreated to a safe distance, to avoid being blown over. The scuttle lurched forward. With each pull on the oars, Sproutly leaned back so far he seemed about to fall right over the side. They rose slowly, until the carriage was above the rhubarb glade. Sproutly dipped an oar sharply, and the scuttle turned in a great sweeping arc. They drew level with the top of the Willow Tree, and then completed a full circuit of it. Nan, Marigold, and Papa, stood in the front garden, waving. The scuttle swooped away and Tatty lost sight of the willow for a second, spinning in her seat until she saw it again, smaller now. She felt a hand on her arm so turned to face the front, determined not to cry.

The scuttle soared over the meadow where the cows grazed, and over the next field, and the next. Sproutly rowed the vessel smoothly through the blue sky; the Whump – Whump – Whump of the oars was loud. Tatty felt lost among these strangers and wished Will was with her, but he still slept, and would for another five or six hours at least. *What's he goin' to do when he wakes and finds me gone?*

A deep voice interrupted her thoughts: 'Beggin' your pardon, Sir Edwin, but would you and the guest mind fastenin' yer seatbelts – case we hits a bit of turb'lence, like?'

'Of course, Sproutly. Quite right, we wouldn't want anyone falling to their deaths now, would we?' Sir Edwin chuckled and looked at Tatty.

Not that she *would* fall to her death, having a perfectly good set of wings, but she decided she would watch Sir Edwin closely from now on. She draped the straps across her lap, not bothering to tie them, in case she had to make a quick getaway.

A harsh sound filled the sky: Kraar! – Kraar! – Kraar! Three huge carrion crows rose from the treetops and circled the scuttle.

'Lert!' screeched Tatty into Sir Edwin's ear. 'We've got to find shelter!' To her amazement, Sir Edwin stifled a yawn.

'Not to worry, lass,' said Sproutly, still rowing hard. 'The guards will sort out them ne'er-do-wells. You wait an' see.'

They flew over a field of ripe corn. The crows got closer. One struck out on its own, veering away from the others. Sir Edwin snapped his fingers and the guards unclipped two crossbows from a harness and hoisted them under their chins. The large weapons were each loaded with a row of six arrows. They didn't fire, but remained as still as statues.

Now. Fire now, Tatty silently pleaded.

The crow came closer.

Now. She crouched on the seat, peeking out from beneath the canopy.

The crow's legs came forward as if to strike.

'Please now,' she whimpered, as the bird let out another harsh

Kraar!

'Please ... *Now!*' she yelled, as the crow bore down on Sproutly.

The bird was a moment from striking, when the guards let their arrows fly. The crow was hit. An arrow had struck it through the heart and it hung in the sky for a moment, and then plummeted to the field below, where it came to lie with wings spread wide in the golden corn, like a shadow.

The other crows soared away.

Tatty was jubilant and shouted at the guards, 'It's dead! You actually killed it!'

'Of course they did.' Sir Edwin chuckled. 'You don't think we'd travel without proper protection, do you?'

Even Sproutly grinned.

Then Sir Edwin said, 'Ah, I think we've arrived.' He waved a hand towards a sparkling shape emerging from the side of a gorse-covered hill. 'My dear,' he turned to smile at her, 'the Palace Over Yonder.'

All her life Papa had told her of its beauty, but his words hadn't properly described the glittering jewel. The palace was made of glass: beautiful domes nestled amid soaring bottle-towers of purple, green, red, blue, and brown, topped by differently shaped crystals. Stained glass windows were fused together to form the outer battlements. As they passed over the tallest tower, Sproutly stopped rowing and pulled the oars across in front of him. Descending towards a courtyard below, the scuttle seemed to weigh less than a feather, landing with barely a bump. The guards jumped from the footplate and opened the doors.

Tatty stepped onto the cold pearl courtyard, instantly regretting not wearing the satin slippers. Beneath overhanging balconies and in shadowy corners, richly-dressed courtiers whispered and stared. Tatty tried to pull her crusty feet under her skirts. She'd thought her mother's dress had been lovely, but it was dowdy compared to the richly costumed creatures gliding about.

As if sensing her discomfort, Sir Edwin said softly, 'You look wonderful. Truly. Shall we?' He offered her his arm.

Tatty noticed for the first time how his eyes crinkled kindly in the corners. She placed her hand on his arm and they walked across the courtyard. She turned and waved to Sproutly, who polished greasy fingerprints off the brass scuttle. He bowed and went back to his task. She shook out her wings, still brilliant-white after her bath. A murmur of voices came from the shadows as they walked towards two huge arched glass doors, which swung silently inward as they drew closer.

'The Great Hall,' said Sir Edwin as they entered the palace.

CHAPTER TWENTY TWO

The Rat Wheel

Because the palace was made of glass, Tatty braced herself for a blast of hot air. It was like Sir Edwin could see her thoughts. 'Underground spring,' he stated; 'runs right under the floors, keeps the place deliciously cool, don't you think? Except for the kitchens, they're always an inferno.'

Tatty felt nervous. She shivered.

'I agree,' he said, laughing. 'Sometimes it's a little *too* cool.'

Then, from a galleried landing, came a voice: 'Edwin, I'm so glad you're back. It unnerves me so when you're away. I trust all went well? Oh, it *did*, for you've brought the darling creature with you.'

Sir Edwin chuckled. 'It would be more than my life was worth if I'd left her behind. Before I could blink Queen Maeve would've severed the wings from my body.'

Tatty was horrified. What a tyrant the Queen must be to even *think* of cutting off somebody's wings! She watched a tall figure glide down the sweeping staircase. Sunlight shone through the glass behind the elf, making her appear almost transparent. On her silver hair she wore a circlet of gems the same colour as her crimson gown. She swept across the floor to Tatty.

'You're very young, Titania,' she said. 'I expected someone older.'

'I'm past thirty, and please call me Tatty. Nobody calls me Titania, 'cept Nan … usually when I've annoyed her.' The beautiful elf smiled.

Sir Edwin said, 'This is my wife, Lady Miranda.'

'Plain Miranda will do,' said the elf.

'Plain Miranda,' echoed Tatty.

'*Just* Miranda,' said Sir Edwin, his mouth twitching on one side.

'Oh – yes … course,' Tatty mumbled, blushing.

'I thought we'd take some refreshment,' said Miranda.

With all the rushing about, Tatty had forgotten she'd missed lunch.

'Splendid idea, Miranda, it was a rather dusty trip.' Sir Edwin took them through an archway that led into the base of a tower. 'Shall we take the stairs, darling,' he asked his wife, 'or would you rather go by rat-wheel?'

Lady Miranda gave off a nice glow, Tatty thought; it shone around her head and shoulders like a hazy silver cloud. She still couldn't see Sir Edwin's.

'I'd rather not climb any more stairs, if you don't mind, dearest,' said Miranda, wearily. 'I've had quite enough of them today, what with the preparations for this evening's banquet.'

'Rat-wheel it is then.' Sir Edwin led them to a golden cage in the middle of the floor. 'After you,' he said, following them inside, before closing the little door. He tugged on a cord hanging through the top of the cage. Somewhere, a long way above, a bell rang. A moment later the cage gave a jolt and began to rise.

Looking up, Tatty noticed the rope pulling the cage upwards seemed a bit frayed, as if something had chewed it. She looked down and wondered if she'd be able to get the door open before the rope snapped and the cage hit the ground in a mangled mess. *Doubtful.* Above them, a circular opening had been cut into the glass ceiling,

124

where the rope disappeared. There was a horrible creaking, grinding sound. Soon after, the cage passed through the opening and Tatty saw what had made the noise: a *rat*, scratching around inside a wooden wheel that turned shafts and cogs attached to the rope, raising the golden cage. When the cage was level with the glass floor it juddered to a halt and the passengers alighted.

Sir Edwin gave the rat a handful of oats from a bucket. 'Good old boy,' he murmured, scratching the rodent behind a tattered ear.

Tatty thought it was sweet, the way Sir Edwin petted the mangy creature, and that he must be nice, after all; even if she couldn't see his glow. 'How did he lose his eye, Sir Edwin?' she asked, noticing the rat wore a faded black eye-patch.

Edwin answered softly, 'He lost it when he was a hairless babe; found him beyond the palace walls, terribly injured. No sign of his mother. He'd been attacked by something, thought we were going to lose him at one point. Sproutly nursed him back to health ... He would've kicked the bucket without Sproutly and his ointments.' Sir Edwin spoke to the rat. 'Once, when you were young and more presentable, you were a great favourite of the Queen, weren't you, old chap?' He turned the rat's moth-eaten head, so he could look into its remaining eye. 'She had a silver chariot made for you, and you wore a silver eye-patch, too. You were magnificent then. How times have changed, Nibblit, eh? I hated to have to plead for you to be given this task, to stop you from being ... you know: "put out to pasture", as it's politely called.' Sir Edwin looked at Tatty and drew a hand across his throat in a slicing motion.

Tatty gulped and stared pityingly at the old rat, at the bald patches in its dull fur, and the way its tail kinked in the middle. She was about to pat Nibblit on his back, when Sir Edwin did just that, sending up a billowing cloud of choking dandruff. Sir Edwin coughed and thumped his chest.

Tatty let her hand drop to her side.

Nearby, Lady Miranda held a heavily jewelled curtain aside. Sir

Edwin and Tatty passed beneath and entered a magnificent room. Its rounded glass walls were draped in luxurious fabric, and the glass floor was covered in warm woollen rugs, soft under Tatty's bare feet. A window had been left ajar, letting in a slight breeze. On a gilded table sat a tray of drinks and sweet pastries. Tatty was told to help herself. As she bit into a strawberry tart, she thought, guiltily, that it tasted better than anything Nan could have ever baked.

★ ★ ★

Willum Patch slept like the dead. Unlike a corpse, his brain swirled with feverish dreams:

It was night. Brambles hung all around. Sharp and cruel, they tore at his clothing. Then, through the snagging tendrils came a horror: a hideous mouth yawed towards him. Cracked lips smacked together, licked by a yellowed tongue. Strange words came from the mouth: 'Num – num – num.' Drool pooled on the ground in a thick puddle. The lips parted to reveal two rows of jagged teeth, which blurred, then transformed into odd-sized gravestones. One, right at the front in the bottom row, had Will's name and year of birth carved into it. Eerily, the place where his year of death should have been had been left blank … Then he was pulled down into a dark hole. Earth clogged his mouth and he choked. His head banged against roots and stones as he sped along a tunnel. He was being carried … by who, or what, he didn't know. Then there was nothingness.

He slept on; black hair clung damply to his forehead, like clammy fingers.

CHAPTER TWENTY THREE

Bridget Sproutly

Lady Miranda pulled aside another curtain, this time to reveal a tangled network of copper pipes, each ending in a mouthpiece with a paper tag attached. She selected a pipe with the written tag *Ned and Bridget Sproutly*, and spoke into it: 'Tatty is ready for you now, Bridget.'

A faint, tinny voice answered, *'Who?'*

'Oh, I meant, Titania.'

'Yes, right away, m' Lady.'

Tatty was wary. 'Ready for what?'

Lady Miranda let the curtain fall back. 'The housekeeper, Mrs Sproutly, will help you prepare your toilette for this evening's festivities.'

'I don't need help with the *toilet!*' said Tatty, horrified. 'I can manage that on my own, thank you!'

'What my wife means,' explained Sir Edwin; 'is that Mrs Sproutly will help you with your hair; washing, dressing and such – for the banquet this evening.'

'Washin'?!' said Tatty in a panic. 'I had a *bath* this mornin'. Wet all over I was! I won't need another till The Long Sleep.'

'Well, in that case,' said Miranda, 'a swift rinse of hands and face should be sufficient. Don't you agree, Edwin?'

'Oh, yes, quite agree … don't think I'll bother bathing either – complete waste of time and effort if you ask me. Sweaty business banquets, merry-making, and such.'

Just then, a red-faced, breathless figure bustled through the curtained entrance. The elf clung to the back of a chair for support. 'Oh my,' she gasped. 'If d'ose stairs don't finish me off one day, den me name's not Bridget Sproutly, so 'tisn't.'

Sir Edwin sighed in exasperation. 'My dear Mrs Sproutly, why you don't save your legs and use the rat-wheel, I'll *never* know.'

'Sir, oi don't hold wid dem new-fangled contraptions. Oi'd no sooner trust dat sorry-looking rat dan oi would floi.' She looked from Sir Edwin to Tatty. 'No offence.'

Sir Edwin shook his head in bewilderment. 'Well, anyway, I'd like you to meet Titania Moon, though she'd prefer to be addressed as Tatty. Tatty, this is Mrs Sproutly, palace housekeeper.'

'Nice to meet you, Mrs Sproutly.'

Bridget Sproutly grasped both of Tatty's hands. 'Oh, choild! It's a happy day, so it is. And ye're much younger than oi expected. Not dat age should be a barrier, for oi'm sure ye'll defeat him.' She dropped her voice and leaned closer. ''Cause if ye don't, we're all doomed, so we are.'

Tatty stared at the housekeeper with a creeping feeling of dread. She pulled her hands free and turned to Sir Edwin. 'What's she on about, defeat him?'

Mrs Sproutly grew flustered. 'Oh, oh, oi'm so sorry … oi've spoken out of turn …'

'Don't be silly, Bridget,' said Lady Miranda. 'You weren't to know the child hadn't been told about … Well, the Queen is going to explain the details personally to Tatty, after the banquet – which, if we're not careful, will soon be upon us. Bridget, please take our guest to her quarters.'

'Yes' m' Lady. Please follow me, Miss.'

It was clear to Tatty that Sir Edwin and Miranda would tell her nothing. *Why?* she thought. *What's the big secret?* And why couldn't they get rid of the magpies and Gnomes themselves? She mumbled a 'thank you' and followed Mrs Sproutly past the rat-wheel, where Nibblit now snored, and down steep steps to the bottom of the tower.

★ ★ ★

Alone in their chambers, Miranda Popplewhite said, 'Can that little country bumpkin really be the next queen, Edwin? It's hard to believe that she has even a *spot* of royal blood; though, I admit, she does have charm.'

'The Queen insists she's the rightful heir,' Edwin answered. 'The wings confirm it, and in her hand I saw evidence of the third eye. It was troubling her.'

'Then we must hope she's fit for the task, for it won't be easy.' Miranda went to the window, pushing it wide. She looked out over the palace, home for most of her life. In her mind she tried to picture it smashed to thousands of glinting shards. She shook her head. *No! It couldn't happen – it mustn't!* She gripped the window ledge tightly and whispered: 'She must defeat him. She must.' *Him, from her earliest memories it had always been about Him.*

★ ★ ★

Tatty followed Mrs Sproutly across the Great Hall, noticing the ceiling for the first time. A human's image was etched into the colourful glass: rounded ears; short, curly yellow hair. The kneeling figure wore golden armour from neck to toe. There was writing on the glass. Tatty squinted, trying to read the elaborate script. *St. Jeanne d' Arc. Funny name,* she thought; *a proper mouthful. I'll call her Jeanie.* She was startled by Mrs Sproutly's loud voice:

'Ye girls will need more wax on dat floor. Have ye had a delivery today?'

Three faery maids whizzed across the floor, dusters tied to their feet, wings beating at lightning speed. 'Yes, Mrs Sproutly,' they called.

'Ye'll definitely need more.'

One of the maids took a small flute from her apron pocket and

129

blew into it.

Nothing, no sound. Broken, thought Tatty, absently. They had only gone a few more steps when a droning began in the distance. It grew louder and louder. Next, the Great Hall's doors swung open and a dozen enormous bumblebees swarmed inside like fuzzy balloons, their legs loaded with great globs of beeswax, which they dropped in evenly spaced, creamy splats. Once they'd dumped their cargo, the bumblebees left. The maids skated through the wax with duster-wrapped feet.

Mrs Sproutly smiled. 'Dat's more like it. When ye've finished dis floor ye can start out in da courtyard – and hurry up! Ye've only an hour till de tables are brought in for de banquet.'

The maids skated faster, until they were blurred shapes whizzing around the hall.

Satisfied, Bridget Sproutly bustled on with Tatty close behind. Next, the housekeeper turned a corner so fast that Tatty almost fell headlong into gurgling blackness. She wheeled her arms to keep from falling in and wondered how Mrs Sproutly seemed to hover over the gushing dark water.

'Don't look so worried,' Mrs Sproutly said, laughing; ''tis only a glass floor bewitching yer eyes, not'ing more. Old Bridget hasn't learnt to fly yet, mores de pity.'

Tatty edged along the slippery floor. They had entered the hillside. A gloomy rock tunnel disappeared into the darkness. Mrs Sproutly clapped her hands and, instantly, hundreds of lanterns lining the tunnel walls lit up, casting a flickering glow. Tatty could see flashing scales from fish, darting about in the water beneath the glass floor. *The underground spring …*

Hurrying after the housekeeper's rustling skirts, gooseflesh prickled Tatty's arms in the chill air. Ahead in the gloom, too far to see, she could hear water splashing on rock.

'Here we are,' said Mrs Sproutly, unlocking a small door in the right-hand wall.

They entered a candlelit room. It reminded Tatty of her bed-chamber in the Willow Tree, with its curved walls. The room was warmed by a stove whose chimney vanished through the rock ceiling. Her trunk had been placed at the foot of a narrow bed. A small side-table held two candlesticks, a mirror, and a large jug and bowl.

Tatty stood by the bed. 'Are you related to Sproutly, who brought me here in the carriage, if you don't mind me askin'?'

'Oi don't mind. Yes, Sproutly's me husband,' said Bridget.

'Where are you from, Mrs Sproutly?' Tatty asked, sitting down on the bed. 'It's just that you speak … different.'

'Call me Bridget, dearie. And no, oi'm not from around here. Oi'm from across de Oirish Sea. Have ye ever heard of de Emerald Oisle?'

'No, I haven't, but it sounds lovely,' said Tatty, 'very … green.'

'Oh tis beautiful,' Bridget agreed, 'but ever so damp.' She suggested Tatty might benefit from a nap before the banquet, 'To see ye t'rough dis evening's shenanigans.'

Tatty agreed, though she couldn't see how she'd ever sleep. The thought of appearing at the banquet in front of strangers made her stomach lurch. The housekeeper helped her out of her dress and turned back the bedclothes. Tatty slid between crisp, cool sheets. The housekeeper blew out one of the candles, before tiptoeing out the door. Tatty thought she heard a key turn in the lock. But why would Mrs Sproutly lock her in? She wasn't going anywhere, *can't even remember the way home* … She yawned and listened to the crackle of flames inside the stove as she fell asleep.

She dreamed of mallow clouds and a toffee river, with fish striped like mint humbugs. Tatty laughed as she sat on sherbet soil, watching them leap from the thick swirling toffee. Someone approached on the far sherbet bank.

The figure was hazy at first, but as it got nearer Tatty could see the person was pale and looked sad. He had a short pointed beard and long, untidy, black hair, with a shock of white at the temple. She smiled to cheer him up, but that just seemed to make him angry. His mouth opened and meaningless words that she didn't understand came out. One of his arms grew longer, until it reached across the toffee river. His warm dry hand gripped one of hers. *Too hard.* He squeezed the hand with the scar. It hurt.

'C'mon, Tatty, time t' get up.' Bridget patted her hand and brushed hair off her forehead. Hairpins dug into her scalp.

'Is it time?' Tatty mumbled.

'Yes, dear.' Bridget lit the candle. She poured water into a bowl on the table and guided Tatty to a stool. Tatty gazed at her reflection. It stared back, a pale statue. She watched numbly as Bridget dampened her hair and teased it into place, reattaching some loose Forget-Me-Nots. Next, Tatty put on the satin dress. Once Bridget had eased Tatty's wings through the wing-slots in the back and fastened the buttons, she said: 'Ye've a small tear here. Oi didn't notice it before. Not to worry, oi'll pop in a couple o' stitches and ye'll never know it'd ever been torn.' She scratched her head. 'Now, where did oi put dat needle?'

Tatty frowned as Bridget peered up her sleeves, down her bodice, and rummaged in her apron pocket. Finally, she reached into her frizzy hair and pulled out the longest needle Tatty had ever seen. How it had ever fit under her mobcap in the first place was a mystery? The needle looked as if it would damage the dress rather than mend it.

'Ha, oi know what ye're t'inking,' said Bridget, 'dat dis needle's going to do more harm dan good. But ye'd be wrong. Dis needle belonged to Oona, da great Sea Witch. It's made from a spine of da Lesser Oblong Sea Urchin. Ye have to be swift to catch 'em, dey're one of de fastest creatures on da seabed. Keep still, oi'll be done in no time.' Within moments of touching the dress with the needle, the mending was complete.

Tatty swivelled round, straining to see the stitches in the mirror. None were visible. The tear had vanished. 'Neptune's kneecaps, thank you, Bridget.'

'Ah, tis not'ing.'

After a pause, Tatty said, 'Bridget …?'

'Yes, choild.'

'I … I had a weird dream before you woke me. Lately my dreams have been ever so clear, like they're happenin' in real life. I saw a stranger, with a pointy beard and scruffy black hair; there was a white streak in it, right here;' Tatty touched her temple. 'He seemed really angry.'

Behind her, Bridget appeared to freeze. Her eyes locked onto Tatty's. For a while the housekeeper was silent. 'Oi recollect a young fellow matching dat description … da white streak seems familiar. Mind, oi t'ink ye'd be better off asking Sir Edwin about it, ra'der dan me.' She avoided looking into the mirror again. 'Right, ye're about done. Ye look gorgeous.' Bridget stood back and smiled. 'We'd best hurry along. De Great Hall was filling up quickly when oi passed t'rough earlier.' She ushered Tatty out the door and into the cold tunnel.

Tatty noticed that the tunnel was dark; a lot of lamps had gone out.

★★★

Deep in the hillside, inside a cavernous chamber, where the drip, drip, drip of water echoed, a withered crone stared into her enchanted rock-pool. She watched The Next follow the housekeeper along the tunnel, not far from where she and Jeb now stood.

'See Jeb – see The Next,' she crooned. 'How young she is. How innocent.' The shrunken hag stroked the back of his smooth brown neck with a yellowed fingernail.

'I see her,' he said.

'Is she strong enough that is the question? Cormac grows in strength every day, with more minions joining him.' She sighed. 'We may lose her yet. Pity.' With a twitch of a bony finger the image in the pool faded, and the empty eye-socket in her palm closed its wrinkled lid.

'Come, Jeb, and help an old lady prepare.'

★★★

Some lamps blinked on and off. Tatty heard Bridget Sproutly mutter something about how 'dey don't breed glow-worms like dey used to,' and how she was 'always changing de dratted t'ings.' Reaching into her apron pocket, the housekeeper took out a fat wriggly glow-worm. Her pocket hadn't bulged at all, but remained quite flat, even when she reached in and pulled out another insect, tucking this one into her armpit. 'Good job oi've got deep pockets – odderwise dis place'd be in constant darkness.'

Tatty nodded. *Bottomless pockets, more like.*

The first glow-worm shone brightly, Bridget took a glass jar from one of the recesses in the wall, unscrewed the lid and tipped a dead insect onto the floor. She thrust the new glow-worm inside and screwed the lid on quickly. The second glow-worm received a smack before it began to glow, and Bridget slid it inside another jar. She picked the two dead glow-worms off the floor and dropped them into her pocket. 'Waste not, want not – I'll make a nice broth for Mr Sproutly's supper.' She turned to Tatty, 'Oi'll do de odders later. We'd better get a move on, wouldn't want ye to arrive after de Queen.'

As they neared the end of the tunnel the noise and chatter grew loud. Tatty hung back.

Bridget said: 'Brace yerself and gird yer loins, choild. Hold dem wings up straight and proud. Take a deep breath. Yer audience are waiting for ye. Now … go on!' Bridget shoved Tatty into the brightness of the Great Hall.

In a daze, Tatty repeated in her mind, over and over, *I'm girdin' my loins – I'm girdin' my loins – I'm girdin my loins'–*

~CHAPTER TWENTY~FOUR~

Horace Hemp and His Performing Woodlice

The chatter of guests dwindled to silence as Tatty entered the Great Hall. A few slow handclaps turned to applause, mixed with loud cheers. Tatty felt like her legs weren't moving; that it was only the noise from the guests carrying her along. She turned to find Bridget, but the housekeeper had vanished. At the far end of the vast room, where a long table sat upon a raised platform, Sir Edwin Popplewhite beckoned. As she walked towards him, guests bowed and curtsied. She looked up. Moonlight had dulled the colours in the glass ceiling, so that Jeanie seemed to be sleeping. The Great Hall looked magical: rows of tables were lit with hundreds of candles; glow-worms drifted overhead like wandering stars. Finally, Tatty stood in front of the platform. She circled it and stepped up. Sir Edwin pulled a large ornate chair back from the table and Tatty sat on the velvet cushion. The chair on her right was even bigger.

Sir Edwin announced in a booming voice: 'My Lords, Ladies, and esteemed guests, would you please be seated!' The glimmering crowd jostled to be the first at their places. On the tables, named place settings were used so that sworn enemies were kept separate.

Tatty twiddled the heavy cutlery and checked that the plates really were made of solid gold. She realised that it had grown quiet, and that everybody seemed to be staring in the direction of the rock tunnel. A horrible screeching came from the entrance, followed by lots of harsh curses. Sir Edwin laid a hand on Tatty's shoulder and whispered, 'Queen Maeve approaches.'

'What's that noise?' she asked, imagining a fearsome ogre.

He sighed. 'Beelzebub.'

'Beelzebub?'

'Yes, the Queen's chariot rat – most unpredictable. I advised Her Majesty to use Nibblit. We haven't had such a large function in the longest time, but Her Majesty said he didn't look the part any more and she'd be a complete laughing-stock if she used him. Poor old lad. Though I think Nibblit's finest hour is yet to come, I'm sure of it.'

A small procession emerged from the tunnel. Everyone stood to attention.

Even from a distance, Tatty could see the Queen was tall. As the chariot came closer she saw a towering silver crown perched upon silver-grey hair. White gloves covered the Queen's hands, and a sparkly veil hid her face. Over her shoulders hung a heavy looking, high-collared, white cloak; magnificent white wings trembled behind. *Like mine,* thought Tatty. Queen Maeve shone in the soft light of the Great Hall.

The rat pulling the chariot let out another grating squeak. A groom yanked the silver bridle to quieten him. Beelzebub tossed his glossy head, lifting the elf off his feet. Footmen rushed forward to help as Queen Maeve wobbled in the back of the chariot. Tatty gasped. Sir Edwin's grip on her shoulder tightened for a moment. Thankfully, the Queen remained upright and relieved sighs echoed around the hall. Tatty thought she could see someone else riding with the Queen, but only the top of the person's head was visible over the side of the chariot.

Minutes later, a white gown crumpled into the large chair next to Tatty's. Then the other guests sat. The Queen's white-gloved hands rested together on the table, the left had a huge ring on one of the fingers; Tatty dragged her gaze from it, turning to see a boy seated on her other side. He had dark brown skin and eyes that were almost black. She smiled. He didn't. She looked away and her empty stomach rumbled.

The Queen tut-tutted.

Tatty stared at the endless sea of faces around the hall. A longing for the Willow Tree brought a lump to her throat.

The Queen drummed her fingers on the table.

Gloves and a veil, thought Tatty, idly twirling her fork. *Maybe she's ugly or horribly disfigured?*

Queen Maeve turned and gave a huff of disapproval.

She heard me, thought Tatty, horrified, *but I didn't speak! Surely she can't tell what I'm thinkin'?*

'Yes – I can, actually,' said Queen Maeve. 'MindSpy is a gift few possess, though you'll have *some* elements of it at present.'

Tatty stared open-mouthed. 'M – MindSpy?'

'Yes, I just told you. *Do* speak clearly, I cannot abide mumblers!'

Silence followed, interrupted again by Tatty's stomach. The Queen turned away to speak to Sir Edwin, seated beside her. Tatty wished the food would hurry, she'd only eaten a few small pastries earlier. Her mind drifted to thoughts of Will, and Mr Patch … She hoped he wouldn't be too upset when he woke to find her gone.

Sir Edwin, wearing a smart scarlet coat, stood up. 'Would you all join with me in singing the first verse of the anthem to our beloved Queen Maeve?' A group of musicians up in the gallery began to play a dreary tune. Everyone stood and began to sing, including Tatty, who lagged behind because she didn't know the words.

'Good Queen Maeve, your praises we sing,
'Good Queen Maeve, your braids we singed,
Health and happiness, to you, Majesty,
Health an' crabbiness are your … tragedy,
Let your reign be triumphant and proud,
Let Lorraine blow trumpets out loud,

And may you always stay brave and true,
 Annie-May, you've a stain on grey shoes,
For you, our lives we would willingly give,
 Forsooth … Olive's a flibber–ti–gibbet,
For centuries more we hope you will live,
 For centipede lore is hopeless ol' drivel,
We pledge that all shall serve you forever,
 Green veg's what we'll serve you forever,
Great Queen, till your fi–i–i–nal breath.'
 Grapes and swill on fly–y–blown bread.'

Everyone sat and dinner was finally served. Great silver platters were carried from the kitchen by elves dressed in black and white tunics; some of the dishes were so large that it took two to carry them. The Queen's table was served first. An enormous stag beetle – complete with antlers – was slid on to each plate.

Tatty tucked a napkin into the front of her dress. She'd never eaten stag beetle before. They were supposed to be a delicacy. It looked like it was still alive; she prodded it with her fork, expecting it to lunge, but it remained politely still. Her knife barely made a mark on its armour. She abandoned her cutlery and wrenched one of the insect's legs off, biting it and nearly breaking a tooth. She sighed. From the corner of her eye she realised that she was being watched. The dark-skinned boy shook his head and nodded towards a pincer-like tool beside her plate. She picked it up. The boy smiled for the first time. He wasn't eating the same as everyone else, Tatty noticed. His plate was pile high with vegetables. *Fussy so-and-so* she thought. *He'd never get away with that if he lived with Nan.*

The Queen was using a pincer-thingummy too. Tatty copied, cracking the thick shell to get at the juicy meat inside. She reckoned it must be a bother having to keep lifting a veil every time you wanted to put food in your mouth. Then she remembered MindSpy, so concentrated on her meal. She managed to finish nearly all the stag beetle. One leg remained on her plate; she grasped it with the pincers and gave it a squeeze. The limb made a whooshing sound as it flew through the air, before coming to rest at the feet of a guard on the other side of the hall. He kicked the leg under the nearest table before anyone noticed.

Suddenly, the Queen said, 'Ah, my favourite part … lovely pudding.'

Waiters cleared the tables and placed massive sponge puddings, topped with fruits and whipped cream, in front of each guest. While she ate, Tatty glanced at the boy again. He sat hunched over, his shoulders covered in a heavy cape. She wouldn't dare slouch like that at home. Nan had no time for slouchers.

Sir Edwin made another announcement: 'May I have your attention, please!' He continued once the chattering had died down. 'Back by popular demand, I'd like to present, Horace Hemp and his amazing performing *wooooooooodlice!*'

The crowd roared as a skinny elf, dressed in a yellow and red all-in-one suit, with matching puffball hat, ran to the middle of the Great Hall and somersaulted, while juggling six greyish-brown balls. Usually, anyone performing this sort of act without using magic was thought extraordinarily gifted. The audience were mesmerised.

Horace Hemp lifted a leg high above his head and juggled with one hand. The audience went *'Ooh'*. The balls travelled so fast they were a brown blur. Horace flipped one ball on to his knee, where it remained as if stuck with glue. Next, there followed a dazzling display of ball-skill, using elbows, forehead, feet, and chin. The audience went *'Aahh'*.

In a flash, Horace scooped the balls into his arms. When he gave the command, 'Unroll!' the balls uncurled to reveal six woodlice. They scuttled up his arms and squeezed on to his shoulders. One woodlouse climbed to the top of his hat. Standing upright on their hindmost legs, the crustaceans waited for their next command. 'Alee – *up!*' barked Horace. Immediately all the woodlice scrabbled on to Horace's hat, where they balanced on top of one another until they had formed a wobbling tower, their segmented bodies creaked and clunked like rusty armour. Horace walked rigidly among the guests, enjoying their gasps of wonder.

Tatty yawned. It had only been a few hours since she'd arrived, but she still felt sad when she thought of the Willow Tree. This was the furthest she had ever travelled from home.

'If you wish to ... write a note ... I shan't object,' said Queen Maeve, sluggishly.

'Eh?'

'You *should* say, "I beg your pardon, Your Majesty," actually,' said the Queen. 'You'd like to contact your kin? It's understandable, I suppose ... Your family have been informed that your little, um, *stay* might take longer than previously planned ... perhaps by as much as two or three, or four days ...'

'And they were all right with that, were they?' Tatty longed for Nan and Marigold to appear, to demand that she be sent straight home.

'Oh, yes ... more than all right,' drawled Queen Maeve. 'They were honoured.' Her veil puffed outward as she gave a huge sigh. 'Now, the note ... you'll find writing implements in the kitchens ... over there.' She waved a hand vaguely towards a set of swinging doors that the waiters had used all evening.

Tatty slid off her chair and gave an awkward curtsy. 'Thank you, Your Majesty.' She followed a waiter carrying dirty dishes. As he elbowed the swing doors inward, she darted through behind him.

The kitchens were hot and steamy and the glass walls ran with moisture. There were lots of raised voices. A plump elf in a tall white hat – and with the pointiest ears Tatty had ever seen – was doing most of the shouting.

'This air conditioning's playin' up again, Ethel!' he yelled. 'How I'm supposed to get my creative juices flowin' is beyond me! The only juice flowin' at the moment is the sweat runnin' down my face. It's a wonder they haven't dried up completely, what with this heat. I'm tellin' you, if conditions don't improve soon I'm going to leave!'

'Tell me about it, Cook,' agreed greasy-haired Ethel, gesturing upward with huge muscly arms. 'Look at 'em, they're droppin' like flies!'

Up on the glass ceiling moths and butterflies wilted like old lettuce leaves, trying hard to cool the stifling air with their wings. Some lost their grip on the wet glass and fluttered to the stone floor below.

'Porter! Porter! Clear this lot up will you?' barked Cook, grabbing the arm of a younger elf as he passed. Waggling his knife, he added: 'Don't bruise 'em too much; I'll turn any that don't recover into rissoles for lunch tomorrow. I can't stand waste, sign of a badly run kitchen.'

'Yes, Cook.' The young porter grabbed a broom and swept the twitching insects into a heap in the corner. As he wiped the sweat from his brow, he spotted Tatty near the doorway. 'Beggin' your pardon, Miss,' he said, removing his hat as he spoke, 'but you're not allowed in here – health an' safety.'

'S – Sorry,' Tatty stammered. 'I was told you'd have some writin' stuff … bit of charcoal and a scrap of paper …?'

'Over there,' he said, pointing to a small table. 'It's where we write down any special dietary requests. 'Cause some folk have allergies, an' that.'

'Thanks,' Tatty said, going to the table. 'I'll be out of your way in a minute.'

'No problem.' The porter leaned on his broom to watch her – until Cook snapped at him to stop idling and get on with his work.

Tatty picked up a long quill and dipped it in some ink. She wrote:

Dear All,

Food is very nice but not as nice as Nan's. Folk are very posh, but nice. The Queen, Lady Miranda & Sir Edwin have been very nice, as is the Palace Over Yonder.

Not sure when I'll be home, soon I hope. Miss you all and love you (even Mealy),

Tatty X X X

Reading it through, Tatty realised her note contained rather too many 'nice's, though it would have to do as there was no more paper on the table, and she was too tired to remember the spell that wiped paper clean. She shook the note to dry the ink, then returned to the Great Hall.

Horace Hemp and his woodlice had finished their act. The Queen still chatted to Sir Edwin. The hunched boy was nowhere to be seen. She headed towards the raised platform; then went around it, going through the arched, glass doorway and into the pearl courtyard beyond. Tatty looked up at the sky. The moon shone down and the stars seemed close enough to touch. She creased the scrap of paper into folds, brought it to her lips and whispered. Then she opened her hands and watched the note flap skyward, up towards the moon, higher and higher – until it faltered. She blinked. The note beat itself against an invisible barrier, like a little white moth against a windowpane.

Behind her, a voice said: 'It's no use; the Curtain will be in place 'til morning, hopefully. Nothing can get in or out at night. Even our guests will be staying 'til first light.'

She turned to see the hunched boy. He looked up at the tattered note and smiled wryly. 'I don't know why Queen Maeve told you to send it? It was naughty of her. But then – she has been a little odd lately, since …'

Tatty stared at him, anger burned her cheeks. 'What is she – some kind of *numbskull*? What person in their right mind would do such a spiteful thing!' she yelled.

'Ah,' said the boy, 'and there you have it. She isn't always in her right mind. There are lapses in judgement from time to time – comes with great age. Anyway, we mustn't dwell on it or she'll see our thoughts and have us both de-winged.'

Tatty was horrified. 'What?'

The boy interrupted: 'I'm only jesting. Calm down.'

'Oh, that's all right then,' Tatty sniped. 'I've a good mind to tell her to sort out her own problem!'

He cleared his throat. 'But it isn't just *her* problem, is it? The raid on Little Upham might have been your first. For us, it's the fourth such event. The Queen can't always maintain the Curtain over the palace to shield us from human eyes, and from attacks. Queen Maeve's powers are failing. Sometimes she hasn't the strength to conjure the Curtain at all during the day. It's only by chance we haven't been spotted yet.' His voice softened to a whisper. 'She can't do it *all* by herself.'

Tatty sighed. '… Just tell me the details and be done with it.'

'That's why I'm here,' he said, smiling. 'It's time.'

He held out his arm to her, and as Tatty linked her arm through his, she saw why he hadn't eaten stag beetle at dinner. For a fleeting second, his cloak swirled away from his body as he twisted. She glimpsed a greenish-brown beetle carapace, which reached to mid-thigh. 'Oh. Well I … You can fly, too,' she said.

'Of course.' He drew back his cloak, opened his wing cases and displayed transparent wings. Moments later he closed them and let the cloak fall back.

She stared at his face for several heartbeats.

Together they hurried back inside the Great Hall.

CHAPTER TWENTY FIVE

Methuselah

Tatty watched as Sir Edwin and several servants helped Queen Maeve into the chariot. The Queen looked like she might keel over at any moment.

'She's drunk,' Tatty whispered in disbelief.

'Her Majesty most certainly is *not*!' replied the boy. 'She hasn't touched a drop all evening.'

Tatty wasn't convinced.

'And careful what you're thinking.' He tapped his temple. 'Remember – she *knows*.'

Queen Maeve gripped the handrail. The rat, Beelzebub, pawed the floor, keen to set off. He squeaked and gnashed his sharp teeth. The groom had trouble holding him, so Sir Edwin grabbed the rat's bridle. 'Who's been eating too many oats with honey on, then?' he said, glaring at the groom. 'Walk on, Beelzebub. Walk on.' The feathered plume on the rat's head bobbed jauntily as they filed past the courtiers, then carried on down the rock tunnel towards the Queen's private chambers, passing the small door where Tatty had slept only hours before. Tatty and the boy followed. The groom trailed behind, a sulky expression on his face.

'Well done Edwin,' trilled the Queen. 'Remind me to reward you with a knighthood.'

'You already have, Your Majesty,' answered Sir Edwin, batting away Beelzebub's feather.

'Oh, good … should think so too,' she mumbled, sagging dangerously. One of her wings hung out of the chariot and dragged along the floor.

A damp chill seeped through Tatty's thin dress and she shivered. The boy swept off his cloak and draped it over her shoulders. She smiled her thanks, and said, 'By the way, what's your name?'

'Jeb,' he answered.

'Jebediah?'

'No, Jebeneezer.' He laughed. 'Supposedly, my mother couldn't decide between Jebediah and Ebeneezer, so she chose a jumble of both. It's the only thing I remember her giving me.'

'I like it,' said Tatty; 'it's unusual. And call me Tatty, everyone does. My real name's Titania, but I think that's too prissy.'

His face was serious. 'Titania was the name of our very first queen. You should be honoured to share it.'

Tatty raised her voice over the sound of rushing water. 'But it's not *me*. I mean, do I look like royalty?'

He stared. 'Very well, as you wish. I shall call you Tatty – for now.'

They walked in silence. The air smelled damp and musty, like an unwashed face flannel. The hiss of running water grew louder. At the end of the tunnel was a huge cavern, where the glass floor ended; replaced by smooth rock. In the centre of the cavern a fountain spouted water into the air from a pool. On the far side of the pool was a massive, iron-studded, wooden door, with a brass door knocker.

Edwin handed the reins to the groom, jumped into the back of the chariot and prised Queen Maeve's fingers from the handrail. He and Jeb helped her down.

Tatty sat by the edge of the pool, trailing her hand in the clear water. Looking up, she saw that the cavern was topped by a beautiful glass dome, spoiled by a jagged hole on one side. She guessed it had been damaged in one of the attacks. She stood, and noticed huge bubbles bursting on the surface of the pool, wending their way up through the water from the gloomy depths. She leaned closer and called: 'Somethin' strange is goin' on in this pool. There're these big bubbles. Come an' look.' The bubbles burst rapidly now, as if whatever made them was rising from the darkness below. Feeling uneasy, Tatty stepped back from the pool's edge.

'Don't be alarmed,' called Jeb, 'but come over here – and hurry about it!'

Tatty turned her head. Both Jeb and Sir Edwin seemed frozen. She took another step back. Her legs felt like they belonged to someone else. Something followed the trail of bubbles. Something *huge*...

A warty hump rose from the churning water; unrecognisable at first, but slowly it grew, emerging like an algae-covered island, until golden eyes appeared above the waterline.

The island was a monstrous toad.

The amphibian wiped its toes across one enormous eye. The movement was hypnotic. Tatty was unable to move or utter a sound. The toad opened its mouth and took a lazy gulp. Then, it shot its tongue out and captured Tatty in a sticky hug, before drawing her into its mouth. Inside was pitch black, and wet. She felt powerful muscles pull her towards the toad's throat. She panicked, couldn't think of a spell. Her mind was blank. *Come on you idiot! THINK!* 'Help!' she yelled instead, trying not to be sick.

Thankfully, Queen Maeve shouted: 'Methuselah, spit the child out at once, do you hear! She – is – a – *friend!*'

The toad blinked twice and spat Tatty at the far wall. She slid to the floor in a crumpled mess. 'Nan,' she wailed, 'don' wanna go to the palace ...'

Jeb ran over and helped her to her feet. 'Tatty, can you hear me?

146

It's, Jeb.' When she didn't respond, he slapped her face – hard. She was instantly alert, looking over his shoulder toward the pool.

'Ow!' She rubbed her stinging cheek.

'Sorry.'

She fumbled with her hair. 'Look at me,' she sobbed. 'It's only gone an' ruined my hair! I looked so n – nice, too …'

'Never mind your hair,' said Jeb, 'at least you're in one piece.'

Tatty eyed the toad, still at the water's edge. She gripped Jeb's sleeve. 'Come on. Let's get out of here before it eats us all.'

'He won't. Methuselah's been guarding the royal chambers for a thousand years. He's never seen you before, probably thought you were a danger to Her Majesty, what with everything that's happened.'

'Do I *look* dangerous?' Tatty asked, plucking at her saliva-soaked skirts.

Jeb's voice was cool. 'You'd be surprised. Come, we must hurry, Queen Maeve is weary.'

Tatty snapped: '*She's* weary? I'm bloomin' done for!'

CHAPTER TWENTY SIX

The Mermaid Knocker

After a sound telling off from Queen Maeve, Methuselah sank back beneath the crystal water. Beelzebub and the groom were also dismissed, leaving Sir Edwin, Queen Maeve, Tatty and Jeb, standing by the door to the royal chambers.

The door … was much larger than the doors to the Great Hall, made from solid oak, with knobbly iron studs and fitted with a huge brass door knocker almost as big as the door itself. The knocker was in the form of a mermaid sitting on rocks and looking out to sea, her face hidden by long windblown hair. Leaving Jeb to support the Queen, Edwin grasped the mermaid's tailfin in both hands.

Three times he lifted the tail and let it fall.

The clanging was loud enough for Tatty to have to cover her ears. As she studied the mermaid, she could have sworn that a lock of hair moved, as if blown by a breeze? She blinked several times. It happened again. Next, the rest of the mermaid's hair began to ripple and billow. There was a horrible sound of metal grinding as the head began to turn to face Sir Edwin. The mermaid's eyelids creaked open, a blue fire burned deep in the sockets; when her cold lips parted she spoke with a gargle, as though from the depths of the sea:

'Many wish to pass this way,
Some succeed, and some I slay,
Be ye friend? Or be ye foe?
This I'll learn afore I go,
A secret word ye must proclaim,
To step inside yon domain.'

Edwin Popplewhite glanced about, before whispering: 'Titania.'

The mermaid's tail uncoiled and flopped on to the rock floor with the slapping sound of a wet fish. *'Ye may pass,'* she gargled, her tail pushing the heavy door open.

'Come along, let's not dawdle,' Sir Edwin said, as they entered an inner chamber that had an eerily silent waterfall at the far end. It ran from the rock ceiling like a liquid screen. Sir Edwin checked Queen Maeve's slow progress. 'We're almost there, Your Majesty.'

Perspiration speckled Jeb's forehead with the effort of holding the Queen upright, while Tatty helped support her other side. She was surprised at how bony her arm was, and at the great lumbering steps Queen Maeve took. Eventually, they reached the wall of water, which vanished before hitting the floor, leaving the rock dry. Sir Edwin touched the water with a finger and it parted like a pair of curtains, allowing them to pass.

Tatty was disappointed. Queen Maeve's chambers were not what she'd expected.

'I suppose you expected jewels, silver, and gold as far as the eye could see, did you?' Queen Maeve cackled.

Tatty nodded, surprised at the bare rock walls and plain furniture. Glow-worm lamps hung from hooks and candles shone out from alcoves. A rug lay before the massive inglenook fireplace. The only decorative things were an engraved, four-poster bed, and a huge portrait hanging on one wall.

'I wasn't always Queen, you know,' said Queen Maeve, sighing.

'Like you, I came from humble beginnings. I've never felt truly comfortable with the trappings of wealth. Speaking of comfort … Edwin, would you help me out of these infernal vestments of torture?' She plucked feebly at her heavy robes.

'I'll summon the maids,' said Sir Edwin.

'No, no, no. I don't want the fuss. *She* can help me.'

'Me?' Tatty gasped.

'Yes,' said Queen Maeve. 'Jeb will assist. And do hurry; I'm ready to collapse. This crown is giving me chronic neck ache.'

Jeb smiled at Tatty and knelt at Queen Maeve's feet. 'Hold Her Majesty's hands, Tatty, and I'll start by taking off her footwear.'

'Why're you wearin' her footwear?' Tatty blurted.

Jeb gave her a withering stare and muttered, 'Just hold her hands.'

Sir Edwin coughed to cover a snigger.

The Queen's bony hands reminded Tatty of a bird's claw, the way the gnarled fingers curled around her own. *Don't think that! She'll see your thoughts.* She tried to focus on the Queen's feet instead. Or, what she'd thought were the Queen's feet.

Once Jeb had lifted the robes, Tatty could see why the Queen had appeared so tall. She stood on wooden blocks attached to each foot with straps, which Jeb unbuckled. He and Tatty helped Queen Maeve step down to the floor. She was tiny, the top of her head barely reached Tatty's shoulder.

She pointed to her crown. 'Quick, Jeb, get this off … before my head disappears into my shoulders.'

So Jeb lifted the crown from her royal head – along with the royal hair.

Tatty was surprised to see crown, hair, and veil, placed on a chair. She hardly dared look at the Queen, couldn't be seen to stare … *but it would be ruder not to look, wouldn't it?* Lively eyes in a wizened face regarded Tatty with interest. A few tufts of white hair were all that remained on her ancient skull. Jeb slid the heavy cloak from the

150

Queen's shoulders. Her wings were false too, sewn on to the pearl-studded material. The Queen's natural wings were white, but any similarity with Tatty's ended with the colour. In places there were ragged holes, and when they moved dust and scales showered the floor. The cloak bunched around Queen Maeve's feet. She reminded Tatty of a little child playing dress-up.

So, *this* was the tall, proud, queen who'd ruled over the folk of Little Upham for so many centuries, nothing more than a crone in a greying shift.

'I'll have more strength to speak if I retire to bed,' said Queen Maeve, wearily. 'Not what you expected am I?'

Tatty hesitated. 'I, well, um …'

The Queen waved dismissively. 'Oh, it doesn't matter. I know what I look like and it isn't impressive. That's why we have all the …' She nodded towards the chair where the wig and crown lay, '… paraphernalia.' As she swung her stick-thin legs into the bed, Jeb covered her with an eiderdown and plumped the pillows. Queen Maeve appeared even more child-like in the huge bed. She sighed and looked at Tatty. 'Now … I understand you have an irritation?'

'Beg pardon?' Tatty flushed with embarrassment.

'Your *hand*, child,' said Queen Maeve, sighing. 'Your *hand*!'

Sir Edwin looked away.

'Oh, that … yes.' Tatty inspected the ridged scar in her palm. 'It does burn a bit sometimes – I can't remember how I got it.'

Now it was Queen Maeve's turn to look flustered. 'It isn't an *injury*, dear. It's your third eye, the second sight.'

Tatty was puzzled. 'Third … second …'

'Please tell me you aren't feeble-minded?' said the Queen. 'Or is it that your family has kept it from you?'

'Um, kept it from me ….'

Sir Edwin said, 'Tatty had no knowledge of her destiny, Your Majesty. It came as a great shock to learn that she is your heir. I think it's to her great credit that she readily agreed to come here today–'

Hardly agreed, thought Tatty.

'–without once complaining.' He looked at Tatty and winked.

'Good, good … glad to hear it,' muttered Queen Maeve, looking like she might drop off to sleep at any moment. 'Dear, oh dear,' she went on, 'I do wish people would take their … responsibilities seriously. Why, I was barely hatched when I was told that I was The Next. Never did *me* any harm. You and I have the same gift … or affliction, depending on how you look at it. Though, I must confess to being without my own third eye at the moment … sadly.' She opened her left hand so that the palm faced Tatty. A scar, identical to Tatty's own, was scored across it. The edges parted, and Tatty saw that it wasn't a scar at all, but a pair of withered eyelids. The eyeball was missing. All that remained was an empty, raw-looking socket.

'See. Gone. Stolen,' said Queen Maeve. 'I'm sure it was an inside job, someone who knew the password. How else could they have snuck in to my chambers to steal it and slip me a sleeping potion? Of course it was *made* to look like a break-in; that's why the dome over the fountain was smashed. But, for the life that's left in me, I can't seem to root him, or her, out. Without the eye's powers I can't use MindSpy effectively … or shield the palace properly. It's only a matter of time before we're discovered by the human populous.' She sighed, and let her bony hand fall back to the coverlet. 'There's a spring … over there. Look into the pool, there's someone I want you to see. Take a good look at your adversary – see what you're up against.'

Tatty went to a deep recess in the rock wall, where a bubbling spring whirled, never once overflowing, never drying out. The water appeared to boil; vapour dampened Tatty's face, but when she dipped in a finger the water was cool to the touch. Moments later, the pool grew flat and dark, until it resembled the surface of a mirror.

The Queen said, weakly: 'Concentrate on the centre of the pool, to the very bottom … and try not to blink … blinking distorts the image.'

Tatty stared until her eyes stung. A faint glow, like a gold coin,

152

glimmered at the bottom of the spring. It grew larger, and brighter, until an image appeared inside. Tatty could see a Biggun. Rapidly, the image faded and woodland emerged, with wooden houses joined by what looked like rope bridges. And there was someone inside one of the houses, at a window. *A figure, all in black; a crown of bones on his head.* His face looked cruel, made more so by its pallor and the blackness of his beard and hair, with the streak of white running through it. *The same fellow I saw in my dream,* she thought. He turned away, and all that remained of his wings were two twitching stumps. Then his face was replaced by another, the new face had huge, white, saucer-eyes. *A Gnome.*

A sudden pain seared her palm.

Her concentration broke, and the image in the pool wavered then vanished. The spring bubbled and flowed again. She straightened and saw them studying her. At the Queen's bedside, Tatty told them what she'd seen.

Queen Maeve listened intently. 'So, you saw Cormac, my beloved nephew.' The Queen described him: 'Pale complexion; beard; black hair with a white flash here,' she pointed to her own temple, 'and with two mutilated appendages which used to be wings ... I did that to teach him a lesson ... didn't work, mores the pity.' Her eyes were almost closed as she spoke. 'He's joined forces with Gnomes and magpies ... but then magpies are such silly, silly birds, I find. They'll do anything if thrown a shiny bauble. Cormac wants my throne, always has, I could see that from an early age, though he had no idea then ... simply yearns for power ... not quite right in the head, that one. I blame his accident ... and the Gnomes. They want a rich food source, plenty of elves round these parts. Somebody slipped me a draught to make me sleep ... and pried my third eye out; stole it clean away ... I do need it back so ...'

That's why I'm here, thought Tatty, her shoulders slumping, aware for the very first time that she had no choice but to confront this Cormac, find the Queen's eye, and try to rid the district of Gnomes –

though the mere thought made her feel ill. But how could she possibly expect Queen Maeve to do it? She looked at the Queen again, lost in the oversized bed. *I'll be in that same bed someday,* she thought, *havin' to deal with the sorts of things she's had to deal with.* Now it was *her* turn to take the burden. She felt a pang of home-sickness, not just for the Willow Tree, she wished more than anything that Will was beside her … 'When do I leave?' she said flatly.

Sir Edwin went to her side, lifted her hand and kissed it. 'Within the hour,' he said solemnly.

Tatty nodded. 'I'll want everyday clothes from my trunk.'

'No need,' said Jeb. 'Everything you require is here.' He went to the big portrait of Queen Maeve when she was young. She had been painted astride a rearing white mouse. Tatty thought the mouse's tail looked very lifelike – even more so when it twitched. Jeb grasped the tail and pulled. One side of the portrait swung away from the wall with a creak. It was a secret door, and hidden behind was a smaller chamber. Jeb led Tatty into the Queen's dressing-room.

Wooden mannequins stood around the room wearing different coloured robes with false wings attached. On shelves sat carved heads, each wearing a wig and veil. On the lowest shelf were wooden platforms for the Royal feet, starting off low and getting taller as the Queen shrank with age.

'These are yours,' said Jeb, showing her a neat pile of clothes on a chair. 'I'll wait outside.'

Alone, Tatty struggled out of the blue gown and hurriedly dressed in the clothes left for her. She pulled on woollen stockings and a pair of breeches. Next was a cotton shirt, then a jerkin, each cut to accommodate her wings. She removed the hairpins and brushed out her hair. Lastly, she pulled on a pair of stiff, lace-up boots. She carefully laid her mother's toad-stained dress over the chair, then pushed on the back of the portrait and re-entered the Queen's bedchamber.

Queen Maeve sipped a hot bedtime drink. Jeb sat at the end of the bed. There was no sign of Sir Edwin. 'Oh, *yes,*' said the Queen, eyeing Tatty's new clothes, 'very practical. Sir Edwin is waiting near the fountain to see the two of you off.'

Tatty looked at her questioningly.

'Yes, that's right – I did mean both. Jeb will be going with you too. He has reasons of his own to want to see the demise of Cormac. I think it would be most unfair to deprive him of the chance, don't you agree?' Queen Maeve peered over the rim of the large goblet.

Tatty laughed with relief. 'Oh. I'm so glad. I would've got lost on my own.'

Queen Maeve bade Tatty a solemn farewell. But with Jeb, the Queen's manner was quite different. She hugged him tightly. 'Come back safe, my dearest boy,' she said, her voice catching.

'Of course I will,' he replied, stroking the faery's hand. He straightened and said to Tatty: 'We'd better go. It won't do Her Majesty any good to get upset.'

'Upset! Me? *Piffle*! Hurry along now, the both of you. Don't keep Edwin waiting. It's time for my beauty sleep ... And goodness knows I need it.'

So Jeb and Tatty passed beneath the cascading water, back through the mermaid door, to where Sir Edwin Popplewhite stood by the fountain.

He held the halter of a moth-eaten rat:

Nibblit.

CHAPTER TWENTY SEVEN

Simon the Sticklebrat

The dark shape glided against the black backdrop of trees. It could have been mistaken for a hunting owl the way it flew so silently. By all appearances it was a raven, swooping and landing close by The Patch, instantly transforming into a tiny, human-looking figure. Agatha Pottage entered the cottage as silently as she'd flown moments before. She climbed the stepladder to the floor above. Going to the sleep-sack, she placed a cool hand on the sleeping elf's forehead. Agatha stared at the child, noting the way one of his pointed ears curled over at the top. 'Well, that didn't take long, did it, Willum?' she whispered. 'I've brought it back to you – sooner than I would ever have anticipated – but, there you are.' She took his hand and slipped the luck-stone into it. His fingers curled around the talisman. 'It's high time you were up,' said Agatha. 'It's way past the witching-hour and you've a long way to go before morning. Come to Pottages when you wake. Do you understand?'

'Mmm ...' Will moved restlessly in the sack.

Agatha left him then. Once through the garden gate, she transformed into the image of Chorley once more, hopping on to The Patch's wicker roof and launching into the night sky. She flew over the roof of Mould Cottage, on up the lane, then in through an open upstairs window of the store.

In her sitting room, Agatha changed back to her usual self. Croaking and scratching came from her bedroom, so she opened the door. Chorley sat on the broomstick-headboard of her bed and plucked black, downy, feathers from his breast, scattering them over the pillows. 'Please don't do that, Chorley,' she said soothingly. 'I know. You wanted to come with me, didn't you? It was quicker for me to go alone this time, that's all.'

The raven cocked his head to the side and stared meaningfully at her. Agatha sighed and went to her bookshelf. She had to read him three whole chapters of *Gulliver's Travels* before he finally settled for the night, leaving her free to dash down the stairs when she heard the shop's bell jingle. Moments later she had shrunk to her small size again. 'There you are, Will. My commiserations on the loss of your father ... terrible, shocking news. Do come in. I've something to tell you. Don't be too worried. It's about Tatty. I went to the Willow Tree after doing a bit of divining with some entrails and the Moons' told me something interesting. To tell you the truth, I'm rather worried ...'

★★★

Nibblit was weighed down with baggage: food sacks and pots and pans hung from his back. The hilt of a sword poked out from beneath a blanket. Tatty found it difficult to tear her gaze away from the weapon; she hoped it would remain unused.

'You will take care of him, won't you? And yourselves, of course,' said Sir Edwin Popplewhite. His eyes looked moist.

'We'll try our best,' Jeb assured him.

'I'm sure you will. I wouldn't trust any other creature to be as reliable as Nibblit.' Edwin gave the rat's tattered ear a last tug. 'Well, I think you've got everything you'll need.' He went to the water's edge. 'Now, where *is* that toad?'

'Toad?' Tatty's stomach lurched. She turned to Jeb. 'What do we want the toad for?'

'We need Methuselah. A bubble is the only way we're going to get out of the palace without drawing attention to ourselves. Don't worry – it's been done loads of times before.'

Tatty was more than a little puzzled.

They peered into the water, trying to see past the ripples. On the pool bed, Tatty could make out a dark shape. From what she could see, the creature looked in discomfort. Suddenly, Methuselah belched. The loud burp rumbled through the deep water. The toad opened his mouth and a massive bubble emerged and floated upward. When it broke the surface the bubble was so big that only the top half was visible.

'Right, inside,' instructed Edwin. 'You'll have to hurry. A belch-bubble only has a short lifespan before it bursts: no more than fifteen minutes at best.' Then he addressed Tatty. 'Push your way through the bubble. It'll be tough, but you'll manage. Let me look at your nails? Good. Nice and short. We don't want the thing bursting prematurely. It takes Methuselah hours to produce one of these dimensions. You fly to the bubble, Tatty, and Jeb will go with Nibblit. Once you're inside, start walking, otherwise you'll sink right through the bottom.'

Edwin turned to Jeb. 'Up on to his back now, Jeb. That's it. Easy Nibblit. I know you've a lot to carry, but it's only for a little while.' Jeb sat astride and clung to Nibblit's fur. Sir Edwin led the rat into the shallows, until water threatened to flow over the top of his boots.

Tatty hovered above the bubble. Over the roar of the fountain, she yelled: 'Cheerio then, Sir Edwin.' He waved back. She landed on the bubble and started to sink inside.

Edwin slapped Nibblit on the rump and the rat leapt into deeper water with the wood-sprite clinging on. Jeb had to lean far forward over Nibblit's neck to try and stay clear of the icy water. Seconds later, the rat pushed his pointed snout through the bubble's membrane, eventually the tip of his tail passed through too, and the bubble sealed itself once he and Jeb were inside.

Tatty dropped beside Nibblit.

'Start walking!' barked Jeb urgently, sliding from the rat's back. 'If we don't, we'll sink right out again, remember.'

Nearly overbalancing, Tatty did as she was told: the bubble rolled over and downward and sank beneath the frothing fountain.

Soon they were near the bottom and quickly sped past Methuselah, zooming out of the pool and into an underground stream, which cut through the centre of the hillside. Rocks were covered in luminous green algae, lighting everything with an eerie glow. Tatty felt sick with nerves. She looked at Jeb. His face appeared pinched, his jaw clenched. The only one who seemed to be enjoying the adventure was Nibblit. 'Bub-baw,' he squeaked. 'Preeeeeeetty bub-baw.'

As it journeyed on, the bubble travelled into deeper, darker water. The luminous algae vanished, and lights appeared, glittering in the rock's black walls. The lights shone out from the windows of an underwater city. Tatty could see figures moving in the gloomy water. At first she assumed they must be fish, until she saw arms and heads. She looked at Jeb enquiringly.

'Sticklebrats,' he told her. 'Or water-sprites. They live here. We should be meeting one of them any moment, a good friend of mine. He'll come with us a short way so we don't get swept off course. There are loads of tunnels branching off down here; it would be easy to get lost.'

She stared at him. 'But we won't though, will we? Get lost, I mean?'

'No,' said Jeb. 'Not with Simon guiding us. Ah, speaking of Simon … here he is now.'

Out of the gloom a boy appeared. But, only a boy from the waist up; below the waist, Simon was a fish. He had pale, blue-tinged skin, pondweed-green sinuous hair and green eyes to match. He spoke clearly under the water, with hardly any distortion: 'You're late. For a while there I thought you weren't coming.' He looked straight at Tatty, his pondweed hair billowing in the current. 'It's an honour,' he said, bowing.

Tatty blushed. 'Thanks,' she mouthed.

She liked Simon's face, though it was a little narrow: the way his chin tapered to a point. Also, his nose was slightly, *indistinct*. Overall, she thought he looked quite kind.

'Well, if we're *that* late we'd better get a move on,' said Jeb, loudly.

Simon grinned and swam behind the bubble, placing webbed hands against it to push it along, making them walk faster to keep up. Simon changed position often, to adjust the bubble's course.

Gaping crevices and black caves appeared every now and then, where the underground stream veered off to goodness-knew-where. Time seemed to pass slowly, making Tatty feel sure that the bubble would burst at any moment. *Fifteen minutes, Sir Edwin said we had.* Muscles in her legs ached, unused to so much walking. Just as she was about to ask when they would rest, the surrounding water lightened. The bubble began to rise. She saw Simon positioned below the bubble, helping it upward with great sweeps of his tail. They headed towards a bright light. It was only when they broke the surface that Tatty saw the moon, and that they'd left the hillside completely. Simon struggled against a strong current, but managed to push the bubble to the shallows, where it suddenly burst, leaving them waist-deep. Tatty howled as the icy water seeped through her clothes.

'Shush!' Jeb hissed. 'Do you want every predator in the area to know where we are? We have to be quiet. Grab hold of Nibblit.'

Tatty clutched a handful of the rat's fur and was dragged from the stream and up the bank. She sank to the ground and watched Jeb say goodbye to Simon. After a few words, the water-sprite waved, then dove beneath the water, leaving barely a ripple. Jeb waded to the stream's edge and crawled up the bank, collapsing on his front beside Tatty. Nibblit shook himself dry, making the pots and pans clank together, which also earned him a telling-off. He peered at Jeb with his good eye and gave a loud snort in response.

Tatty asked, 'Where to next?'

'Bicuspid Cottage. We can rest there for an hour or two. Come on.' He stood and helped Tatty to her feet. Her legs felt wobbly. They took off their boots and emptied the water out, before putting them on again and setting off in the direction the stream flowed.

On a rocky hilltop outside the palace walls, the traveller thanked the stars that his luck had held. His mount was agitated, so he patted its back to calm it. He'd caught a glimpse of movement a second ago, down on the water, and heard a definite squeak. It wouldn't take him too long to catch them. He dug his heels into his mount's flanks and set off down the side of the hill in pursuit.

CHAPTER TWENTY EIGHT

Bicuspid Cottage

'Creeeeeeeeter!' squealed Nibblit, again and again, each time louder than the last. 'Creeeeeter! Creeeeeeeeeter – creeeeeeeeeeeeeter!' The rat's high-pitched utterances rang through the night.

'Oh … for pity's *sakes*,' muttered Jeb.

'What's he on about?' moaned Tatty.

'How should I know,' said Jeb, yanking on the rope. 'It sounds as if he might be saying *critter*? He doesn't annunciate his words properly, so I can't be sure.'

Tatty was tired and feeling a bit ratty herself. It was hard going, walking a deep stony furrow in the freshly-ploughed field. 'You try annunciatin' your words properly when you're a rat. I think he's doin' rather well!' Just then, a big rabbit bounded out of nowhere, startling them. Once Tatty realised it what it was, she laughed with relief. 'He *was* sayin' critter … It's a rabbit. What a clever boy, Nibblit.' A wingtip brushed the top of Tatty's head as an owl swooped, grabbed the rabbit, and carried it away.

Nibblit squealed triumphantly: 'Seeeee – creeeeeeeeeter!'

Jeb and Tatty stared silently at the owl's shrinking silhouette.

'Next time he keeps going on about somethin', I think we should both pay attention,' Tatty said.

They hurried on, sighting a wooden stile in the distance; soon passing beneath the large structure.

'Bicuspid Cottage is just down here somewhere,' said Jeb. 'Ah, yes, there it is.'

Nestled inside a stone wall, close to the ground where some large stones were missing, was a strange little dwelling. Its walls were made entirely of teeth. Human teeth, held together by clay. There was a turf roof, though the cottage hardly needed one as it was set deep in the wall and shielded from the worst of the weather. Teeth hung down from the edge of the roof, clunking hollowly together.

'There's no door?' Tatty stated, baffled.

'I was very young the last time I visited; Sir Edwin had to remind me how to get inside. Um, you'll have to excuse the bad manners,' he said, spitting on to teeth set in the front wall of the cottage. There were grinding sounds as two rows of teeth parted as if they were still rooted in a human mouth. Leading Nibblit, Jeb stepped over the lower row of teeth and went inside. Tatty jumped quickly over, in case they decided to snap shut on her.

Jeb tied the lead rope to a nail in the corner; then removed the rat's heavy load. He lit candles and leaned the sword against the wall, next to the bed. Tatty felt queasy each time she looked at the sword. She kept putting the fact that they were going into some sort of combat to the back of her mind. *Two of us, against how many?* The thought of Gnomes worried her most: the jagged teeth and towering height … Why was it just the two of them? Why hadn't Queen Maeve sent an armed escort?

Tatty glanced around the cottage's only room. Most of the furniture was constructed from one sort of tooth or another, animal and human. Candles dripped wax in tooth candlesticks; even the table legs were fashioned from pointed canines. The bedstead was made from grimy tusks bound together by coarse twine.

Jeb said a quick spell and a fire burst into flame in the fireplace.

He coughed when some of the smoke curled back down the chimney; it obviously hadn't been swept for a very long time. The whole place appeared neglected.

'Whose cottage is this, anyway?' Tatty asked.

'It belonged to the Queen's elder sister. She was a Tooth faery and has been dead for decades. Shame, she was funny; had no teeth herself – not one.' He pulled off his boots and placed them near the fire to dry. Then he took off his stockings and draped them over the back of a chair. He advised Tatty to do the same. 'They won't dry out properly in a couple of hours, but they'll feel better than they do at the moment.'

She sat on the bed and took off her stockings and boots. Jeb placed them with his, next to the sputtering fire. Tatty stared into the flames and asked: 'How is it that you live at the palace? Do your parents work there?'

Jeb was silent for a moment. 'No, I wish with all my heart they did.' He sat facing Nibblit, as if talking to the rat. 'I was only a babe when I was found near Woebetide Wood, close to starvation. Sir Edwin found me. He has a habit of picking up waifs and strays; doesn't he Nibblit, old chap?'

Tatty thought she detected something in his voice.

'Oh it isn't that I don't appreciate what he did … it's just that … well, it can get a bit wearing, I suppose, feeling grateful all the time. I think Queen Maeve latched onto me because she hasn't any children of her own.' He looked down at his hands, his voice a whisper. 'I was desperate to go back, you see.'

'Go back? Where, Woebetide Wood?'

'Yes. It's where my people are from. Or *were* from, I should say. I don't know if there's anyone left. I can sort of remember my parents, my mother mostly … By all accounts, Cormac's wiped out most of the creatures in the wood. Mainly I'd like to see him get his comeuppance.' He sighed. 'We were the last, you see – the last wood-sprites in the district, the last stronghold. Maybe I'm the only one left on Mother

Earth?'

'No,' she said, 'you're not – I'm sure of it. And don't forget,' she waggled her hand at him, 'I have the third eye. I *know* stuff.'

He laughed and saw her expression change. 'What is it?'

'In the Queen's chamber, when I looked into that spring … I saw houses in the trees, all joined together by rope bridges.'

His face glowed in the candlelight. '*Scarabia* – that's where I'm from.'

'Can you find it?'

'The wood, yes; I've been over and over it with Sir Edwin. There was a map; once I'd learned it by heart he destroyed it – said we couldn't be too careful, that eyes might be watching. *Somebody* got into the Queen's chambers to remove her third eye. It *had* to have been done by someone very close to the Queen, someone who knew the password; they gave her some kind of sleeping potion … I mean, to have *prised* it straight out of her hand. It must have been a person she trusted.'

'She should've used that MindSpy,' said Tatty.

'Nobody could use MindSpy constantly. And the Queen doesn't have the strength these days to use it for more than a few minutes at a time.' He sat up and stretched. 'Anyway, we need rest. You can have the bed.'

'Thanks,' she replied, eyeing the grubby coverlet. She took off the jerkin and laid it over the end of the bed, then slid between mouldy-looking sheets. The pillow was covered in thick dust, making her sneeze.

Jeb blew out the candles, so that their only light came from the fire. 'Sneeze once – sneeze twice – thrice will bring the Devil's lice.'

'Thanks for that,' Tatty said, feeling itchy straight away. She watched Jeb remove his heavy cape. He climbed the wall easily and settled onto an overhead beam to sleep, curling his legs beneath him, his back to her. In the firelight, she watched his carapace slowly change colour so that it blended against the enamel of the tooth ceiling and the grainy wood of the beam, until he'd almost disappeared.

A couple of minutes passed before Tatty spoke. 'Jeb?'

'Mm,' he murmured.

'Why *are* we goin' alone? Why haven't we got any guards with us?'

'Would've drawn too much attention,' he murmured. 'We needed to leave quietly, without fuss. Anyway, there aren't enough guards to defend the palace properly as it is these days. We little folk are getting scarce … The fewer who knew about our leaving, the better. Besides, the Queen doesn't trust anyone, and that includes her guards.'

'Oh,' she said. 'I see.'

He yawned loudly. 'Do you mind if I sleep now?'

'Sorry – yep. Night then.'

'Good night – and don't let those bedbugs bite.'

But bite they did; and she had to perform an insect repellent charm to keep them at bay, horrible hissing things. But it wasn't too strong a charm: she didn't want Jeb dropping dead from the ceiling now, did she?

CHAPTER TWENTY NINE

Dorcas Gumble

The Romany waggon lurched over bumps and dips in the lane. The vardo had been built by Dorcas Gumble's great-great-grandfather. He'd painted it black, except for the white horses on the sides and red roses trailing their stems down its wooden struts. Dorcas didn't know who'd painted those, but they'd always been there. No other waggon was decorated in such a way. Dorcas's husband, Arthur, said that it looked like a funeral waggon. *But,* she often thought, *what did he know?* He didn't know that it possessed magical abilities. Ordinary black paint had been mixed with black pigments found in an ancient tomb in Egypt, where the word 'Gypsy' was thought to have originated. The tale had been passed generation to generation, down through her family tree. Dorcas felt it was safer that Arthur and their only child, Little Arthur, were unaware of the vardo's special powers. Too many folk would be after her to sell it if they knew the truth; though she'd finally decided to tell her son all about the waggon when he was older, seeing as he possessed 'gifts' of his own. Dorcas sat up front in the vardo, driving her white cob mare, Emma, while the skinny lurcher, Red, trotted along behind. She had trouble keeping weight on the dog now that he was thirteen-years-old, but if he fell too far behind, she'd lift him into the waggon to sit beside her. Red was happiest travelling under his own steam, growling at anyone who came too close to his mistress.

She steered Emma and the waggon on to a dirt track, lined with overhanging trees. The track led to a grassy clearing beside a lake. The land had once been part of the estate of the long dead Earl of Upham, the manor house now divided into posh flats, with the farm and parkland sold off in smaller chunks. A wildlife trust purchased the lake and surrounding parcels of land, including Woebetide Wood, and gave the Gumble family permission to stay there for two months each year.

Arthur and Little Arthur arrived at the clearing first, in a Land Rover that towed their modern caravan. They'd already set up camp by the time the elderly vardo rolled onto the grass. Arthur switched on the TV to watch the local weather forecast. The boys slept in the modern caravan, but Dorcas preferred the cosiness of the waggon.

She unhitched Emma and tethered her out to graze, then fed old Red. After, Dorcas joined her son by the campfire, sitting on a deckchair. She watched Little Arthur stir a pot of stew. He was a good lad. The only times he'd ever got into bother was when folk mistook him for a grown man. Once, she had to fetch him from a pub, scolding the men who'd led him astray. They'd protested that any thirteen-year-old who had the cheek to grow to six-foot-three was asking for trouble and only had himself to blame! *Fools, the lot of them! Why,* thought Dorcas, *you only had to look into his baby-blue eyes to know he was still a child.*

Dorcas smiled as her son's dinner plate-sized hand brushed away sandy-coloured hair, which flopped down over his eyes. She realised that she'd have to take a trip into Pratchester, to buy him new jeans. He'd grown so quickly that there were now several inches of exposed sock between his jeans hems and the tops of his trainers. She leaned forward, resting her hands on her knees. 'Little Arthur, have you fed that owl yet? I don't want to be kept awake again tonight with its hootin'. You know owls are night birds. I think it would've been best if you'd have left it where you found it.'

'Couldn't,' he said earnestly. 'He was all on 'is own in the storm. He was shiverin' with cold and would've died if I'd left him, Ma. I gave him some rabbit liver just now an' he's gone to sleep. He's almost full-grown. I'll let 'im go in a week, when he's a bit stronger.'

Dorcas nodded, confident of her son's nursing of the young owl, and pleased at his gentle ways. He had no idea that he was a Healer. But *she* knew – always had. She'd lost count of the sick and injured animals he'd tended. And many more had lived than died. Little Arthur definitely took after *her* side of the family, the Larks. Her husband's side, the Gumbles, weren't gifted, apart from being successful horse dealers. She was lucky; she'd been blessed with second sight: tea leaves and crystal were her instruments for dukkering. Her two eyes were in the vardo. *No, not two eyes. Not any more. Only one remained.* Dorcas frowned, recalling when the storm had first hit. They'd camped over on the other side of the village …

★★★

The day before, Dorcas had dukkered for some village folk. Her last customer of the day had been a thin, pink-haired woman: *Dorothy Bottom-somethin'-or-other? Mind, she'd insisted on being called Dot.* The Dot-woman had wanted to know if she was going to win the lottery, and became annoyed when Dorcas told her that the eye couldn't predict the winning numbers, and everybody would be a millionaire in that case. 'Otherwise I wouldn't be here doin' this, love, would I?' Dorcas had said, laughing. 'I'd be off sunnin' myself somewhere foreign.'

Dorcas had gone on to tell the woman that she would suffer a sad loss soon, whereby the woman had argued that she most certainly would not! She'd screeched: *'That wasn't what I came 'ere for!'* and demanded her five pounds back. Dorcas had been certain the reading was correct, and that Dot's loss would be restored to her in time, but the silly woman hadn't listened or let her explain, so Dorcas had finally lost her patience and said: 'What do you expect for five measly quid!' The Dot-woman then stomped down the waggon's steps, loudly announcing that *'Upham doesn't want* your *sort around here, anyway!'*

Dorcas had laughed when the woman's spiky heel snapped off on the uneven ground. She'd staggered into the distance, carrying the broken shoe and muttering the whole way. But Dorcas forgot to put her crystal ball away after, leaving it lying upon a velvet tablecloth. It was her most precious eye, and had belonged to her Granny Rose. She preferred using Granny Rose's eye: it was more accurate. Her other, younger, crystal ball was stored safely at the back of her china cabinet.

The first clap of thunder brought the thieves. Still agitated from the Dot-woman, and noticing the approaching black clouds, Dorcas had hurriedly unpegged laundry from the washing-line and slung the dry clothes over her arm. Fat raindrops sploshed onto her head. In moments her dark hair was plastered to her scalp in sodden tendrils. Arthur and Little Arthur were out and she'd rushed to the caravan, pulled the door open, and thrown the laundry on to a chair. It was while she folded the clothes that she'd glanced at the window and noticed the bird.

A lone magpie had landed on the roof of the vardo. *One for sorrow. That's not a good sign,* she'd thought. She searched frantically for more of the birds. One on its own was a bad omen. Oh, the relief she'd felt when another came into view! *Two for joy!* Dorcas had been amused when she saw the second magpie had orange plastic netting in its beak. Then, another bird followed the first two. Soon more came along: *five, six, and seven. Seven for a secret ne'er to be told,* if the old saying was to be believed.

And Dorcas *did* believe.

Amazed, she had watched the birds pull and tease the crumpled plastic netting until they each held a section. The birds rose from the wet roof, flying inside the vardo through the open door. Before Dorcas left the caravan, the magpies had flown away, struggling up into the rain-drenched sky, carrying something inside the netting. 'No!' Dorcas had shrieked when she realised what it was: *Granny Rose's crystal eye!* She'd watched, helpless, as the black and white birds vanished over the treetops. The crystal – used by her family for over two hundred years –

had gone.

That night there wasn't just a storm raging outside, another raged deep inside Dorcas Gumble.

★ ★ ★

'Stew's ready, Ma,' said Little Arthur, rousing Dorcas from her thoughts. He handed her a bowl and spoon. 'I'll give Pa a shout.'

She sniffed the stew appreciatively. As she ate, Dorcas decided she'd try her very best to get the eye back. There was something else too … she *knew* help would come soon. She had seen them in that morning's tea leaves. She sighed and her mood lifted.

'Cor, that smells right cushti, Little Arthur,' said Arthur Gumble, emerging from the caravan. He ruffled his son's hair and sat in one of the fireside chairs. Dorcas dished up dinner for her husband and Little Arthur, and then sat down again. They ate in silence, listening to the wildlife. When he'd finished, Arthur wiped his curly moustache and loosened his Union Jack braces – which he wore *all* the time, even over winter pullovers. He stretched his legs out and watched Dorcas clear away the dinner things. She made big mugs of steaming tea, even though the evening was warm. Darkness crept in and the fire cast long dancing shadows all around the campsite.

Later, Dorcas said: 'Going off to bed now. Got to be up early.' She yawned noisily. ''Specting visitors. They'll likely be hungry time they get here.'

'Not Uncle Van and Auntie Flossie?' said Little Arthur, scowling.

'Nope.'

'Who then, Ma?'

'Oh … you'll see,' Dorcas said, mysteriously.

'But, Ma, I–'

'That's enough,' interrupted Arthur. 'Your ma won't tell and that's all there is to it. You know how she is with her secrets.' He tapped the side of his sunburnt nose. 'Time we was all turnin' in anyways. Come on, Sonny-Jim; say night-night to your ma.'

Little Arthur sighed, got up and trudged to the caravan, following his father inside. 'Night, Ma,' he called, before closing the door.

'Night, son,' said Dorcas quietly, leaning back in her chair. She stared out over the lake, a silver sheet across the land, and thought of the coming morning.

Red slept, stretched out on his side underneath the vardo. More grey hair than red speckled his coarse coat these days. Four paws twitched as he chased a dream hare. Suddenly he woke and emerged from beneath the waggon. Red stood motionless while his nose searched the night air. *Nothing yet.* His misty eyes looked away from the lake and out over rolling farmland. Then he raised his head and howled into the night sky for several moments.

'Shurrup, Red!' came Arthur Gumble's muffled shout from the caravan.

Dorcas shook her head sadly. Arthur would never understand the language of beasts. Red knew they were coming. She called the dog to sit by her side. Human and animal looked at each other; both nodded in agreement.

CHAPTER THIRTY

The Cruel Streak

'CURSETHEMCURSETHEMCURSETHEM!' raged Cormac Viperian. He hurled a lit candle, hitting a magpie on the side of the head. The bird hopped about madly as burning wax ran through its feathers. 'Curse them,' Cormac added, softly this time. His mood quickly switched from rage to sadness. He stared into the glowing depths of the crystal ball, at the children asleep in the old cottage. 'They have no idea *who* they're meddling with, no idea at all. Look at them ... I don't know *what* my aunt was thinking, sending babes to do her bidding? I really thought she'd come herself. She must be sickly, eh lads?' He looked about the treetop house. Nobody answered from the gloom. *Talking to myself again – first sign of madness!* He smiled at his observation, but carried on talking to himself anyway: 'She should have died – swallowed enough Deadly Nightshade to kill a hundred souls. All she did was sleep.' Already tipsy, he took a long swallow from a cup of mead. 'Managed to get the eye out ... fat lot of good *that* did! Wouldn't work, would it. Stitched it to my hand ... nothing. Strapped it to my forehead ... nothing. Look at it now, lads.' He held up a withered object, turning it in his hands. 'Useless, utterly, utterly *useless*!'

A magpie's head loomed in through an open window. Sad again, and close to tears, Cormac shrieked and snatched his hand away. 'No, Pip! You *shan't* eat it! It's still mine; even if it *does* resemble a mouse dropping ... I may keep it as a memento.' A sudden grin burst on to his face. 'On the positive side, Aunt Maeve grows weaker without it. It's only a matter of time now, and I've always been patient.' He sniggered. 'Well, not *always*.'

His once handsome face was now etched with deep lines. Why did everything have to go so wrong? Why couldn't everybody see that he, Cormac, was the rightful heir to the throne? He was strong, wasn't he (in his mind he answered his own questions)? *Yes, definitely strong.* And wasn't he noble? *Most certainly.* Worthy? *Of course.* And wasn't he good? *Mm, well, three out of four wasn't too bad, was it?* Besides, no one's perfect.

He slumped back on his makeshift throne and pulled the bone crown from his head, dropping it on the floor. Why did his head ache so? It was true that since he'd got the Cruel Streak he was prone to headaches, and lately they'd been getting worse; so had his violent outbursts. He rubbed his temple where a shock of white hair sprouted amongst the black. *His 'Cruel Streak' – that's what mother had called it when it first started coming through.* And the name had stuck. Another of Queen Maeve's sisters, Cormac had adored his mother. But that was before he'd had to … get her out of the way. When he was younger, she'd heard him plotting to overthrow his ageing aunt. So he'd no choice in the matter: *One simply didn't go around bumping off one's parents willy-nilly!* He'd had to make it look like an accident so as not to arouse suspicion. A magical shove under the wheels of the blacksmith's cart did the trick: she'd perished immediately, turning instantly to bright dust which blew away on the wind. She hadn't known a thing about it. *Well, I wouldn't have wanted her to suffer; she* had *been an excellent mother, after all.* Despite his throbbing head, Cormac managed a smile as he remembered the day, long ago, when he'd first acquired the Cruel Streak …

★ ★ ★

He'd been playing in the palace garden with his friend, Philomena: a pretty child, with blue-black wings and bouncing, black ringlets. The nursemaid was called away on an errand, leaving them alone. Before the *accident*, Cormac had been a sweet, lively child: quick to learn, but

174

even quicker to get into scrapes. The game they chose to play was forbidden to faeries their age – and rightly so – what with its pyrotechnic element. Lightning took a lot of mastering.

'Your turn, your turn!' Philomena squealed, after producing a tiny squirt of white light from her fingertip. It had fizzled to nothing, travelling barely an inch.

Cormac was uneasy. His eyes were huge with dread. What if something were to go wrong? What would his mother say? 'If I get hurt, or anything gets damaged, Mother will have f – forty fits!' he spluttered.

Philomena's eyes narrowed. 'Mm, you're a *mummy's* boy.'

'No I'm not!'

'Cormac is a mummy's boy – Cormac is a mummy's boy – Cormac is a mummy's boy!' She skipped around him, flicking his pointed ears.

He reddened. 'No I'm not! And you always repeat everything you say – at least twice!'

'No I don't!'

'You do, all the time!' He'd gulped down a sob. 'And I'm definitely *not* a mummy's boy.'

'Yes, you *are*,' Philomena lisped. 'Who wouldn't let you stay for the masked ball last month because it was past your bedtime? Your *mother*, that's who; of course, *my* mother let *me* go. She said it would be a good experience for me, for my future life at court. Oh yes, and I almost forgot – whose mother won't let him have his own riding mouse in case he falls off and hurts his little botty? *Your* mother, I believe.' Philomena placed her hands on her hips and sneered. 'At least I've got my own pure black riding mouse – to match my hair. *My* mother wouldn't *dream* of letting a servant carry me around. Poor old *you*.'

Cormac squirmed with embarrassment. Everything Philomena had said was the truth; his mother *had* molly-coddled him. She'd banned him from performing anything but the most basic of charms.

175

Even his aunt, the Queen, scolded her for it. But he couldn't go against his mother's wishes, so he had stood up straight and answered haughtily: 'Perhaps my mother *does* forbid me to do certain things, but it's only because she loves me dearly, and it's for my own good.'

He hadn't cared for the way Philomena held her head on one side. 'A – Anyway,' he'd gushed, 'since the Queen had a word with Mother, she's been positively neglecting me, so *there*. And if you think you're so high-and-mighty – watch *this*!' With resentment seething to get out of his small body, Cormac produced a crackle of lightning from the tip of his outstretched finger. His target had been a flagpole on the top of a turret, but, instead, the zigzagging lightning bolt had missed, somehow managing to pierce the protective Curtain over the palace, travelling onward across fields, even striking a poor grazing sheep stone dead.

Cormac and Philomena stared.

'Neptune's kneecaps!' Philomena had gasped. 'Who'd have thought you had *that* in you, Cormac Viperian. Your powers are out-standing!'

Cormac's chest had swelled with pride. He was actually *good* at something. Maybe his mother's reluctance to let him use his magical abilities had enabled them to be stored inside his body somehow, so that now he had too much of the stuff!

Those precious few minutes were to be the happiest of his life. Sadly, they weren't to last. Out of sight the lightning bolt still fizzled and sizzled on its haphazard way, setting light to rooftops; a haystack; and even a clothesline of drying sheets. Then, quite by chance, it struck a weathervane on top of Upham church (causing the Great Fire of 1890), sending it speeding back towards the Palace Over Yonder. One moment Cormac and Philomena were talking excitedly, and the next, Cormac was enveloped in an inky blackness. When he finally awoke two weeks later, he'd changed. Gone was the chatty, sweet child, and in its place was a brooding, selfish being with no thought for anyone but himself. The lightning bolt had left a big scar on his temple, running into his hairline. The hair that had burned away grew back pure white.

A deeper scar was seared on his soul.

★ ★ ★

Cormac drifted back to the present, his aching head resting on his hand. *Bad luck was all it had been*, he thought, *not fate*, as others said: *They keep on saying that fate has your life mapped out for you before you're even hatched. No, no, just bad luck, simple as that.* Bad luck that he'd stood in that precise spot in the palace garden; bad luck that Philomena hadn't been struck instead! *Well, a pox on the backside of luck!* From now on he'd make his own luck, and it would be on *his* side! Wasn't the tide of luck already turning in his favour? His servants found him an eye to replace the one he'd stolen from the Queen's hand. Granted, the crystal was cumbersome, and he hadn't the spell to shrink it as yet. Also, he hadn't quite figured out how to read the future in the thing, simply the happenings of the moment, but those were getting clearer the more the eye got used to him, and he to it. Time *would* tell.

The wing-stumps protruding from his shoulder blades dug painfully into the back of the rough wooden throne. *Never mind*, he thought, *she'll soon pay for my mutilation.* And his aunt thought *him* cruel. 'More mead!' he yelled suddenly.

An elf rushed into the room to refill his cup. Cormac took great gulps, before falling asleep where he sat, spilling the remaining liquid into his lap, where it soaked into his dirty black robes.

CHAPTER THIRTY ONE

Eye Don't Lie

After a quick breakfast of oat biscuits and honey, they left Bicuspid Cottage at first light. Tatty had cast a muting spell on the pots and pans that Nibblit carried, leaving them silent. That was hours ago, and though it was still early it was another blistering day despite the storm. Following a hedgerow, Jeb led the way around stones and tall clumps of rough grasses. Nibblit was misbehaving, dragging the rope out of Tatty's hand each time he spotted a blackberry hanging near the ground. She wished Jeb would lead him for a while to give her sore hands a rest. The grasses and brambles grew thick. They kept close to the stream so as not to lose their way. Jeb used the sword to hack through undergrowth.

'As soon as we get through this bit,' he said, 'we'll stop and rest.'

Thank you, thought Tatty with relief. She was hungry again.

Nibblit began whinging. 'Wants oats!' he squeaked. 'Wants oats 'n' honeeeeeeeee!' No one bothered answering him. 'Wants oats 'n' honeeeeeeeee 'n' a cuppa teeeeeeeeeeeeea!'

'Will you belt up!' hissed Tatty finally.

Jeb told her quietly: 'He doesn't even drink tea. He's only saying it for something to say.'

'Well, he's gettin' on my nerves! He's not the only one who's hungry.'

'I wish you'd *both* be quiet,' Jeb whispered sternly. 'We're supposed to sneak in, retrieve the Queen's eye, do … whatever we have to do, then sneak out. You two are going to get us killed!'

Tatty felt her face burn. 'Sorry,' she mumbled. Even Nibblit looked ashamed.

Jeb hacked his way through the last of the brambles. Thorns tugged at their clothes. A clearing opened in front of them and Jeb dropped to the ground, sweat covered his face. He laid the sword down and spat on his blistered hands.

Tatty let go of Nibblit's lead-rope. Jeb was bleeding. She hadn't realised. Her thoughts had been for her own sore hands and empty belly. She took his hands in hers and spoke the healing spell:

'Callin' Spirits from North, East, South and West,

Come an' do what you do best,

Conquer blood, fever and pain,

Make this child whole again.'

One by one the blisters healed, until the skin was perfect again. 'Thank you,' said Jeb, relief on his face. Tatty smiled and let go of his hands.

They made camp close to a clump of brambles. Tatty filled a bowl with oats for Nibblit. Jeb collected twigs and made a fire. He brewed tea with dried dandelion and mint leaves. Tatty watched him, until something squirmed beneath the eyelid in her palm. She closed the hand into a fist, not wanting to see an eyeball that had no place being where it was. She spun around and faced the bramble thicket. Something approached, getting closer every second. Then Tatty heard a noise. She called Jeb.

He stood in front of her, protectively. 'What is it do you think?'

'I don't know? Though … that sound …'

Jeb stepped closer to the thicket.

'Come here.' Tatty grabbed his sleeve and pulled him back.

The noise grew louder, making the bramble thicket rustle.

Jeb said, 'It sounds very big.'

Tatty looked up, shielding her eyes. Something blotted out the sun, casting a shadow over the camp. Only then could Tatty finally see what it was: *Blue*. The dragonfly landed near the campfire and Will leaped from his back.

Tatty's surge of pleasure at seeing her friend quickly vanished when she saw the grim expression on his face. He looked very, very cross.

'Thanks for goin' off an' leavin' me behind!' He strode towards her. 'Goin' to tell me all about it when you got back, were you?' His burning gaze took in Jeb. 'And who's *that?*'

Tatty was outraged. 'If you *must* know, this is Jebeneezer – or Jeb, to his friends – which I most certainly am. And don't be rude, Willum Patch. Jeb's in the same situation as you. He doesn't know if his parents are … if they're alive or …'

'We were about to have some tea before you arrived,' Jeb cut in quickly. 'Would you like some?'

Will looked at the ground and nodded, silent.

Jeb added: 'Sorry, we've only brought two cups. Will a bowl do?'

''S all right,' Will muttered, 'I've brought my own.' He gestured at Blue, who was loaded with bags.

Once Will had got his cup, Jeb poured the tea and unpacked biscuits to dunk. Will told them what Agatha, and the Moons, had said: of Tatty's summons to the Palace Over Yonder; and the fact that she was of royal blood (he kept glancing sideways at her), and that she was on an errand for the Queen. He told Jeb of the moment in Pottage's, when he'd first looked through the hole in the stone and saw Agatha Pottage with the head of a raven. He'd no idea of the power that lay within the luck-stone, but Aggie insisted he take it with him. It hung from his belt once again. 'She told me: "The luck-stone is an instrument and it is up to you to choose how to play it". Whatever that means?' Then he spoke about his father, and how his mother had refused to return to The Patch without her husband there.

'Looks like we've both got a score to settle, doesn't it? Do or die, eh?' Will said, holding his hand out to Jeb.

Jeb shook Will's hand. 'Do or die,' he agreed, and grinned.

Tatty's chest hurt. 'Do or die,' she whispered. After a moment, she asked: 'How did Aggie know where we were headed?'

'Well, she *is* a witch, she's got her methods. I know it had somethin' to do with innards,' said Will.

Tatty grimaced. 'I wish we had some mead, or wine, so we could drink a toast to her.'

'We've got tea,' said Will. 'Aggie loves tea.'

'Tea it is, then.' Jeb refilled their cups.

'You do it, Tatty,' Will said. 'I can't think of anythin' to say.'

'Oh, right. Wait a minute.' She bit her lip, thinking, then picked up her cup and raised it in the air. The two boys did the same. 'To Agatha Pottage, a witch of unrivalled ability … and a friend of unequalled loyalty.' They tapped their cups together and all said: 'Agatha Pottage!'

Soon after, Jeb advised that they'd better set off again, that going by the sun's position it must be around ten o'clock. 'It's hot now,' he said, 'but in another hour it's going to be unbearable.'

They washed their cups and threw earth on the fire to smother the embers; then left the safety of the thorns and followed the stream. As they walked, Will asked many questions, so Tatty told him about Queen Maeve and of the long ago predictions of the court astrologers, and of having the third eye. Even when she'd shown him the sealed eyelid, he was still unsure. It took a lot of persuading from Jeb before Will finally believed.

★★★

Dorcas finished scrubbing the clothes. She straightened and flexed her aching spine then scanned the trees around the camp, but saw nothing out of the ordinary. *They'll be here soon, the little 'uns. I 'spect they'll be hungry. Once I've done the washing and put it through the mangle, I'll cook 'em a nice breakfast.*

A washing machine was something Dorcas missed when they were on the road. It was difficult, scrubbing dirt out of denim jeans by hand. She looked at the iron mangle nearby and smiled as she recalled a younger Little Arthur forcing one of his hands through the wooden rollers whilst turning the handle with the other. He would scream his head off in pain – then do the very same thing the next day. She sighed. *Kids.*

It was while she was feeding wet clothes through the mangle, that Dorcas felt the first prickle of unease tickle the back of her neck. She tried to ignore it but the feeling persisted. She carried the laundry over to the line and pegged it out to dry. Then she climbed up into the vardo. What she saw in the depths of her remaining crystal ball made her eyes widen in horror. *No, it's not possible!* She sat back and thought about the vision. A minute later she was calm and determined. 'Eye don't lie,' she murmured. 'Nope, eye don't lie.'

CHAPTER THIRTY TWO

Spartacus

Bert had been foolish. He knew that now. Why couldn't he have just kept quiet? He sighed. Mind, it had all been the fault of that silly Gypsy, telling Dot that she was going to suffer a sad loss. And then when the storm had hit and Delilah had gone missing ...

The previous day, Dot had seemed to settle down and started planning the big advertising campaign to find Delilah. She'd said, 'You never know, the Gypsy could've been wrong ... Come to think of it she did try changin' her mind, I think; but I wasn't really listening. We might get Delilah back yet.'

Bert closed his eyes and rubbed his forehead. He'd blabbed about finding fur and blood out on the decking. *Stupid – stupid – stupid!* Of course, Dot had gone completely ballistic: sobbing, shouting, blaming him for not liking the cat in the first place. 'How *dare* you!' she'd shrieked. 'Fancy lettin' me think Delilah was still alive somewhere, when all this time you'd been pretendin'!'

That was yesterday.

Since then, Dot had taken her revenge. He'd woken early. Dot's side of the bed was cold and empty.

It was Bert's day to play golf with his friends. Dot had placed his golfing clothes on the chair in the corner of their bedroom. He showered and started to dress when he'd noticed something on the sleeve of his best golf shirt. *A black armband?* It had been sewn onto his shirt with tiny, tight stitches, giving him no time to unpick them.

He decided to wear something else and had flung open the wardrobe doors to find – *nothing!* He hurried to the chest of drawers and dragged open each drawer. The only garments remaining were his underwear and socks, everything else had vanished, even his non-golfing clothes.

She'd taken them all!

Bert had inspected the lemon-coloured polo shirt, the one with a little pink golfer embroidered on the front. *How could she!* He realised that she must have been up half the night sewing and hiding his other clothes.

Time marched on too swiftly. He couldn't be late to meet the lads. So he'd dragged on the clothes, wolfed down a bowl of cereal, grabbed his golf bag and car keys, and slammed the front door shut behind him. He limped to the car, threw in his bag and flopped into the driver's seat. The car's wheels squealed and kicked up lots of gravel as Bert sped out of the driveway. He glanced at the black armband. *Maybe they won't notice? Just don't draw attention to it …*

Minutes later, Bert pulled into the car park at Upham golf course. The boys (both in their late fifties) were already heading towards the first hole when they saw him arrive. Cheering, they practically dragged him out of the car. 'What time d' you call this?' asked Dougie Hamhock, slapping Bert on the back with a big meaty hand, as befitting the village butcher.

'How's the ankle?' asked Sid Dawber, weasel-faced owner of a scrapyard.

'Um, yes, sorry I'm a bit late,' Bert mumbled. 'I – I couldn't remember where I'd left my ... um ... car keys.' He jangled them in front of his face. 'The ankle's gettin' there ... mendin' slowly ... thanks.' He grinned suddenly. 'Are we here for the golf, or what?'

In reply, Bert received another round of backslapping.

After they had played for a while, Sid blurted out of nowhere: 'What's with the black armband, Bert?'

Bert froze and went red.

'Fancy askin' him that!' said Dougie Hamhock, outraged. 'He's not wearin' it for the good of his health, is he? Someone's obviously passed away. I don't know, Sid, sometimes you can be so ... so ... *insensitive!*'

Sid had the grace to look shamefaced. 'Sorry, old chap. No offence. I could kick myself, I really could.' He gently placed a hand on Bert's shoulder. 'Who was it, family?'

'S – Sort of,' Bert mumbled, staring at the ground.

'What it expected, or sudden?' asked Dougie.

'Sudden,' Bert whispered, unable to look at his friends.

'How old?' enquired Sid.

'Eight.'

'*Eight-years-old!*' Sid exclaimed. 'Aw, that's a cryin' shame ... Isn't it Dougie?'

'It is, Sid.' Dougie grabbed Bert in a tight hug. When he let go there were unshed tears in the big butcher's eyes. 'Poor little thing,' he said, a sob catching in his throat. 'Thank goodness it was quick.'

'If – If you don't mind,' Bert whispered, 'I'd rather not talk about it any more.'

''Course not,' said Sid.

'Absolutely, whatever you say,' said Dougie. He cleared his throat. 'Come on. Let's play golf! Oi, Bert, give me those clubs. I'll carry 'em as well as my own. Can't 'ave you doing yourself another injury.' He'd grabbed Bert's bag and hitched it over his shoulder to join his own.

'No,' said Sid. 'Dot would murder us if we let anything else happen to you. She's scary when she's in a tizzy, is Dot.'

'She sure is,' Bert agreed, looking down at the armband.

★ ★ ★

Bert played the worst round of golf that day than he ever had before: gouging great divots from the turf each time he tried hitting the ball. He knew Dougie and Sid were trying their best to look the other way, to give him a chance, but Bert had taken so many shots they'd finally lost count of the score.

Soon it was midday and boiling hot again. The golfers were all heading home. Bert unlocked his car and threw the bag on the back seat. Trapped heat inside the car blasted his face. He felt a twinge in his back so stretched, glancing toward Woebetide Wood. Magpies covered the treetops.

He shivered.

He'd only ever noticed the birds in small groups before, certainly never in such vast numbers. *Creepy.* They were close enough that he could hear their cackling calls: *It sounds like they're laughing. Maybe they're laughing at your pathetic attempts at golf!* He dragged his gaze away from the birds, got into his car, and drove the short distance to Cooper's Close. He parked in the drive, retrieved his bag, and limped to the front door. With the heavy bag dangling from his shoulder he found it difficult to get his key in the lock, until he realised he was using the garage key by mistake. He dropped the golf bag on the ground and fumbled for the correct key.

The door opened suddenly. Dot held some ginger fluff. 'Look, Spartacus,' she cooed. 'Daddy's home.'

The warm, tingly feeling Bert had felt since his Chopper was returned, fizzled away in an instant. Perhaps he should have continued to carry the note in his breast pocket like a lucky charm, instead of leaving it in a corner of his sock drawer.

It was too *soon!*

It wasn't *fair!*

He was getting used to having hairless trousers!

The kitten's head swivelled to face him. Its emerald-green eyes locked on to Bert's and held, unblinking.

'Aw, Bert, take that look off your face. You look like you're suckin' a lemon!' Dot waggled one of the creature's tiny paws in his direction. 'Isn't he the most precious thing you've ever seen? Look at his dear little feet.'

A nasty reply hovered on the tip of Bert's tongue. *No, actually – its little feet aren't dear! I don't think the thing's precious, at all! Why can't I have a couple of goldfish, or a nice budgie –* a blue *one? Oh, yes, I forgot – you don't like birds: they flap an' leave seed all over the place. Well, I don't like hairy trousers or havin' my favourite chair used as a bloomin' scratching post!* He took a deep breath and closed his eyes. When he opened them again Dot's face wore a pleading expression. In a heartbeat, he noticed the way she cradled the ginger kitten, as if the slightest gust of wind might break it.

And for the briefest moment, the tingly feeling came back.

A smile twitched at the corner of Bert's mouth. 'Spartacus, you say? Mm, puny little thing, looks more like a Runtacus. Or Titchacus.' He rubbed the top of the kitten's tiny skull with his fingertip.

Dot giggled. 'Oh, he's definitely a Spartacus. He's been answerin' to it all morning. Oh, Bert, you wouldn't believe how bright he is.' She nuzzled the kitten's soft fur. It raised a minuscule paw and batted her nose.

Bert even managed a laugh. 'Suppose Spartacus is as good a name as any.' In truth, he wasn't against Dot getting another cat; it was just that *he* would've liked to have chosen the next one …

Dot was gushing now: 'I know it's only been a short while since – you know – since Delilah, *went*. But Mrs Openshaw – you know, who's got the cattery – well, she had a cardboard box dumped on her doorstep the night of the storm. I mean, it seemed like *fate*, and these four kittens were inside. She was *desperate* to rehome them. I could've had all four if I'd wanted, but I know you're not that keen … Well anyway, I picked the smallest. Mrs Openshaw reckons it was meant to be, what with losin' Delilah; then gettin' a litter of free kittens …'

Bert picked up his bag from the doorstep and followed Dot inside.

'Maybe there *was* something in what that Gypsy said, after all: havin' a loss an' then resolving it. What do you think, Bert?'

Bert thought that the new cat toys scattered around the kitchen floor looked as if they were waiting to trip him up, and over by the back door, next to the cat-flap, was a soiled litter tray.

'What do I think ...' Bert thought he'd better get that special little note and put it back in his pocket. 'I think ... I think I'd like a cup of tea. A really strong one.'

CHAPTER THIRTY-THREE

Too Much Mead

Woebetide Wood didn't appear to be getting any closer. 'How much further before we stop?' asked Will. Even Blue's wings had shrivelled in the heat.

'We haven't been walkin' long enough yet,' Tatty said.

'Oh.' Will stared at his dusty feet, the luck-stone bumped at his hip.

'Stop!' The urgency in Jeb's voice brought them to a halt.

'What's the matter?' Will asked.

'A *human* – over there in that field!' Jeb pointed to a figure, visible through a gap in the hedge.

'Why's it stood with its arms stuck out like that for?' Will said.

'Don't know,' said Tatty, a squirm of dread in her stomach. 'It's not movin'.'

Jeb squinted into the distance. 'Maybe it's dead.'

Will had the keenest sight. He handed his lasso to Tatty, and Blue let out a chirp of protest. The elf went towards the field.

'Will!' Tatty hissed.

He turned. 'What?'

'Don't go,' she insisted. 'It's all … *wrong!* And we're supposed to be goin' *this* way!'

'I quite agree,' said Jeb, with a worried frown. 'You'll add too much time to our journey, and you'll be out in the open.'

'Come *on!*' Will laughed. 'It'll only take a minute. Can't you two see that it's not even *real?*' He ran down a slope and into the field, disappearing amongst the stubble left from the harvest.

'There he goes!' Tatty wailed. 'Off and runnin' like a fool! Go after him, Jeb, will you? I don't like it, somethin's goin' to happen. My hand's burnin'. Why's it burnin', *Jeb?*'

'I – ah – think we should just let him look,' said Jeb, licking his lips nervously. 'He'll be back soon.'

Tatty approached Jeb slowly. Her face almost touched his. 'Go after him,' she hissed.

'I – um – of course, wait here.' Jeb flicked open his wing casings and took off. In moments he'd disappeared from sight.

Minutes later, Tatty grew restless. *Where were they?* It was no use; she couldn't wait any longer without knowing what was happening. She told Nibblit and Blue to stay until she returned, and launched herself towards the eerie figure with an unshakable feeling of doom.

★★★

Cormac woke with a nauseating headache. He plucked the bone crown from the floor. Blearily, he stared at it. *Rodent bones, lashed together with twine. Unseemly.* Even so, he placed it on his head. One day his crown would be of the finest silver, or perhaps *gold,* and studded with precious jewels …

One day very soon.

He was alone, his feathered servants off feeding somewhere. The sudden thought of food made his stomach churn sickeningly. *Always, always, too much mead … Never know when to stop, that's your trouble.* He licked his cracked lips and peered into the crystal eye.

Something was wrong.

How was it the babes still slept in gloom? *But here, in the wood, it's daylight?*

In the swirling image inside the eye, all appeared peaceful. Candles warmed the darkness inside the tooth cottage. *The eye is trying to trick me!* Anger surged inside him. 'No!' he yelled, kicking the crystal, jarring it so that the image wavered and snuffed out. When the crystal ball stopped rocking, he stared into its depths again. Another image began to form, bright and luminous. 'Ah, better,' he purred, as dazzling sunlight showed him the babes zooming across farmland. And what's this? *Another one has joined the first two. Three times the fun!* He laughed loudly.

The elven urchin stared upward. *What at? What at? I need to* see ...

Then it was as though he were seeing through the elf's own eyes: a skull peered sightlessly down, a human skull to all appearances, attached to a misshapen, lifeless body. *Lifeless to be sure, but a body nonetheless!* Gleefully, Cormac rubbed his grimy hands together. *Remember – remember – remember ... Head's all fuzzy. What is it, again? Ah yes, there it is. I see it now.* Calmly, he mouthed silent words while his hands flew in all directions, as if he were conducting an invisible orchestra.

His wild, black hair sprang outward, crackling with energy.

And in the field, not far away at all, the scarecrow twitched.

CHAPTER THIRTY FOUR

The Scaredycrow

'It's a scaredycrow,' Will explained. 'Bigguns use 'em to protect their crops.'

'A what?' asked Jeb, staring up at the strange figure tied to a wooden frame with mouldy-looking rope.

'A scaredycrow. They scare away crows and rooks.'

Jeb touched one of the scarecrow's battered boots; the toes were turned comically inward. 'Well I never. It's an ugly-looking brute.'

Tatty landed beside them on the scarecrow's boot. 'Are you deliberately tryin' to get yourself killed, Will?' Her eyes flashed with anger.

'Look,' he said, placing his hands on his hips. 'I knew it wasn't a Biggun. I'm not as stupid as you think.' He tugged on one of the scarecrow's tattered trouser legs as if to prove a point. 'See – not real.'

'Don't!' snapped Tatty. She grabbed her hand. '*Ow!*'

'What is it?' asked Jeb.

She gasped: 'My *hand*!' They stood transfixed as the scar began to peel apart. And *open*. She shook and slumped to her knees as the third eye appeared. The eyeball was black and glossy, shot through with golden flecks. The raw upper and lower lid healed in moments.

Tatty closed her eyes and held her left palm out in front of her. She groaned.

Will froze at the sight of his friend's new eye; its golden flecks swirled with each roll of the eyeball, making him feel sick.

Jeb appeared calm. For him this was nothing unusual. It was identical to Queen Maeve's lost eye.

As the eyelid in her palm closed, so Tatty's true eyes opened. 'We have to move – *now*!' she shouted, taking flight.

'Eh?' said Will, still standing on the boot.

'Get down from there!' Tatty screamed. 'Run, as fast as you can!'

Jeb flicked out his wings and rose in the air. 'She's seen something,' he said, almost to himself. Louder, he added: 'Do as she says. Jump!'

Preparing to leap, Will felt the boot judder, as if the earth beneath it lurched. He grabbed a leather tassel to keep from falling. He looked up. The scarecrow's skull leered down at him and snapped its jaws. It looked … *hungry*! Will jumped then. He had never run so fast, dodging big stones poking from the soil, leaping some of them in his terror. He knew he shouldn't look back, that it would slow him down. But he *had* to look, found his head turning on his shoulders. At the same time there was a sound: a snapping and rending. His head whipped around to see the scarecrow breaking free, the rotten rope giving way against the wooden frame. And judging by the way it strained against the last rope, it would be after him any second. Will's head snapped forward. Pieces of sharp flint in the ground sliced into the soles of his feet.

He felt nothing.

Another sound flooded his veins with ice. *The last rope's gone.* This time Will didn't turn. He couldn't see the gap in the hedge; the wheat stubble was too high. He *thought* that he was travelling in the right direction ... It hadn't seemed this far before? *Why's it always me? I should've stayed near the stream with the others. We might've been able to see Woebetide Wood by now* ... He couldn't blame Tatty or Jeb for wanting to save their own skins. *Wings. Wish I had wings* ...

Behind him the earth shook in pounding waves as the scarecrow gave chase.

Will's scalp prickled. He half-expected an enormous boot to come crushing down on top of him. He knew he couldn't afford to check to see how close the scarecrow was. Every second counted. The pounding of the earth changed to a booming. The booming turned to a thundering. The scarecrow was so close that the flapping of its long waxed coat hurt Will's ears with deafening cracks, like somebody cracking a whip next to his head.

Then the sky went dark. A shadow passed across the sun ... But it wasn't a shadow. A massive leather-gloved hand reached over him, fingers spread wide, like the bars of a cage. Will darted to his right, just as the hand was about to grab him. The old motorcycle gauntlet grabbed nothing but a fistful of dusty soil. Will risked a quick glance as he sped away, in time to see the scarecrow sprawl on to its front in a heap. He slowed, breathing raggedly, and then howled with despair as the thing started to rise, forcing itself upright, lurching after him once more. His lungs burned. He knew he couldn't keep running much longer. Pain signals from his cut feet finally made it to his brain. A sort of acceptance crept over him then: he hoped the others were safe and that he led the monstrous thing away from wherever they were. It would all be worth it, he thought, to have given them a greater chance of survival.

Will slowed his pace.

His legs felt boneless as he staggered to a halt.

Bending over, he gripped his knees and gasped for air. Tears streamed down his face; he clasped his luck-stone. He felt the scarecrow skidding to a halt behind him, felt the dusty earth sting his back as it was sprayed up by the massive boots. He closed his eyes and held the luck-stone to his chest.

Make it quick, Aggie, he pleaded silently.

Something grasped him under the arms. *Almost over now ...* He felt suddenly weightless as he was borne upwards.

★ ★ ★

'He's heavier than he looks.'

'I shan't be able to keep ... this up for long; my arm's killing me already!'

Will's eyes snapped open. He glanced back and forth at Jeb and Tatty. They flew with him dangling between them. He laughed and cried in disbelief.

'Shhhh!' said Tatty sharply. She turned to Jeb. 'There – can you see it? In front of the wood ... a lake! We'll ... be safe if we ... make it to ... the lake.'

'I see it!' yelled Jeb, as they soared higher.

The lake. Each time they gained height, Tatty could see it shining in the distance like a shimmering beacon, urging them on. They lost height suddenly. 'Will! Stop wrigglin',' puffed Tatty. 'You're makin' this ... a lot harder than it need be.' She hooked the crook of her arm more securely into his armpit and they flew higher.

A crashing from somewhere close meant that the scarecrow was still following.

'Can't you stop that thing?' Will yelled.

'I tried!' Tatty shouted. 'But whatever ... enchantment it's under ... is too strong! Couldn't muster ... enough *oomph* at ... such short notice.'

'I must tell you,' said Jeb, 'that I really ... ahhh ... think I'm going to have to ... urghhh ... drop him in a minute.'

Tatty glared threateningly at the wood-sprite. 'You ... drop 'im an' I'll drop you ... We fly ... or die *together!*'

'All right ... I was just, *saying*, that's all ... He'd be a lot lighter without that ... urgh ... cursed stone.'

195

'*No!*' yelled Tatty and Will at the same time.

'Aggie made me promise to bring it. She – *Ouch* – said I'd need it.'

Heavy footfalls behind them sounded even closer.

Nearing the lake, they left the farmland behind, narrowly missing a wire fence bordering an overgrown lane. Something up ahead howled mournfully. They headed towards it and veered through a gap in the trees, which led down a rutted dirt track. A grassy clearing opened up in front of them and a figure stood there: A *human*. The howling came from a big dog standing at her side.

'Don't be scared,' the woman called. 'Come here, little 'uns, out of harm's way.'

Tatty could feel Jeb stalling, slowing. She almost lost her grip on Will.

'It's a *human*!' Jeb yelled, pulling in the opposite direction. 'Quick! This way!'

Will shrieked in pain.

'Stop it, Jeb!' Tatty shouted. 'It's *safe*! The Biggun's a friend! Come *on*!'

'But–'

'Don't argue!' she snapped.

Jeb gave up the struggle. Of course the wire fence pinging and twanging in the background may also have helped change his mind. Speeding past the human, Tatty and Jeb dropped Will on to the grass, before both collapsing close by, exhausted.

'Stay back, my loves,' said the human, 'an' don't you worry. Dorcas Gumble's goin' to mangle-ise him!'

Blundering footsteps came from the overgrown track. Dorcas stood beside the old mangle, its wooden handle gripped tightly in her clammy hands. 'I know what's comin',' she said, 'saw it in my crystal eye.'

Tatty looked at the Biggun. Close up, she was huge. There was a bright yellow glow around her. Tatty saw the glow when her third eye

196

had opened. She'd known this Biggun was good.

The dog growled. Wiry hair along its back stood on end.

Dorcas hissed through clenched teeth: 'Here it comes …'

The twitching, jerking, scarecrow reeled into the clearing. 'Good grief!' Dorcas exclaimed. 'What a sight. It's wearin' cowboy boots … *Pink* ones!'

The scarecrow loped towards Dorcas with its lower jaw hanging by a loop of wire. Its long greatcoat fanned out behind like giant bat wings.

'Get them under the waggon, Red. *Now!*'

Red picked up each of the faery creatures in his soft mouth, dropped them gently beneath the vardo and lay with them between his front paws.

The door to the caravan opened suddenly. 'What's Red howlin' for, Ma? I was trying to have a lie-in, what with the owl keepin' me up all … Ahhh! A *zombie!*' Little Arthur froze when he saw the figure weaving unsteadily across the clearing.

Dorcas had no chance to reply. She smacked the scarecrow's plastic skull. As it reached out its straw-packed gauntlets to grasp her throat, she managed to side-step and grab its collar. With her other hand, she turned the mangle's handle. 'No you don't,' she said, as the scarecrow tried to squirm away. She shoved its body against the mangle's spinning rollers, until one of its sleeves slipped between them. Strangely, as it had no voice box, the scarecrow began to shriek and wail. Dorcas let go of the collar and used both hands to turn the handle faster. It took immense strength to get the scarecrow's bulky shoulder between the rollers, but Dorcas was determined *and* strong.

Little Arthur's mouth hung open, while his father's snores rumbled on inside the caravan.

Then the scarecrow's plastic skull, pitted and perished from years outside, splintered into thousands of tiny pieces as the rollers crushed it, stopping the shrieking abruptly. Once the rest of the freakish figure slid through the mangle it was as though the nightmarish creature never was, except for a pile of mildewed clothes; mouldy straw; bits of plastic, and on top, a pair of battered, pink, cowboy boots.

★ ★ ★

In the treetop city of Scarabia, inside the largest house, Cormac looked into the crystal and allowed himself a smile. Who'd have thought a human so resourceful? A surprise, indeed. *You win this time, human, but I'll trounce you sooner or later. And I'll butcher and eat your mangy old dog, too.* Then, as he watched them shelter under the waggon with the hound, he noticed something for the very first time, though it had been glaringly obvious all along. How on Neptune's nose-hairs could he have missed it! 'Careless, careless, Cormac,' he murmured. 'Who else would Aunt Maeve send … but her successor!' The faery-child's wings were blindingly bright, branding Cormac's eyes with their perfectness. He felt a pang of envy. 'Why wasn't I blessed with such specimens, eh? Then all the bloodshed and upheaval would have been unnecessary.' He laughed bitterly. 'I can't even fly. A wingless faery is nothing short of an abomination! Not to mention ridiculous.' He made up his mind to make his aunt put it right. She would restore his wings, though the effort of doing so would probably kill her. *So*, he thought, *she wants me dead. It would simply be self-defence.*

Cormac suddenly felt light-headed and realised that he hadn't eaten anything that day; or the day before. He went to the window, pushing the shutters wide with a crash. He blinked. He didn't much care for sunlight: it brought on his headaches. Gloom suited him best these days. His stomach cramped painfully so he bellowed 'Food!' into the treetops, to nobody in particular.

A pale-looking elf poked her head from a rundown dwelling opposite. 'Yes, Y – Your Majesty,' she said, timidly. 'I'll bring food, right away.' She darted along a connecting rope bridge, disappearing through a doorway in the large turreted house that Cormac had claimed as his. Within moments he heard the satisfying sounds of pans clanking together. He stroked his empty belly and watched as his slaves went about their daily toil. He'd allowed some elves to live, providing they were useful. Some were cooks; others were Healers; most useful were the carpenters, of whom there were a dozen or so. He'd set them to work repairing the dilapidated city. The replacement of rotten timbers and wooden roof shingles seemed a never-ending task: no sooner had one dwelling been mended than another would be found, sometimes on the brink of collapse. *And what would be the point of ruling over such a city?* The battle to prevent the magpies fouling the place seemed well and truly lost. No amount of scolding and beating the birds had worked, they still left their droppings everywhere. Although, Cormac thought, the white-encrusted roofs had a certain *charm.* He'd only seen snow a handful of times, so Scarabia seemed a permanent enchanting winter wonderland, without the nuisance of cold weather.

He'd already decided that when the city was repaired, he would rid himself of most of the elves. One cook, for his own needs; one Healer, and two or three carpenters to keep on top of repairs would be sufficient. The rest he would give to the Gnomes. *The Gnomes.* He could see them now, skulking through the dry bracken on the woodland floor, keeping to the most shadowy areas. They hated sunlight as much as he did; their sensitive eyes preferring the cover of night for scavenging. But the lure of elves had brought them close. Cormac guessed that their food supply had run out again. *Serves them right,* he thought, *if they can't make their rations last.* He would let them have the companions of the faery-child once they were captured. They were of no importance. *Ah, the young, everything is oh–so–romantic when one is young and fearless. You think that you'll live forever ...* He laughed and went back to look into the crystal eye. But his laughter died on his lips when he saw that the image had vanished. He cursed his weakness and lack of ability. It seemed the eye still did not trust him yet. But it was only a matter of time until he made it see things *his* way. One day it would forget where it came from, of that he was certain.

A sound by the doorway made Cormac swivel on his throne; the elven female carried a tray of food. It rattled in her shaking hands.

Cormac's lip curled in annoyance. 'Come on in, my dear,' he urged gently. 'And don't be afraid, *I'm* not going to eat you.'

CHAPTER THIRTY FIVE

The Kelpie

After throwing the scarecrow's remains onto the campfire, Dorcas cleaned Will's cut feet with a cotton-bud, then cooked breakfast. Little Arthur had hurriedly dressed and rushed back to the vardo, watching as Tatty, Will, and Jeb sat cross-legged on the rim of a plate, spearing bits of sausage and egg with pared down cocktail sticks. Between mouthfuls, Tatty told Dorcas about the night of the storm; the magpies and Gnomes; then of the moment she'd first had the vision of the lake, and of Dorcas.

Dorcas expressed her condolences to Will at the loss of his father. At first the elf didn't reply. Then he blurted: 'He *has* to die!'

'It's the only way,' said Tatty, through a mouthful of sausage. 'None of us wants to do it; but he's already had his wings cut off, an' that didn't teach him.'

Jeb was full and sleepy. 'Cormac stole her eye.'

'He did – he stole my eye!' Dorcas exclaimed, outraged.

'Not yours,' said Jeb, 'the *Queen's.*' He then went on to explain that Tatty was the rightful heir, and that she too had the third eye. At this point Tatty held up her palm; the lid opened and the tiny black eyeball rolled wildly.

'That's it then. I'm coming with you.'

'Me too,' said Little Arthur.

'No you won't,' said Dorcas.

Her son's face fell. 'But—'

'No buts, young man. I said no an' I mean no. You're going to the New Forest pony sales with Pa. I don't want him getting suspicious. If you don't go along he'll want to know why. I can't have 'im knowing what I'm up to can I? He'd have forty fits if I told him I was off on some high jinks with little magic folk, now wouldn't he? Why, he don't even believe in Father Christmas.'

'Nor do I,' Little Arthur mumbled sullenly.

'Hush, don't let me hear you talkin' like that again.'

Dorcas explained that her crystal eye was stolen too, and that, apart from the vardo, it was her most treasured possession. 'Belonged to my Granny Rose,' she said sadly.

Jeb was concerned that Cormac was allowing his raids to spill over into the human realm: 'It seems there's no boundary he's not willing to cross in his hunger for power.'

'Sounds a right plonker,' remarked Dorcas, draining the last of her tea.

Someone clomped about in the neighbouring caravan.

'And it sounds like Pa's up an' about,' said Dorcas to Little Arthur. 'You'd best go and chivvy him along. The quicker you both leave for the sales, the better. And remember, not a word.' She turned to the faery-folk. 'I'd love to introduce you to Arthur, I really would, he's the dearest man … but we've been married nigh on twenty-four years an' I'm not even sure he believes in *my* powers. So what he'd make of you three, I don't know.'

'It doesn't matter,' said Will.

'We understand,' Tatty assured her.

Little Arthur stooped beneath the low ceiling. He rocked the waggon as he left, blocking the doorway, plunging them into momentary gloom.

'Soon as they both leave,' said Dorcas, 'I'll get the 'orse and we'll set off ourselves.'

An hour-and-a-half later, when the three were fast asleep, Arthur Gumble and his reluctant son were ready to leave. From the Land Rover, Arthur called: 'Did your visitors turn up? You know, the ones you was expectin' for breakfast?' He tapped the side of his nose and winked.

'No,' she answered, crossing her fingers behind her back to ward off bad luck; 'waste of bloomin' time.' She'd also kept the loss of the crystal ball from Arthur. Not that he'd believe it had been stolen by a bunch of magpies. He'd think her doolally. When he waved and turned away to look through the windscreen, she gave Little Arthur a meaningful stare. In reply, he stuck his thumb up, meaning that she needn't fear, he wouldn't tell.

Once the Land Rover disappeared out of sight down the track, Dorcas set about harnessing Emma to the vardo. Red wound himself around her legs, tail thrashing the air. 'Get out of it, you pest,' she scolded affectionately, pushing him away with her knee. While she secured Emma's last buckle, Dorcas noticed something flitting about above her head. She looked up and saw an enormous dragonfly as big as a bird. It carried tiny pots and bags on its back.

'Mornin',' said Dorcas. 'You must be Blue. Will told me about you – but not how lovely you are.' The insect settled on Dorcas's head. 'Now, where's the other one? Nibblit, isn't it?' She looked at the ground around her feet. Dorcas didn't much care for rodents, especially rats. But she was prepared to believe the little folk that Nibblit was the most gentle, intelligent rat anyone could wish to meet.

A soft woof told her that Red had found Nibblit. Dorcas was surprised to see the dog gently lick the rat's face, as he would normally killed rodents. Dorcas bent closer and peered at the creature. *What a sorry-looking individual*, she thought. *So moth-eaten; an' it's even wearin' an eye-patch*. The rat looked up at Dorcas with its remaining eye. And, strangely … she found herself smiling at it! She thought there was something very wise about its little pointy face. She almost collapsed in shock, however, when it opened its mouth and squeaked: 'Wants oats, pleeeease!'

'I – I 'spect you do. Come here an' let's get that clobber off you.' She untied the rat's bundle and put it on the waggon's footplate. Then she gingerly lifted the rat and placed him there too. She sprinkled some of Emma's oats in front of him and watched as he gobbled them up, his tiny claws making scratching sounds on the wood.

Dorcas climbed inside the vardo to wake her guests. The sight of them, lying asleep on a cushion, took her breath away. What amazing creations they are, she thought, with their tiny hands and sweet little pointed ears. Not that she could see much of Jeb, because his carapace had blended against the cushion, so that it had adopted the same burgundy and gold swirly pattern. Dorcas gently nudged Will with a finger. His grumbles woke the others.

Tatty sat up quickly and rubbed her eyes. 'Is it time, Dorcas?'

'Reckon it is.'

Will sat up and grinned at Dorcas. Though it wasn't the human who made his face light up, but the dragonfly perched on her head.

'Nibblit and Blue have turned up. Isn't that good news? I don't know whether you'd like to ride up front with me,' asked Dorcas, 'or if you'd rather travel inside? But I must warn you, it gets *really* bumpy.'

They each agreed that they would rather ride with Dorcas. After a few more minutes, the vardo was ready to leave. Dorcas held the reins; beside her, on a little wooden doll's chair, sat her new companions. Dorcas had secured the chair to the vardo with a strap, just in case. Red was on the ground, with Nibblit clinging to his back. On top of Dorcas's head, Blue had dozed off in the sunshine, not that anyone had noticed, seeing as dragonflies don't have eye-lids.

'Right then,' said Dorcas. 'Are we all set?'

'Yes!' everybody, including Nibblit, shouted.

Dorcas turned her attention Red. 'Get ready for a swim, ol' boy!' To her passengers, she said: 'There's a chance you might get a bit wet.'

'Wet?' yelled Tatty.

Dorcas laughed. 'You lot aren't the only ones what knows a thing or two about magic.' She slapped the mare's back with the reins. 'Walk on, Emma!'

The horse pulled the waggon towards the lake.

Tatty was worried. *Somethin' this big's goin' to sink.*

A second later, the vardo rolled down the bank and in to the shallows. Emma whinnied and thrashed at the water with her hooves, throwing mud and weed up onto her belly.

'That's enough, Emma,' said Dorcas. 'She's bound to be excited – hasn't been in water deeper than her fetlocks for … well, must be ten months.'

Tatty, Will, and Jeb looked back blankly.

'You'll see her change,' Dorcas went on, 'as soon as the water gets above 'er knees.'

Emma dragged the vardo deeper. The water quickly rose to her shoulders. The mare stood still, dunking her head repeatedly under the surface. She arched her neck and whinnied again; but mid-whinny, her horsey voice changed to something else: a *roar* came from between her rubbery lips. ''Ere she goes!' called Dorcas excitedly, as Emma's long, square, teeth rapidly sank into her pink gums and in their place long fangs appeared. Then her flowing white mane shrank back into her skin and her neck became elongated and serpentine in appearance; also, where Emma's ears had once been, there sprouted fins. Her eyes changed from a chocolate brown colour to a vivid red, the lids closing from side to side instead of up and down. As Emma pulled the vardo farther into the lake, her fine white coat disappeared, the hairs retracted so that her skin resembled that of a white Beluga whale.

Suddenly, the vardo also began to change. Black timbers popped their nails and shifted. The sides of the waggon began to curve outwards. Where Dorcas and the faery-folk sat, apointed prow took shape. Next the wheels flipped sideways and disappeared beneath a hull. The vardo was now a boat. 'Quickest way to Woebetide Wood,' said Dorcas. 'It beats goin' the long way round.'

Emma swam freely now; the final changes were that her stout

legs had morphed into flippers and her tail had become broad and flat like a beaver's.

A splash from the rear meant that Red had entered the lake. Soon he was swimming close to Emma, though safely out of chomping distance from her sharp teeth. Nibblit clawed his way up to the top of the old dog's head, where he remained quite dry.

'You see, she's a Kelpie,' Dorcas explained. ''Course, nobody knows about it 'cept me. I'll tell Little Arthur one of these days. She looks like a horse, but get her wet … Well, then she becomes a different sort of a beast altogether. You wouldn't want to get in 'er way when she's turned – she'd have you with them teeth in a flash. Swim on, my Emma.'

Soon they were in the middle of the lake, and they heard the first cackling magpies, though no birds were visible yet. Tatty thought the landscape looked *too* perfect: the way Woebetide Wood was mirrored on the lake's surface, and the way that fish jumped clear of the water, as though they were trying to catch a glimpse of the craft cutting through their aquatic world. No, something else about the scene felt strange.

'Did you see–?' Will began. 'No, don't worry … my mistake.'

'What is it?' asked Tatty.

'Thought I saw somethin' over on the far bank. But there's nothin' there now, just giving myself the heebie-jeebies.'

'I know what you mean,' said Tatty. 'I've got them too.'

Emma swam swiftly. The far side of the lake came close. Soon she could swim no longer and hauled herself through the shallows like a walrus. As she flopped up onto the bank she began to change. The boat shifted and bent too, quickly transforming into the vardo. When Emma's legs were sufficiently horse-like, she pulled the waggon out of the mud and on to the grass. Horsification complete, Dorcas drove the waggon under the cover of the trees, then hitched up her floral skirt and stepped down to the ground. She passed the reins over the mare's head and looped them over a strong-looking branch.

Red dragged himself from the lake and staggered up the bank. The swim had tired him more than he would admit, so he shook the water from his coat, sending Nibblit sprawling in to the long grass. The dog went towards the trees, but Dorcas grabbed his collar. 'Oh, no you don't,' she whispered. 'You're to stay here and guard the vardo. And there's no use showin' me those soppy eyes, I've made up my mind. Anyway, you'd scare those magpies and I need to get Granny's eye back.'

Red slunk under the waggon and sulked.

'Good lad,' said Dorcas. 'I don't want you gettin' hurt, that's all, you mean too much to me.'

Jeb and Tatty helped Will down from the little chair.

'I could heal those feet for you,' said Tatty.

Will winced as he placed a cut foot onto the wood. 'No, it'll use up too much of your energy. Can't tire you out, you'll need to keep as strong as possible. We don't know what to expect from Cormac … I'll be fine.'

Tatty started to protest. 'But–'

'He's right,' Jeb stated. 'You save your strength for what's coming.'

'Up here then, Will,' said Dorcas, lifting the elf onto one of her shoulders. 'No need for you to walk at all.'

He clung to one of her large earrings for balance. Carefully, Dorcas picked Nibblit up, placing him into a pocket in her skirt. 'Otherwise 'is little legs won't be able to keep up with us,' she explained. Again, Dorcas told Red to stay, and then walked into the wood as if she knew which direction to take, picking her way over fallen branches and tree roots without making the slightest sound. Tatty and Jeb followed, flying close behind. Dorcas looked back often, to make sure they were keeping up. After a while, Tatty saw Jeb tugging on Dorcas's skirt. The wood-sprite landed on a branch. He'd tucked the heavy sword into his belt.

'What is it?' asked Dorcas.

'We're nearly there,' Jeb said. 'There was something familiar about that twisted oak tree we just passed. I *know* I've seen it before.'

Will interrupted. 'Shh!'

'What's the matter?' asked Tatty, landing on Dorcas's other shoulder. 'I don't hear anythin'.'

'Exactly,' said Will, with a worried frown. 'The wood's silent.'

Dorcas offered a hand to Jeb and he stepped onto it. She placed him on her shoulder, next to Tatty. He wrapped a hand in her hair. Dorcas walked on.

Tatty thought that, so far, Woebetide Wood looked neglected and sad: trees had fallen and been left to rot where they lay; weedy saplings sprouted in every little patch of sunlight. A snap of a twig over to Tatty's right made her whirl around. Nothing lurked in the shadows, even though the feeling of being watched was over-whelming. A slight breeze shifted the thinner branches. Nothing else moved. She realised she'd been holding her breath, so let it out slowly. Then she saw something in the branches. She whispered in the Gypsy's ear: 'Dorcas, up there …'

Dorcas looked up.

Far above, Tatty could see the undersides of countless small wooden houses, linked together by bridges made from rope and wooden slats. There was life up there, too.

'Magpies,' said Dorcas.

Hundreds of birds watched. Silent sentinels.

'There goes our chance of takin' them by surprise,' Dorcas muttered.

'What shall we do, Dorcas?' Will whispered.
'I'll take the catapult out of my pocket and shoot 'em down one at a time till I get my crystal back – I *swear* it!'

'My dear lady,' said a voice so oily that it could have deep-fried doughnuts, 'I really think you'd be wasting your time. You see, there are so many of us and so few of *you*.'

Dorcas spun around. On a branch, sitting astride a magpie with a waxy-looking substance clogging its feathers, was a pale, straggly haired person dressed all in black. A rustic crown sat crookedly on his head.

'Salutations,' he said, giving a brown-toothed grin. 'In case you hadn't heard, I am Cormac, Viscount Viperian ... Am I to understand that *you*, human, are looking for something? Is that right?'

'You know it is,' Dorcas hissed. 'And if you don't give it to me I'm goin' to– '

'Do what exactly, dear lady? Do *what?*' Cormac leaned back and laughed. 'You have no authority here. This is *my* Kingdom. Yes, yes, you heard me correctly – I said *King*dom!' He looked straight at Tatty when he added: '*Males* take precedence here, girl! And that's as it should be, and will be from now on!' Cormac's complexion had taken on some much-needed colour as his temper flared.

'What *are* you anyway?' Jeb's outraged voice rang out now. 'The king of the magpies, that is all! And it isn't your kingdom, but *mine!* Scarabia belongs to *my* people, and you and your – your *scavengers* have murdered hundreds of innocents to get it! Well, My Lord, I've come to take it back!' Jeb stood and pulled the sword from his belt. A shaft of sunlight glinted on the blade.

'And me!' yelled Tatty, standing.

'Me too!' called Will, rising awkwardly on to his sore feet.

Nibblit jumped from Dorcas's pocket and landed on the leaves at her feet. He stood upright on his hind legs and bared his sharp yellow teeth. Blue was awake now too; he shifted on Dorcas's head and shook his wings angrily, rattling the cooking utensils tied on his back.

Dorcas took a step towards Cormac. 'I – want – my – eye,' she said, quietly.

'Queen Maeve wants hers too!' Tatty shouted.

Cormac chuckled. 'What this old thing.' He took something from his robes. 'She's welcome to it. Sadly, it died far from the haven of its owner's hand.' He laughed hysterically. 'Fancy it just dying like that ... Oh dear, never mind.' He grinned wolfishly at Dorcas. 'Good job I've got yours then, isn't it! I grant you, it isn't organic matter, but it works awfully well, and it's getting better all the time. So much for loyalty, eh?' He stroked the neck of the magpie with a grime-engrained hand. The bird flinched at his touch. 'You were very clever, Pip, finding it for me. Funny, isn't it, how these birds will do almost anything on the promise of shiny trinkets? And once I get rid of my aunt they will have treasure in abundance.' He sat up straight and tugged his beard. 'What to *do* with you all, that's the thing?' A lazy grin spread across his face. 'I know … you,' he pointed a finger at Dorcas, 'will skedaddle off to the other side of the lake where you came from, and stay out of that which does not concern you …'

Dorcas fumed. 'I won't! It was you what thieved–'

'… and you,' went on Cormac, his finger drifting across to Will, 'will be turned over to the Gnomes …' his eyes fell on Jeb; 'as will *you.*'

Jeb's mouth gaped.

Next, he addressed Tatty. 'And you, my dearest, will become my bride, when you're of age, of course; which will add, I think, a semblance of legitimacy over my succession to the throne.' He rubbed his hands together with glee. 'There, I think that about covers it! Oh – wait – Pip – almost forgot … You may as well have this dried up old thing. Catch!' Cormac flicked Queen Maeve's shrivelled eye into the air. It arced upward. The magpie caught it and swallowed.

'*No!*' wailed Tatty. She couldn't believe it! They'd come such a long way to reclaim the eye. *Poor old Queen Maeve.*

As if spurred by Tatty's voice, a magpie wheeled away from its perch in the treetops, aiming for her. The other magpies set up a dreadful cackling and hissing. Dorcas dodged sideways and the magpie flew past, turning in mid-flight to continue the attack. With a snarl, Cormac fired a bolt of lightning from his fingertip, hitting the bird. It exploded in a puff of feathers. 'No one is to attack until *I* say so – is that *clear!*' he screeched. The magpies fell silent.

Nobody saw Will throw his luck-stone, least of all Cormac. He threw the heavy stone as if he were aiming his lasso: straight and true, swinging it round and around his head by its cord and letting it fly. His aim was deadly. As the luck-stone soared, a whistling sounded, caused by air forced through the hole? *Perhaps?* Or, could it have been the cries of vengeful spirits waiting to get their own back on the person who had led to their downfall, one of them being Cormac's own mother. The luck-stone hit him with a dull thud, in the same spot that sprouted the shock of white hair. He dropped from Pip's back without a murmur, landing on soft leaves.

No one moved. Each of them expected the pile of rags to rise at any moment, but it didn't. Still they watched, silent, until a full minute had passed. Then Cormac's pale skin began to glow; tiny specks of glittering light peeled away from his body and floated upwards. Up and up they went, all the fragments that had once been The Magpie King, drifting like hot embers up through the outstretched branches of the wood, until all that remained of Cormac Viperian was a bundle of tattered robes and a tiny bone crown.

'He … *died,*' Tatty breathed, shocked. She stared at the others, one by one.

'Is that it?' said Jeb, sounding deflated.

'I – I didn't *mean* to do it,' said Will, hurriedly. 'I only meant to stun him a bit, or somethin', not kill him, not *that!*'

'Don't you go frettin' yourself,' Dorcas soothed. 'Good riddance to bad rubbish, I say! He got what was comin' to him, no more, no less. Fate is what it is, meant to be.'

Tatty tried to reassure him, too, 'Dorcas is right, Will. Why else did Aggie insist on you bringin' the stone? You did it for the Queen, and the folk of Little Upham, remember – and none of our blood got spilled, thank goodness.'

Will smiled weakly, feeling suddenly nauseous. 'Thanks,' was all he managed to say.

'I honestly don't think *I* could've done it,' Tatty said.

'Or me,' Jeb agreed, dropping the sword from his sweaty grip, so that it landed at Dorcas's feet, embedding itself in the soil.

Keen to give her aching earlobes a rest, Dorcas lowered them to the ground.

Nibblit went to Cormac's soiled robes. He sniffed them and squeaked: 'Creeeeeeter!'

Still perched on Dorcas's head, Blue said nothing at all.

Then, almost as one, magpies took off from the treetops and from the roofs of Scarabia. The magpie, Pip, blinked as if waking from a trance and launched into the air. Apart from the sound of many wing beats, they flew away in silence.

CHAPTER THIRTY SIX

Red the Rescuer

The sound of someone shouting made them look up through the branches. A figure ran along one of the rope bridges. 'Your Majesty! The birds! Are you there? They've all flown away! What are we to do?' The person looked down at Dorcas. 'What've you done with 'is Majesty, you *witch!*'

'I ain't no witch,' replied Dorcas. 'Though I reckon we could find one for you, if you want?'

'What the—' Jeb spluttered. 'It – It's *Sproutly!*'

'Who?' said Will.

'Sproutly.' Tatty squinted upward. 'He's the husband of Her Majesty's housekeeper. No wonder it was easy for someone to slip somethin' into the Queen's drink. Who would've suspected those two?'

Jeb said, 'I can't believe it. Not them …'

The elf sped down a staircase that wound around the trunk of a tree. There were nearly a thousand steps, so it took him ages. All the way down he cursed the human standing below: 'I'll 'ave you, I will, you great behemoth! You wait an' see – ruddy rusty jugglers! If you've so much 'as 'urt one 'air on 'is head – I'll 'ave you!' He finally reached the bottom of the staircase, unfurled a rope ladder nailed to the last step and climbed down to the ground. When Sproutly turned around he saw the children for the first time; then noticed the bundle of black rags and the crown. 'Oh, you 'aven't?' He turned his pleading gaze toward Tatty, and staggered forward. 'Please, tell me that you 'aven't? 'E promised me riches – a peerage too. You know, once the old Queen 'ad gone.' He ran a hand over the top of his head. 'She deserves so much; you see ... She deserves so much *more!*'

Even though Sproutly had done a dreadful thing, Tatty still felt sorry for the elf. 'Who deserves so much?' she asked, gently. 'The Queen?'

He rounded on her with hate-filled eyes. 'No, *stupid!* Mrs Sproutly does.' Spit flew from his lips as he raged. 'And now you've gone an' *ruined* it all! Bridget's worked 'ard all her life. All I wanted to do was make it easier. 'Er parents said I wasn't good enough, but she upped an' married me anyway. An' *he*,' he jabbed a finger at the pile of rags, 'was goin' to make me a *Lord!* Bridget would 'ave been a Lady!'

Jeb said, 'Cormac had no power to do th–'

''E *promised!* Now,' Sproutly paced in circles, muttering, 'I've got to think of somethin' ... what to do, what to do ...'

Tatty realised then that the elf was quite mad.

'Got to get away, far, far away ... where nobody knows us. Course, *she* won't want to go an' leave 'er precious *Queen!* Majesty this 'n' Majesty that, all I hear, dawn till dusk. I'll *make* her go ... tell 'er that 'er mother's ill or summat! Yep, that's what I'll do ... Won't want to go, though, nobody else does a good enough job of lookin' after the Queen. Little does she know there's dozens who'd step into 'er shoes, like *that!*' He snapped his fingers.

Tears flowed freely down Will's cheeks. 'Don't you realise what you've done? You helped kill my Pa, you silly, silly – great–'

Tatty placed a hand on Will's shoulder.

'Do you mean that Mrs Sproutly has no idea what you've done?' asked Jeb.

Sproutly shook his head.

Jeb went on: 'So it was *you* who put the poison in the Queen's drink.'

'Who else!' snapped Sproutly. He added smugly: 'Deadly Night-

214

shade and it was easy-peasy too. Bridget 'adn't a clue that I'd already slipped the poison in when she came to fetch the old duffer's nightcap. Like givin' sweeties to a babe, it was. Night of the storm I smashed the dome above the fountain – made it look like someone broke in.' He swayed slightly, as if he might collapse. 'Now, it pains me to 'ave to do this, but I can't 'ave you goin' back to the palace an' spillin' yer guts to folk–,' with surprising speed he darted to the sword and plucked it from the earth, '–so I'll just 'ave to spill some guts right *now!*' Sproutly was powerfully built. He wielded the sword with skill, swinging the flashing blade towards Jeb.

The lurcher loped through the trees. *CHOMP!* went Red's jaws as they closed around the elf. The dog gave two hard grinding bites and swallowed Sproutly whole.

'Good boy, Red!' called Dorcas. 'Even if you was told to stay an' guard the waggon.' She stroked his head and chuckled. 'Just shows how we take animals for granted, doesn't it?' Red looked at Dorcas and wagged his tail stiffly. His lips curled and he spat out the sword. Jeb picked the weapon up and wiped the blade on some leaves, then slipped it back through his belt.

Will went across to the bundle of soiled black rags to retrieve his luck-stone.

The eyelid in Tatty's hand snapped open. In her mind sprang an image of Will sliding into a dark hole. Her dream came rushing back. But it was no dream at all, it was terrifyingly *real!* She spun around.

He was gone.

She ran to where the luck-stone lay and saw a freshly dug hole in the woodland floor. Loose soil and leaves still trickled into it. She heard a distant shuffling coming from deep in the earth and with each second it grew fainter. 'It's got Will!' she yelled.

The others came swiftly and looked down at the large hole. Red pawed at the entrance, dislodging more soil.

'What is it that's got 'im?' Dorcas asked.

'Gnomes,' said Tatty, starting to cry.

'A Gnome, you reckon,' said Dorcas. 'Can't say as I've ever seen one – 'cept at the garden centre.'

'What? Where?' said Tatty.

'Never mind,' said Dorcas. 'This is where Red'll come in useful. He's a top tracker. Come here, boy.' She held the dog by his collar and let him sniff the burrow. 'Find Will, Red. Seek 'im – seek 'im,' she urged. Immediately, the dog began to track and went into the trees, yipping excitedly and zigzagging as the Gnome tunnel veered around tree trunks and roots. Dorcas scooped up Jeb and hurried after her dog.

Tatty took to the air, following as close to the dog as she could manage. She thought of Will in that dark place. She hoped he'd fainted, so that he wouldn't feel afraid.

CHAPTER THIRTY SEVEN

The Gnome Circle

Will hadn't fainted. Not quite. The Gnome (he presumed that's what the smelly creature was) dragged him by the feet down the midnight tunnel, ignoring Will's yells as he hit stones and hanging tree roots. The journey seemed to take for ever; loose earth filled his mouth, choking him. *So this is it*, he thought, suddenly calm, *this is where my fear stems from? It's like I've known where I was headed all along! How strange* … But he didn't want to die, not yet, so he writhed and bucked, but the creature simply tightened its grip. Will stopped struggling then. He attempted to escape the terror by trying on purpose to faint, but couldn't quite manage it, so laced his fingers together behind his head to help cushion his bruising journey.

★★★

The trees grew more densely than before. Red dodged around them, squeezed beneath fallen branches, or jumped over them like a dog half his age. Dorcas couldn't keep up and soon lost sight of Red comp-

217

letely. Snagging branches caught her clothes and scratched her skin. She stumbled, catching her knee on a tree stump. She put out a hand to save herself, letting go of Jeb. He flew off, soon disappearing. 'That's all right, don't you worry,' muttered Dorcas to herself, scrabbling back to her feet. 'I'll be fine … Just gashed me leg open … blood's gushin' out. Never you mind, I'll soldier on …' She stumbled deeper into Woebetide Wood, until Scarabia was left far behind.

Leaving the shelter of the trees, Red squirmed beneath a fence and vanished into a field of tall ripe corn. Tatty flew higher. She could see the stalks moving as the dog ploughed through them. And she noticed something else too, something unusual. Near the centre of the field, part of the crop had been flattened, so that it formed a perfect stalk-circle. Tatty frowned. The dancing corn still rippled as Red hurried on, straight towards the huge circle. She whistled, and the corn became still. She was glad that there wasn't anything wrong with the old dog's hearing. The corn moved again, this time in her direction. She flew low, down to the fence, and Red's grinning face loomed out of the cornstalks. She hovered and he sat in front of her, wafting her with his warm breath. 'Listen,' she said, 'I know you understand me. I want you to stay here. *Stay!*'

Red whimpered and looked in the direction of the circle.

'No – stay here an' wait for Dorcas.'

Red leaned against a post, his pink tongue lolling from his mouth like a banner.

'Good lad.' Tatty left him and flew back towards the circle, zooming low over the heads of ripe corn. The circle was immaculate, unlike the creatures responsible for it. Tatty also sensed Will's presence below ground, and that he still lived; she'd have known instantly if the opposite was true. She pictured the Gnomes scurrying about below the warm soil. *How to get him out though, that's the problem?* Looking around, she could see no entrance; then realised that there were probably many entrances in to the circle, all starting somewhere in the wood. Tatty shivered at the thought of going down there. She was agitated and angry, knowing that Will would be dead if she didn't act soon. *What do I do?*

Slowly, she became aware of a tingling sensation in her fingertips. The tingling soon changed to a burning, spreading up her arms and into her chest, growing stronger all the time. Even the top of her head felt like it was about to burst into flame. The pain made her anger grow ever fiercer, even as she thought she would die from the pain of the burning.

Then, without warning, the pain vanished, and all she felt was warmth enveloping her body. She relaxed, letting the feeling take over. She hung, suspended, above the circle. Her wings were motionless but she stayed airborne. A strange stillness surrounded her. Then her arms rose, straight out, in line with her shoulders, and she started to spin, faster and faster, until she was just a white ball of light. The flattened cornstalks began to rise from the earth, like a lid being removed from a dish; then it too began to spin: a great earthen disc made from baked soil and cornstalks. As Tatty climbed higher into the air, so the crop circle followed.

Jeb reached the fence. His mouth hung open as he watched the huge portion of earth revolving above the field, so high that it cast a massive shadow.

Red let out a long howl.

Dorcas almost ran in to the fence. 'What in blazes is goin' on? I lost Blue back in the woods somewhere ... Um, should we be standin' here?' Dorcas asked breathlessly, pulling twigs out of her hair and staring worriedly up at the spectacle.

'Probably not,' Jeb answered, though neither of them moved.

Above, Tatty gradually slowed her spinning. The huge turning clod of corn and earth seemed close enough for her to land on. Suddenly, tiring of the cursed thing, she flung aside one of her hands and the vast crop circle spun away, hurtling towards the lake like a discarded giant Frisbee. It slewed through the sky, skimming the top of Woebetide Wood and plunged into the middle of the lake, spewing up great gouts of water. Gradually, the lake's ripples stilled, until all that remained of the earthen disc was a muddy stain on its surface.

Tatty looked down on the exposed tunnels. Blinded by the bright sunshine, Gnomes ran haphazardly in all directions, howling in panic. Tatty couldn't stomach the thought of slaughtering the ghastly things, she simply wanted Will back. From the corner of her eye she saw him, curled into a ball inside a cell-like chamber. It was easy, swooping down and scooping him into her arms. Her power felt limitless, like she could do anything, defeat anyone. She stood in the chamber, clutching Will, and noticed a pile of torn clothing stacked against the wall: *Elven clothes*, she realised. Poking from the pile was a shirt she recognised: the letter '*B*' lovingly embroidered on to the collar by his mother. It seemed a lifetime ago that Burnley had vanished. She could do nothing for him now – had known it all along. She launched herself into the sky. Will shifted restlessly in her arms. His face was smudged with dirt; his eyelids fluttered open.

'I *knew* you'd come. And guess what …' he said with a laugh, '… I didn't 'ave a funny turn.' Right then he fainted clean away.

Tatty grinned as a faint violet glow surrounded him. She held him tighter.

Back at the fence a little while later, Will had to put up with lots of fussing from Dorcas. The Gypsy insisted on carrying him back to the vardo. 'I'm not havin' you strainin' yourself after the shock you've had. And we'd better try an' find Blue an' Nibblit. I hope they had the sense to stay nearby.'

On the way, Jeb and Tatty rode on Red's back. It wasn't a very comfortable ride, due to the lurcher's bony spine, but it was better than flying. A numbing tiredness enveloped Tatty, draining her to the core. Even *thinking* was tiring, so she relaxed into the rhythm of Red's long strides and tried not to slide off his back. It wasn't long before they were back beneath the treetop city.

Dorcas retrieved Will's luck-stone from the woodland floor. She passed it to him. He tied it to his belt and rubbed it absent-mindedly.

'Right, where're them two terrors?' Dorcas yelled, 'Blue! Nibblit!' Nothing.

Will put a thumb and finger to his lips and let out a shrill whistle. In seconds, a brilliant bolt of blue flashed among the trees. Swooping down, the dragonfly settled on to his new favourite spot: Dorcas's head.

'There you are,' she said. 'Now it's just that rat.'

A voice, comfortingly familiar to Will, answered: 'I think I might've found him.' A small figure led Nibblit through dry bracken.

Will thought he might faint again. 'Pa!' he yelled ecstatically. Tears rolled down his cheeks.

'Well, well, well,' chuckled Dorcas, lowering Will to the ground. 'It seems that luck-stone's worth its weight in gold. Have to get me one of those.'

Tatty watched through an exhausted haze as Will and his father ran into each other's arms. Jeb patted her gently on the back. No words were needed.

With an arm clasped around his son's shoulder, Alf Patch told them everything that happened. 'Good job I'm handy with a saw an' hammer – it's what kept me alive for so long. Buildings like that,' he pointed upward, 'take a lot of lookin' after.' Alf looked up at Dorcas. 'Someone heard you askin' for your crystal. The others are lowerin' it now.'

'Others?' said Dorcas, bemused, before noticing tiny people lowering Granny Rose's eye by a long length of twine from a balcony. It swung through the trees, cradled in the same plastic netting in which it was stolen.

'Each an' every one of us here was taken by magpies,' said Alf.

'No sprites then,' called Jeb.

'None that I've seen,' Alf answered.

Jeb nodded sadly.

Finally, the crystal reached the ground. Dorcas ran to untie the twine, leaving her heirloom inside the orange netting and carrying it

221

over to Red. She knelt in front of the dog and spoke quietly to Tatty. 'I've been thinkin' … all this time, what with the Queen losin' her third eye an' all, an' it bein' important for a lot of her powers … Well, I want her to 'ave Granny Rose's crystal, as a replacement.'

Tatty tried to protest, but Dorcas silenced her. 'I won't take no for an answer. I've got the spare crystal in the vardo which I can use for my dukkerin' anyway.' She hoped nobody noticed her crossed fingers. 'This one's mainly a keepsake. An' I'm sure Granny Rose would want the Queen to have it.'

'Thank you, Dorcas,' murmured Tatty, barely able to keep her eyes open.

'That's that then. Me an' Red had better get a move on, before those two gentlemen of mine get back from the New Forest sales.' Her knees creaked as she stood up.

An unusual sound came from close by. 'Psst!' it hissed. 'Psst! *Boy*! Is it safe to come out?'

Jeb turned and saw a brown face peering from behind a tree root. 'Y – Yes,' Jeb said. 'It's perfectly safe.'

'It's all right, everyone. It's safe!'

From all around the clearing, small figures peeled away from the trunks of trees and emerged from amongst tangled ivy. *Wood-sprites;* their carapaces had blended with the woodland backdrop completely. They were a small group of about thirty and they gathered together. One walked towards Red and smiled up at Jeb. He slid from the dog's back and went towards her. She reached down and cupped his chin in her hand. 'Welcome home,' she said.

Amazed at her shining face, so like his own, he whispered: 'Are you my mother?'

'Alas,' she answered sadly, 'I am not. But I will be your mother, until you find her, if you wish.'

Jeb gulped. 'Yes, please,' he squeaked.

She reached out and pulled him into her arms. As he sank against her warmth, he knew that even if he never found his real parents, he was home – at long, long last.

Dorcas wiped her eyes quickly and cleared her throat. 'Come on, time to go. I'll 'ave to take you lot home – can't expect you to walk all that way after the trauma you've been through.'

'I'm quite all right,' Alf insisted.

'Me too,' said Will.

Jeb walked towards Alf and Will. 'Vanna,' he indicated his newly adopted mother, 'said that there's a faster way back, so we don't have to go overland. She says it's *under*land.'

Tatty listened quietly. 'A quicker way?' she said wearily, lowering herself from Red's back by grabbing handfuls of his fur.

'So she says,' said Jeb.

'How?' Tatty asked.

'Where you are from, do you have a wishing-well?' Vanna asked.

'A wishing-well?' Tatty's head felt porridgey and heavy.

'Yes, a round shaft that holds spring water,' said Vanna.

Tatty realised that she was reacting dully. 'Sorry. Yes, we have … near Little Upham, Mould Cottage … the Biggun's place.'

'And it's safe, this wishing-well?' asked Vanna.

'Yes, I think so.'

'Come, follow me. There is a well here in Woebetide Wood, near the ruins of a woodcutter's cottage. No human has lived there for a hundred years.' Vanna led Jeb into the trees, and Tatty and Nibblit followed.

Dorcas lifted Alf and Will onto her shoulder to ride in comfort. 'I'll carry this then, shall I?' said the Gypsy, scooping up the crystal ball from the ground.

'Sorry, Dorcas,' said Will. 'Tatty seems a bit … out of sorts.'

'That's all right,' Dorcas said, smiling at the elf. 'Come on. I'm dyin' to see how this wishing-well thing works.'

'Me too,' said Alf with a worried frown.

Whoopsy

They walked until they came to a tumbledown pile of stone blocks bound together with ivy and weeds. Nearby was a smaller pile of stones, where all the wood-sprites and elves had gathered.

'See,' said Vanna, clambering up the stones and pointing; 'here is a gap you jump through.'

Dorcas placed Will and his father on the ground.

'Jump?' Alf looked worried. 'You did say *jump* just then, didn't you?'

'Yes. It's the only way.'

The other wood-sprites nodded in agreement.

'Everything will go well for you,' she said, 'as long as you keep a picture of home in your head and in your heart. In dream-moments you will be back there.'

'That's all there is to it?' said Tatty.

'Yes, that is all.'

Tatty turned to Jeb. 'I'll say goodbye … for now at least. I know you're not comin' back with us, Jeb.'

'No, not for a while,' he admitted. 'I'd like a chance to get to know this place again.' He looked around, at the trees and the leafy canopy above their heads. 'I'll return to the palace very soon; Queen Maeve needs me, though she'd never admit it.'

Tatty nodded and hugged him. An ant-egg-sized lump seemed stuck in her throat. 'Thanks so much for helpin' Little Upham. It means a lot.'

'No, it's I who must thank *you*, for bringing me home,' he whispered. His chin rested briefly upon her shoulder and one of her silken wings brushed his cheek. 'Come along now,' he said and laughed; 'it's time for you to return to your Willow Tree.'

'Yes.' Almost too tired to speak, she wanted to rest against him for ever. Somehow, she managed to climb the stones until she stood on shaky legs by the dark opening.

Will, Alf, and Nibblit climbed next, followed by more elves.

Dorcas knelt close to the jumble of stones and tied the crystal in the orange netting around the rat's middle. 'Just so's you don't lose it,' she said.

'Shan't,' Nibblit answered.

Dorcas laughed. 'It still tickles me whenever I hear you speak, Nibblit, it really does. And by the way, Will, I'll take Blue with me an' release him from the camp. Don't think it'd do him any good travellin' down the well with you. Too skittish. He might get hurt.'

'Yes, good idea. Thanks, Dorcas,' Will agreed.

'I'll take Nibblit to Little Upham with me,' Tatty said to Jeb, 'in case he can't think of a good enough picture of the palace in his head.'

Jeb nodded. 'Write a note to Sir Edwin, he'll send someone to collect him.'

Tatty looked up at the human. 'Thank you, Dorcas, for everythin' you've done for us. You didn't have to.'

Dorcas beamed in reply, not trusting herself to speak. They'd been through such a lot in only a few short hours.

Tatty climbed on to Nibblit's back, so that he travelled with her while she concentrated on a mental image of the Willow Tree. She looked at the others, at all the stolen elves, each standing at the edge of the hole and trying to peer down into the darkness.

'Are we ready?' said Tatty.

'Yes,' they all answered.

'Everyone got a clear picture of home in their heads?'

'Yes,' they said again.

'Right, on the count of three we'll all jump together. One –Two – *THREE!*' Dozens of elves leapt into nothingness.

The cold bit into Tatty's skin immediately: a shock after the pleasant warmth in the wood. Tatty tried her best to ignore it, instead concentrating on the Willow Tree, of Nan on baking day, all hot and bothered; Papa in his rocker, charming his pipe, and lastly, Marigold watching the Stirring-Stick swirl laundry in the cauldron. The blackness was so complete that she wasn't aware of Will or Alf being close by. The water seemed to have disappeared, replaced by chill wind rushing past as she fell. Her wings were flattened against her body as she clung to Nibblit's warm fur, repeating in her head over and over: *The Willow – The Willow – The Willow.*

★ ★ ★

'If you could put this up on your gate, me an' the wife would be very grateful. We don't hold out much hope of seein' Delilah again, but you never know … I promised the wife I'd put the pictures up. The cat's part of the family, you see,' Bert explained.

George Parsons took the home-made poster from Bert's hand and studied the photo of the cat. Not a particularly pleasant-looking animal, George thought, the way its ears were laid back like that, not the sort of animal you'd want to pick up and cuddle. He recalled that he'd seen a similar cat only the other day, by the General Store, probably scrounging for food judging by the size of its stomach.

'Pretty cat,' said Hilda, peering at the picture. 'I used to 'ave a cat when I was little.'

'Did you?' said Bert, wishing they'd just hurry and accept the poster.

'Mm,' said Hilda; 'called it Whoopsy, on account she left

226

whoopsies all over the 'ouse. Never would be 'ouse-trained, that one.'

'Oh ... Dear, dear, me,' Bert murmured, wanting to get away from the mothball-smelling old couple as soon as possible. He had another twenty posters to put up around the village and he'd been here ten minutes already, after the couple hadn't answered his knocking at the door. Strangely, he realised that he'd never actually *seen* the Parsons before, even though he'd delivered the odd bit of post now and then. He eventually found them both in the garden, where the lady had peered down into the well. She told him that she'd often heard voices down there, so Bert had taken a look too, to be polite. He'd listened intently, but heard nothing other than the echoing drip, drip, drip of water.

Hilda took the poster from George's hand. 'Course we'll put the picture on the gate, though we don't get hardly any folk comin' down the drive – 'cept the postman.'

Bert almost laughed, but managed to control himself. 'It doesn't matter,' he said nicely. 'If even *one* person happens to see it ... Well, you never know.'

Hilda smiled. 'That's right, you never know.'

George Parsons wasn't smiling. 'I'll get a hammer and some tacks – put it up on the gatepost.' He wandered off. The sound of heavy objects being moved about in the shed followed soon after.

Bert thought that he'd better wait a while, in case they needed a hand.

After an awkward silence, Hilda said, 'Hot, isn't it?'

'Mm,' said Bert. 'How about takin' that beret off?'

'Ooh, no,' she answered, looking shocked at the suggestion, 'wouldn't dream of it!'

'Ah, right.' Bert looked down at his hands and began picking his fingernails.

Rummaging noises continued from the shed.

'Oh, bless my soul!' exclaimed Hilda, suddenly. 'Look at them little 'uns shootin' out of the well! Did you ever see the like?'

227

Bert swung around. In the middle of the lawn was a manky-looking rat tangled in some orange netting; plus, the same fairy-thingamajig from when his bike had been wrecked: he recognised her wings immediately. And here came more tiny people, without wings this time, fired from the well as if shot from a cannon, followed by even more

'Wonder what they're up to,' gasped Hilda. 'We're lucky, aren't we? Some people would give everythin' to catch a glimpse of just *one* of 'em.' She went forward several paces. 'They live at the bottom of our garden, you know.'

'Do they?' said Bert. 'My word.'

As Bert watched, something else rocketed from the mouth of the well. He couldn't make out what it was – other than it stank! Much larger than the dozens of little people, the thing landed on the lawn with a thud.

Hilda grinned at Bert and pointed a gnarled finger.

However, Bert didn't much like the look of this new, boggle-eyed specimen. He watched as it leapt to its feet and shielded its face from the hot sun. Seconds later, it caught sight of the little people running across the lawn towards the bottom of the garden and loped after them. Thinking quickly, Bert bent down and picked up a pebble. He threw it at the creature – and missed. The thing turned and hissed at Bert, displaying a set of evil-looking teeth. Then the boggle-eyed thing hissed scarily loud. Bert took a step back, sure that he was going to be attacked at any moment.

But it wasn't the creature hissing so loudly at all. From around the side of Mould Cottage came a speeding black and white blur, which hurled itself at the boggle-eyed thing, screeching continuously. At first Bert didn't recognise the blur, because it had no tail. Only when it stood still, the boggle-eyed thing dangling lifeless in its mouth, did Bert recognise Delilah. *Delilah!* He ran to the cat and scratched behind her tattered ears and along her back. As well as the missing tail, Delilah was covered in part-healed scabs and big bald patches. But it *was* Delilah,

228

and she had saved the little people. He looked up, to where they were all disappearing under the fence. The fairy-thingy with white wings paused and looked back. She raised a hand and waved. And … what was this? *Good grief! She just blew me a kiss!*

Bert grinned and waved shyly.

Then she vanished.

The warm tingly feeling stole over Bert again, from his toes to the top of his head, and it had nothing to do with the little note, which had vanished from his sock drawer. Dot had sworn she hadn't touched it and he believed her.

George finally came back from the shed. 'That your cat? Looks a bit worse for wear, don't she?'

Still grinning, Bert said: 'She'll be fine once my wife gets hold of her. She's a good nurse is Dot.' Bert felt a bit guilty about thinking Delilah had died, and that searching for her would be a waste of time. The cat had most probably lain up under a hedge somewhere, or in someone's shed, licking her wounds.

George's face screwed up in distaste. 'What's that she's got an 'old of? A *rat?*'

'Um … Yes, I reckon it is,' said Bert. 'You're a clever, clever girl, Delilah.' He scratched the cat behind the ear again.

Hilda squinted at the boggle-eyed thing; then looked at her husband as if he'd finally lost his marbles. 'Hmm, funny-lookin' rat if you ask me,' she said coolly. 'If that's a rat then I'm the Queen of England, and that'd mean this is a crown on my 'ead – not a bloomin' beret!'

CHAPTER THIRTY NINE

The Long Sleep

Quite a while later, Nan placed an extra eiderdown on Tatty's bed, and insisted her granddaughter swallow all of the hot drink she'd prepared: 'Otherwise you'll look like me when you wake up.'

Obediently, Tatty drained the cup.

Now it was late afternoon and already growing gloomy outside. She burrowed beneath the covers until just her eyes and the top of her head poked out. The Long Sleep had finally arrived and, for the first time, Tatty welcomed it. She still hadn't fully recovered after her exertions in the cornfield. Nan and Marigold had assured her it was to be expected, that in the spring she'd feel her usual self again. Cormac had died only recently, but already it felt like a century ago to Tatty ... *The battle that never was,* she thought sleepily.

A hard frost left a thick crusting of ice at the window. A bitter wind howled around the old Willow Tree, which had shed its long leaves. As Tatty grew drowsier she thought of the Palace Over Yonder, and wondered if Queen Maeve still preferred the crystal eye to her old one. Apparently, as soon as she'd touched Granny Rose's crystal, all her old energy had come flooding back. Even the Curtain shielding the palace was back up to full strength.

She yawned loudly.

As a reward for his bravery, Queen Maeve had reinstated Nibblit as chariot-rat, putting Beelzebub in charge of the rat-wheel (Apparently, the ride to the top of the tower was much quicker now, though with a bumpier, scarier stop). And Bridget Sproutly seemed to have recovered quickly from the terrible news that her husband was eaten by a dog, *and* had been a traitor. Dressed in widow's black – which she'd decided was quite slimming – Bridget had taken only one day off, then gone straight back to organising the daily running of the palace, as she didn't trust anyone else with the task.

Jeb had returned from Scarabia briefly, promising to visit every third week, which seemed to satisfy Queen Maeve. Tatty kept in contact with the Queen by way of their third eyes, but, as she hadn't quite mastered hers yet, they were often very short and confusing exchanges, mainly about the state of the weather.

Tatty hadn't heard from Dorcas Gumble for many weeks. Before she left the area, Dorcas checked that the Gnomes hadn't returned to the cornfield near Woebetide Wood. They hadn't, thank goodness, but Dorcas was told by fellow travellers that two new crop circles had appeared in the neighbouring county of Wiltshire. So, for Little Upham's future protection, a brand-new crossbow was fitted in the Crow's Nest, on the orders of Sir Edwin Popplewhite. Luckily, as yet, they'd had no need to fire the weapon.

She yawned again. *No not yet, it's still too early …*

It was only three weeks before that she and Will had visited Agatha Pottage, handing the witch a jar of honey and a wooden flute, both listed on the I.O.U.; Aggie kindly gave them a big bag of sherbet each, as a gift. And if Tatty concentrated hard, difficult because her head felt as though it was full of soft wool, she could still taste the lovely lemony, fizzy stuff.

Loud snoring came from her grandparents' bedchamber. She smiled at the racket. Nan always blamed Papa, but everyone knew it was *Nan* who grunted and snorted like a foraging hedgehog.

Tatty turned over in the soft bed and peeked from beneath the eiderdown and woollen blankets to see how dark it was. She could barely keep her eyelids open now. Past the window-glass and out over Little Upham, there seemed to be lumps of marshmallow falling from the sky …?

… *Snow!*

It was snowing outside and she couldn't get to the window to look, couldn't move her limbs even if she'd wanted to. She yawned again. Her final thought as she drifted off into The Long Sleep was of Will Patch, and all his brothers and sisters, and what fun they'd have out there tomorrow, playing in the snow.

Aw … Neptune's kneecaps … What a shame …

Also by this author:

HAGCAT
M.J. FAHY

'A quirky middle grade adventure.'

The tale of a boy's longing for a pet of his own ...
Something is hiding in Trevor Talbot's garden shed, placed there
by his very odd neighbour. It is waiting patiently for Trevor's
tenth birthday.

'Is it a birthday cake?' you ask.

'Don't be absurd. Cakes don't hide!'

8579702R00135

Printed in Germany
by Amazon Distribution
GmbH, Leipzig